BLACK LIGHT: CHARMED

JENNIFER BENE

"Cassandra is everything I'm not. Kind, warm, optimistic... happy. If I was less of a selfish prick, I'd walk away. But I can't."

It was supposed to be one night of fun, but ten months after Valentine Roulette Logan can't get the feisty model out of his head. She's invaded his dreams, ruined every session at Black Light, and it's been four months since she even returned a text.

This isn't him.

Logan Chisholm doesn't obsess over women.

He doesn't replay every sweet cry he drew from their lips, doesn't remember the way their smile changes when they laugh, but Cassandra Moreira is different.

He has to figure out if their chemistry was real... or just part of the game.

Luckily, Christmas has come early this year, because she's back in L.A. and he's not letting her leave again without getting a second date.

And this time he won't take no for an answer.

ISBN (e-book): 978-1-947559-24-0

ISBN (paperback): 978-1-947559-25-7

Cover design by Eris Adderly. http://erisadderly.com

Edited by Nerine Dorman.

PROLOGUE

LOGAN

LACK LIGHT WEST

THE NIGHT OF VALENTINE ROULETTE

"That all you got?" Cassandra asked, a laugh in her voice, and Logan grinned, twirling the paddle in his fingers right before he landed it across her perfect ass. She was looking back at him over her shoulder, her brown eyes full of fire, and the sweet little cry he earned from the swat had his dick throbbing… but there were so many things he wanted to do to her, had to do to her, before he satisfied *that* urge.

"You've got a mouth on you, you know that?" he said, trying to sound commanding, intimidating, but something about this girl was already working its way under his skin. It was as if Cassandra Moreira was made of sunshine. She wasn't shy, quiet, or meek like so many subs he'd played with — no, she was brazen. Bold. And sexy as fuck.

It was distracting.

"I've been told that before." Her words started off sassy but ended with a groan as he set the next stroke of the paddle square across her sit spot. Watching her ass bounce, the sparkly faux gem on the buttplug between her cheeks glinting in the light, Logan knew he'd chosen right bidding on her tonight.

"So, you're a brat?" Running his hand over the heated skin on her backside, he squeezed tight and watched her bite down on her lower lip, lifting one shoulder in a shrug.

"I don't like labels."

"You listed yourself as a masochist," he retorted, lining up and smacking the paddle right over the little butt plug. A quiet groan slipped out before she laughed softly, shaking her head.

"That was just a tip that you don't have to treat me like I'm made of glass, *sir*." That last word held way more sarcasm than it should have, no matter how much he liked her sass. Adjusting his grip on the paddle, he brought it down hard. The resounding *pop* seemed to echo off the walls nearby, and he finally got a whine out of her.

"Better?" He was smiling victoriously, wondering if she'd make the same pretty sounds as he worked his fist inside her.

"A little."

The laugh slipped out before he could stop it. He liked her already, and the night had barely begun, but Logan had a feeling that three hours would pass much too quickly with Cassandra as his submissive. Dropping the paddle to the floor with a loud *clap*, he walked over to his bag of toys and took out the oiled flogger. The edges had definite bite when he landed them just right, but he could back off easily as well if he found her limits.

Perfect.

"Say yellow if you need it, I've got plans for you, and I don't need you calling red and ending our fun too soon."

"That won't be a problem," she challenged, glancing back over her shoulder at him, and he wished it was easier to see her expression without her craning her neck back. But… the spanking bench had cuffs, and he liked the way she looked bound to it with her soft brown skin reflecting the lights above.

Plus, it put her in the perfect position for him to light her ass up after all of her sass.

"Good to know it won't be a problem," he snarked in return, and landed the first swat much harder than he normally would. To his surprise, she almost *purred.* If there had ever been a noise that meant 'green light,' that was it, so he kept going.

After a few minutes of the dark falls landing, snapping against her skin, she was whining, but there was no begging, no pleading, no sycophantic dramatics to get him to stop. If anything, she lifted her ass a little higher in the air, wordlessly begging for more even as the marks bloomed on her skin.

"You're definitely a masochist," he said when he finally couldn't resist touching her, stroking over the warm welts, squeezing hard to make her groan. *That's better.*

"I'm many things," Cassandra answered after a minute, but it was a lot breathier this time, less sass.

"Tell me something then." Switching to the other side, he started up with the flogger again, watching her reactions with every slight increase in pressure — but she wasn't backing down.

"I'm a model." It came out like she was rolling her eyes, and he was pretty sure she had. *Naughty girl.* With a flick of his wrist, he snapped the flogger so that the tips of the falls wrapped to the more sensitive skin on the outside of her hip, and she jerked against the bench.

"Want to try again? Maybe a little more politely?"

"Polite could have started with you not tearing my top," she said, in a snippy tone, and he brought the flogger down just a little harder than before. Her whine was like music from the heavens.

"Last chance."

"Fine..." She laughed, turning to look back at him, and he

liked the flush in her cheeks that turned them just a little darker. "I'm not a girly-girl. I grew up with two brothers, and no matter how much my mom dressed me up for pageants, I much preferred getting dirty down at the creek, and I still do."

The sudden, clear honesty made him hesitate on the next stroke, but as he looked over her face, he could tell it was true. Every word of it.

"Thank you for that," he answered, grinning before he swatted her again just to watch her grimace before she laid her cheek on the bench again. "Why'd you go into modeling then?"

"Just because I like to get dirty doesn't mean I don't like to feel pretty sometimes too. Modeling is fun. I get to see the world, and it makes me happy. Isn't that what life's all about?"

Great question.

Instead of answering, he moved out of her line of sight, weaving the flogger back and forth across her ass and thighs, letting her soak in the moderate strokes while occasionally landing them hard enough to make her body jolt in the most beautiful ways.

Cassandra Moreira was more than just a hot piece of ass: she was smart, unique, *interesting.* And she'd asked him a question that was making him way too introspective on a night that was supposed to be pure hedonistic pleasure. A particularly hard strike of the flogger only made her back arch a little, and he cursed himself for not paying attention better.

She was floating, her body relaxed over the padded top of the spanking bench as her hips wavered side to side in a tease that had his hand cupping his dick through his slacks. *Goddamn. I like this girl.* Dropping the flogger onto his bag, he took a step back to appreciate the shine of wetness between her spread thighs.

"You doing okay?" he asked, expecting a witty retort, but all he got was a pleased sigh and a nod that sent the halo of curls around her head bouncing. She was definitely hovering on the rim of subspace, and that was the perfect place to keep her as he moved close to drag his fingers through her soaked pussy. The soft moan that left her lips was fucking heaven.

Damn.

His dick throbbed behind his zipper, wanting to be buried inside her now, but they'd spun fisting, and if he didn't get on track, one of the DMs was going to show up and bitch at him — which would pull Cassandra out of this almost sedate head-space. He wanted to keep her just like *this.*

Sliding two fingers inside slowly, he watched every twitch of her muscles, the way her lips parted, back arching as she pushed back, wanting more. He added a third, reveling in the tight stretch. "You ready for this?"

"For you to finally get started?" she purred, grinning. "Yeah, I'm ready."

"Naughty girl," he growled, pumping all three fingers inside her harder. Cassandra's hands turned into fists, and he knew that was as unconscious as her toes curling. "You better start calling me 'sir' or I'm gonna make this hurt."

"Promises, promises," she said through a groan, and he pushed in all the way to the knuckle, feeling the way her body resisted, and although he knew he needed to grab a glove and the lube from his bag, he just wanted this for a minute longer. The DMs couldn't fault him for enjoying being inside her the first time, and if Cassandra Moreira was as fantastic as she seemed to be, he promised himself it wouldn't be the last.

Not by a long shot.

CHAPTER 1

LOGAN

*R*UNWAY *WEST*
      DECEMBER 6TH

The mansion was packed, and it looked completely different than it normally did when it was functioning as a dance club. All the lights were on, and white tablecloths had been placed over tables scattered throughout the various room, everything decorated tastefully so that the whole of Runway looked like Pottery Barn had been asked to create a minimalistic winter wonderland.

It was... cute.

Or whatever the fucking word was for this stuff, because it wasn't exactly where Logan Chisholm usually found himself. He was only at the release party for Anna Casqueiro's winter clothing line for one reason.

Ten months. It had been ten fucking months since he'd had his hands on Cassandra Moreira, four months since she'd returned a text message, and he was still dreaming about her. Flashbacks to their intense time during Roulette pestered him in meetings and during scenes with other submissives — which was shitty, even for him.

It was why he was here, skipping his afternoon at the office, and surrounded by sprigs of holly and fake snow while trays of champagne and hors d'oeuvres floated past.

I just need to get in front of her again.

She'd been traveling so much during the year that every time he'd tried to get a date, she'd been unavailable. Rome, Paris, New York, Rio de Janeiro. Eventually he'd stopped texting and calling at all. He'd tried to salvage his pride, to move on, find another girl to keep his interest and let him scene out his stress on the weekends… but it didn't work.

Nothing worked.

So, he'd forked over the cash for a VIP seat at this little fashion show, filled to the brim with Jaxson and Chase Cartwright-Davidson's friends, because he'd seen her name on the list of models for the event. Pathetic? Absolutely. But his father had always told him that determination and persistence were the only ways to be successful in life. If you wanted something, you went for it with all you had, and one thing Logan had plenty of was money.

"Chisholm! Is that you?" A male voice lifted his attention from the champagne in his hand, and he scanned the crowd until he saw a familiar dark-haired man headed in his direction. Forcing a polite smile, he accepted his hand when he got close.

"Hey," he replied, trying to place the man's face in his memory. Usually he was good at this, but while he recognized the guy, he couldn't remember from where.

"It's great to see you, man. Wow, it's been, what, fifteen years since Yale?" The man laughed, tilting his head back to finish his glass of champagne, and Logan followed suit as he realized who it was. Derrick Mathers.

"About fifteen," Logan acknowledged, keeping his smile in place even though he wanted to avoid the idiot.

"God, time does fly though, doesn't it?" Derrick chuckled,

spinning to snag a glass of champagne from a passing tray. "Want one?"

"Sure." He took the new flute, letting the young woman take his empty one as she offered him a blushing smile. *Not here for you, sweetheart.* When he turned his gaze back to Derrick, she wandered off, and he turned on the bullshit. "You're right though, it does feel like it's been a long time. What brings you to L.A.?"

"Oh, you know, I've always dabbled in different things." Shrugging, Derrick offered a smarmy grin. "Have to keep busy, but my wife and I are out here right now so that she can sign a deal with a production company to feature some of her products."

"Ah," Logan answered, trying not to sound too interested, but it was already clear that Derrick was going to keep talking.

"Very hush hush, of course." He winked, and Logan took a long drink of his champagne, wishing it was something else. "I really shouldn't even be telling you about it, but Amber's little skincare empire has been dragging us all over the world. It'll be in Nordstrom next year."

"How wonderful for you." Feigning interest was a skill Logan had never quite mastered, but something about him seemed to invite idiots to talk to him.

"That's how I ended up at this show. Amber heard someone talking about it and just had to get us seats. Trying to make some friends out here, more connections. You know how it is. Got to keep working even when you're not." Derrick chuckled. "So, did your wife drag you here as well?"

"No," he answered as a flash of blonde hair moving quickly through the crowd caught his eye, and before Derrick could continue talking, he raised a hand. "I'm sorry, I see someone I need to speak with."

"Oh, sure, sure. We can catch up later!" Derrick called out as he moved past the man, tracking Madison Taylor through the crowd.

The complicated layout to Runway made it hard to keep his eye on her, but he had a feeling she was headed back to where the dance floor usually was, and he side-stepped people as he hurried that direction.

This is different.

The main dance floor had been transformed. No lasers and multi-colored lights today. The bright chandeliers in the ceiling were glowing brightly, and winter sunlight spilled through the huge oval skylight above and the patio windows on either side, lighting up the pristine white runway that was set up in the center of the room. White chairs were already crowded around it in rows, but Madison was skirting the outside of the room, and Logan caught up to her just before she slipped through the doors to the patio.

"Ms. Taylor!"

She stopped on a dime, spinning in her sky-high heels as she turned to face him. The girl was tiny, and she had to tilt her head back to meet his gaze, her brows furrowing. "I'm sorry, sir, you'll need to wait outside until we call everyone in."

"I understand, I just wanted to ask you if Cassandra Moreira was here yet." He tried to sound steady, confident, but he'd felt the nervous tremor go through him as he'd said her name.

What if she had to cancel? What if she's not even here?

Madison Taylor didn't answer immediately, scrutinizing his face for a long moment before her eyes widened slightly. "You were partnered with her for Roulette!" she said too loudly, groaning under her breath before she stepped in close to lower her voice to a whisper. "Look, this is not that kind of event. Ms. Moreira is here as a model, and she's doing this show as a favor to Chase, so if you have any plans to—"

"Whoa, whoa." Lifting his hands, he waggled the champagne

glass side to side, answering in hushed tones. "I'm here as a guest for a fashion show, I'm not trying to drag her off and tie her up."

Rolling her eyes, Madison planted one hand on her hip. "Then, why exactly are you trying to track her down?"

"She travels a lot, I just wanted to see if we could talk. *After* the show, of course." Sighing, he slapped on his most charming smile and shrugged. "Could you just do me a favor and tell her that Logan Chisholm is here? I'll wait around as long as she needs after the show so we can chat."

Madison pursed her lips a little, eyes flicking back and forth between his, and he felt that tremor of anxiety amplify. "Are you, like, stalking her or something?"

"Jesus, no!" Groaning, he swallowed the rest of his champagne just so he could hold the glass at his side without spilling it. "Look, we've tried to get back together a few times, and our schedules never worked out. Yes, I'm here to track her down because I found out she was in town again, but I'm not some crazy stalker. All I want you to do is let her know I'm here."

"That's it?"

"That's it," he confirmed, spreading his arms, trying to look as non-threatening as a guy a foot taller and easily twice her weight *could* look. Then, even though it grated another layer off his pride, he begged, "Please, Madison?"

"Ugh, fine," she finally acquiesced, then her finger came up to point at him sharply. "But if I find out you're being some kind of creep with Cassandra, I'll make sure you get banned from Runway *and* all other clubs associated with the Cartwright-Davidsons. Got it?"

"Understood," Logan answered, taking a step back from her as he turned on his smile again. "Thank you."

"You're welcome." Glancing down at the tablet tucked against her waist, she made a little panicked sound and grabbed the door handle. "I have to go, and *you* need to get back to the welcome party. Go!"

Chuckling, he took a few steps backward and watched Madison bolt out the side door. Through the windows, he could see her heading down the stone steps toward several large, white tents set up on the lawn alongside the pool. They were completely closed, likely to keep out the chill in the air today and keep assholes from peeping at the models getting dressed.

Assholes like me.

Turning away, Logan marched back into the party, immediately swapping for a fresh glass of champagne off the first tray he found. As much as he wanted to push it away, Madison's words were eating at him, digging into his confidence, but there was no reason for it. He'd never been aggressive with Cassandra. If anything, he'd been too casual. He hadn't asked her out *enough…* but what if she felt differently? What if she saw this as creepy?

Fuck, fuck, fuck.

Downing the champagne, he turned to walk back through the rooms of the house, seeking out the little bars that were usually tucked away and active when Runway was open, but they were all empty. No liquor, no bartenders.

If he'd been smart, he would have grabbed the flask from his desk at work. Of course a fancy little event like this wouldn't have an open bar, much less a cash one. It wasn't even two o'clock yet. All of that shit would come out before they opened the dance club tonight, and he had no plans to be upstairs at that time.

Hopefully he'd be downstairs, at Black Light, with Cassandra.

"As long as you don't fuck this up," he muttered to himself under his breath, wandering back to the entrance of the ball-room where the show would be happening in — Logan checked his watch — fifteen minutes.

Yep. Just don't fuck this up.

Try not to be an asshole.

Sighing, he scanned the room for the next tray of champagne, hoping that Cassandra would give him ten minutes to remind her of the night they'd had. A night they could have again, tonight, if she'd only say yes.

CHAPTER 2

CASSANDRA

"*Y*ou look great, Cassandra!" Maritza called out as she walked behind her in the mirror, waving.

"You do too!" Waving, she tried to keep herself as still as possible in the chair, even though she was so full of nervous energy she felt like she might start vibrating at any second. It was always like this before a show though. So much activity, so many people, and it was contagious. Cassandra wanted to be up and moving, *doing* something. Even if all she did was pace the tent like several of the other girls.

"I love your hair," Trina cooed from behind her as she spritzed water on her hair and returned to it with the pick, fluffing her curls higher on the top to create a perfect curve.

"Thanks," Cassandra said, smiling at the stylist in the mirror as she laughed a little. "I'm just relieved someone here knows how to handle this mane. It can be a beast!"

"Oh yeah, you've got a ton of hair, and I'm sure you've met some people who didn't know what they were doing. Don't worry though, you're going to look phenomenal. I promise." Trina winked at her in the mirror as she switched to her hands, patting the edges of the afro until even the most defiant curls were tamed. The woman really was doing a great job, and since she was sure that her natural hair had been part of the reason the designer had wanted her on the runway today — it mattered.

Of course, being friends with Chase and Jaxson didn't hurt, but it wasn't like they were best friends who hung out all the time. They'd ended up at the same shoots a handful of times, hung out, and she and Chase had swapped numbers to chat occasionally... and a few of those more entertaining text convos had led to her being invited to Black Light after it opened.

Okay, so Chase was a good friend.

It didn't matter though. Whether he'd pulled strings to get her on the list of possible models for this show or not, she'd still brought her A-game. She'd owned the catwalk, and Anna Casqueiro had selected her as one of the ten models for today.

"Done!" Trina cheered, clapping her hands together, and Cassandra hopped out of the chair, turning to carefully hug the woman so she didn't mess up her makeup or all the work she'd just done.

"Thank you so much, you're amazing."

"It's my job! Now, I think they want you over by Mrs. Casqueiro. Hurry," Trina said, nudging her hip, and she went where she was told. Half of modeling was just waiting to be told what to do — where to stand, how to pose, smile, don't smile, blah blah blah. But it made the day fly by, and judging by the number of people sprinting around the tent, it was almost runway time.

"You!" A loud, feminine voice shouted, and then she saw Anna Casqueiro marching toward her, eyes already roving over her body. "Let me look at you. Hmm... okay. Yes."

The woman turned, snapping her fingers at someone as she spoke in rapid Spanish, and the young man hurried over to the racks of clothes.

"Walk with confidence, yes? Proud. Chin up. No smiles. Just

like yesterday." Mrs. Casqueiro nodded at her as the man came back holding two long, white dresses. Both were sleek, designed for the winter parties so many of the wealthy in L.A. would be going to, and Anna looked between the two before tapping the one on the left. "This one. The other on that brunette over there, the one with freckles. For this girl, I think the navy one is second. With the gold trim."

Cassandra stayed put as the young man rushed back to the racks of dresses, shoving the ones she would wear during the show in the section of the rack behind her name. The other dress went behind a placard that read *Stephanie*. Mrs. Casqueiro had already wandered off to snap at someone else, and when the young man didn't even glance back at her, she took that as permission to head over to the snack table where several of the other girls were gathered near a heater.

As usual, everyone was standing around in bras and underwear only, so the warm rush of air over her legs felt good. Leaning down, she let it soak into her hands for a moment before she stepped out of the way to snag a strawberry.

"I think the designer is a *little* stressed today," one of the girls leaned over to whisper, and Cassandra laughed under her breath.

"Just a little bit. But this is *her* event, it's not Fashion Week. If we run a few minutes behind, everyone will just wait." Shrugging, she smiled at the other model. "I always try to just go with the flow."

"*That* is something I wish I could do. I'm always worried about what's happening next, what I'm missing. Total FOMO." The girl rolled her eyes. "I just need to chill out."

"LADIES! Time to get dressed!" Sam, the backstage manager for this show, shouted over the bustle of voices in the tent, and the girl laughed.

"Of course, sometimes my anxiety has a reason."

"Yep, that's showtime," Cassandra replied before she glanced down at the strawberry in her fingers. There was no way she'd be able to fix her makeup if she messed it up now. *Damn.* Sighing, she set the strawberry back down uneaten, which made her stomach rumble angrily. She should have listened to Abelita this morning and eaten a better breakfast. A yogurt while running out the door was *not* enough — which was exactly what her roommate had yelled at her as she climbed in the car to make it here on time.

Rolling her eyes at being forced to admit Abelita was right *again*, she gathered near the other girls. The first few to go were already getting dressed, and if Cassandra remembered correctly, she was fifth in line.

"Cassandra!"

Turning at the sound of her name, she saw a familiar blonde girl weaving through the busy tent toward her, and as she got closer, she realized who it was. "Madison!"

"Hey, sorry, I know you're about to get started, and everything is totally ready inside, I just wanted to tell you that this guy named Logan... something, is here to see you. Sorry, I didn't write his name down because I'm insane right now, but he says he'll wait for you after the show." Madison glanced down at her tablet, tapping at something before her eyes came back up. "Look, I'm really sorry, but if I don't get back inside Jaxson will freaking kill me. I hope this is good news, but if he's a creep just tell me, and I'll have him dragged out on his ass."

"No, it's fine," Cassandra answered, but her heart was still racing. *Logan came here? To this?* Shaking herself, she flashed a smile and reached over to squeeze Madison's shoulder. "Really, it's all good. I'll talk to him, okay? You hurry inside!"

"Thanks! You're going to do great!" Madison cheered before she spun and rushed back the way she'd come.

"Cassandra, over here please." One of the dressers called, waving her closer, and like a good model she obeyed. The dress slid on like a glove, cupping her hips, and as they adjusted it and helped her into shoes, all she could think about was Logan Chisholm.

It had to be him, because there was no other 'Logan' that it could be.

Does this mean he's still interested?

The thought made a warm feeling spread through her as various people wearing headsets started to line them up, rushing the ones already dressed out of the tent and onto the stone area at the base of the stairs.

"Shoes!" one of the dressers called out, snapping her fingers to point at all of them.

Grass.

Looking down at her heels, Cassandra couldn't see anything, but when it was her turn, she still steadied herself on the dresser's shoulder so they could wipe off the bottom of the shoes. She needed to be focused right now, mentally preparing to walk the runway, but her eyes kept drifting up to the patio where she could see the tops of the windows.

Could Logan really be in there?

After so many months without a text, she'd figured he had moved on, found a sub who was in town more than she was. Having him show up here, if he was here, was a very interesting surprise — but that was how the universe worked sometimes, bringing the unexpected, changing the winds of fortune. Whether this would be a good thing, or not so much, would be up to fate.

Anna Casqueiro burst out of the tent with two people trailing behind her, one was a makeup artist, and the other was her assistant. He was reading from notecards as she marched across the grass with the kind of confidence that made everyone pay attention. It made Cassandra smile to herself, because in a field that used to be so male dominated — and still was at times — it always made her happy to see another woman be successful.

Absolute badass bitch territory.

"Listen!" Mrs. Casqueiro called out, clapping her hands once. "Remember your order for the change. Be powerful, confident. Do not smile. This is strength in winter! Be cold and bold!"

Cold and bold.

"Yes, Mrs. Casqueiro," Cassandra answered along with several of the other models, but the woman was already heading up the stairs as a dresser chased after her to wipe her shoes.

The heavy bass from the music coming on echoed out over the lawn, and then it was showtime. Applause rolled out of the room above, and the other models began to file up the stone steps ahead of her. Following, Cassandra took a deep breath of the cooler air outside and let her face go smooth.

Strength in winter. She lifted her chin as she entered the tiny backstage space created by the floor-to-ceiling white drapes. *I've got this.*

CHAPTER 3

LOGAN

*I*n some kind of twisted joke from the universe, he'd ended up sitting just in front of Derrick Mathers and his obnoxious wife, Amber. As soon as they'd taken their seats, Derrick had immediately thumped him on the shoulder to introduce him, and after the pleasantries he'd tried to ignore them, but neither of them seemed to take the hint when he kept turning around to look at the runway.

No, they *both* kept talking to him.

Like he wore a sign that read '*please tell me about your bullshit company*.'

Amber had spent the past ten minutes explaining the differences between sourcing organic and non-organic herbs — knowledge that Logan could have spent his entire life without knowing — and it didn't seem like she was winding down.

"See, it's all about keeping your products pure, because if they put those things on the plants then—" She paused to sigh loudly. "*Obviously* it's going in your skin too, and that stuff is poison! Just, absolute poison, so obviously none of that is included in anything my company makes."

"Obviously," Logan replied, deadpan, as he glanced back at the stage.

"And that's why she's so beautiful too," Derrick added, reaching over to squeeze Amber's thigh while she giggled and swatted at his hand.

"Oh, stop. Eating well is a huge passion of mine as well, because you know that's the first place you can really start to impact your skin, it's—" The boom of the bass as the music changed stunned her into silence, and Logan almost cheered out of sheer gratitude.

"Excuse me," he said, straining for polite as he turned all the way back to the stage to block them out. This time, they seemed to get the hint as everyone began to clap and bright lights turned on, aimed at the runway, and a pair of people dragged curtains along the walls to block out the light from outside. It left the runway glowing brightly, surrounded by shadow, and he had to admit that the theatrics were more than he'd expected. When the designer finally walked out through the curtains at the back, the applause grew louder, and Mrs. Casqueiro accepted them with gracious nods as they turned down the music a little for her to speak.

"Welcome, and thank you all for coming," she said with a slight Spanish accent, but he couldn't focus on her. As she began introducing the clothing line, he kept skimming the curtains, trying to catch a glimpse of Cassandra. Unfortunately, the fabric went wall to wall, and there wasn't a hint of any of the models through a gap.

Impatient, he sat back and listened as she talked about the *power of winter* and how capturing that inspired her line of dresses for the season. After what seemed like a ten-minute speech, she finally bowed, and he applauded with everyone else as the music changed.

The show started with a tall, blonde woman who was definitely pretty, but not Cassandra. Plucking at the corner of the card he'd found on his chair, he sat up straighter in his seat, forcing himself to take deep, even breaths as woman after woman walked the runway. The dresses were nice, but it wasn't like he knew much about fashion. He knew what he liked to wear, knew that a bespoke suit was more comfortable than anything off the rack, but beyond that he just bought what he liked.

And he didn't wear dresses.

He was just about to start looking around again when the brunette on stage passed through the curtain, and Cassandra appeared. Everything else seemed to freeze as she walked forward, head held high, eyes glued to the back of the room. Earlier in the day he'd wondered if she'd notice him in the audience, if she might stop to see if it was really him — but he didn't even want that anymore.

This was so much better.

Her warm-toned skin seemed to glow in the lights, and her cheeks were dusted in something shimmery that made her eyes stand out as a vibrant mix of honey and brown sugar. The dress hugged her curves in a way that had him wanting to buy it right then just so he could see her in it again. It was ghostly white, and she looked ethereal as she passed him, moving to the end of the runway to stop, turning to one side and then the other, before coming back toward him.

Fuck.

His memories hadn't done her justice. She was beautiful, gorgeous, incredible.

The only thing missing to make her perfect was her smile. Hell, he'd spent just as much time thinking about the way she'd laughed when they'd gone out for pancakes as he had dreaming of her over that damn spanking bench. That night her smile had been radiant, and even though she'd spent half of their late-night meal at IHOP cracking jokes at his expense… he'd taken every playful swipe at his ego in stride because of the way she looked when she smiled.

Too soon, Cassandra was gone, replaced by another model. Logan almost got out of his seat to find her, but one glance down the row of people intently watching the show kept him seated.

Dammit. How much longer is this thing?

CHAPTER 4

CASSANDRA

he cheer in the tent was loud, interspersed with the popping of champagne corks, and Cassandra leaned into Delilah, laughing as they were peppered with raining champagne.

Glasses were filled almost to overflowing as people passed them out, and Delilah handed one to her with a big smile. "All done!"

"All done!" Cassandra cheered, tapping her glass against Delilah's before taking a sip. They'd ended up chatting during the change since she was only one model behind, and the other girl had still been anxious at that point, but she seemed to have let it all go now that the show was complete.

"Let's do a selfie," Delilah said, squeezing in next to Cassandra as she held up her phone to snap several quick shots.

Laughing, Cassandra dug in her bag to grab her phone. "Here, let me text those to myself so we have each other's numbers!"

"Definitely!"

The other girls crowded around, taking more pictures, swapping phone numbers, posting to Instagram, and everyone was sharing usernames to get tagged when Mrs. Casqueiro's loud voice boomed over all of them. "Attention, please!"

Everyone slowly settled down, and Cassandra caught sight of Chase behind the designer. Jaxson was standing beside him, whispering something in Chase's ear that made him grin ear to ear.

"I want to thank all of you for making my show a success today," Anna Casqueiro started, allowing everyone to clap again for a moment. "Yes, yes, I am grateful to our models, our stage team, and my wonderful design team, today's show meant much to me and I feel each of you are now a part of the Casqueiro family."

"To Anna!" someone cried out, and everyone echoed them, raising glasses high to drink in her honor.

"Thank you," Mrs. Casqueiro said, touching her chest before she stepped to the side to gesture at the men behind her. "And, of course, I owe many thanks to my dear friends Jaxson and Chase for sharing their beautiful venue. We are only the second show to occur at Runway West, but I think it will become popular. Thank you both!"

More applause cascaded around the tent as Jaxson stepped forward to hug her, followed quickly by Chase as Jaxson faced the group. "It's really us that are grateful that you brought your beautiful designs to Runway today, Anna. Thank you for trusting us to give your show the care it deserved and thank you to every one of you who helped us pull it off today. Whether you work here at Runway, or were just here for the day, thank you very much for all your hard work."

"Salud!" Mrs. Casqueiro called out, raising her glass high, and Cassandra followed suit before turning to clink glasses with the other models crowded around.

Everyone started talking again, chatting about the various members of the press who had attended, placing guesses on which publications might feature the show — and therefore, the models too. Just because this show was done, it didn't mean any of them got to rest. Models had to always be promoting, maintaining and building their brand on social media and anywhere else they might appear. Being in one of the shots chosen by a big newspaper could make a career, because like so many other things, it was all about being in the right spot at the right time.

"You were amazing!" Chase shouted, and Cassandra turned to see him beaming next to her. Standing up, she hugged him, laughing when he lifted her off the floor with a tight hug in return. "Oh my God, it is so good to see you again!"

"You too, Chase, but put me down!" Laughing, Cassandra shoved his shoulder as he set her down, but he just shrugged.

"I wanted to sneak out here to see you before the show started, but it was crazy inside. Jaxson was—"

"*Jaxson* was making sure everything went off without a hitch for everyone," Jaxson finished for him, smiling at his husband before he offered his hand. "It is good to see you again, Cassandra. You were beautiful."

"Thanks, Jaxson," she said, shaking his hand before smoothing her dress back down. She'd already changed back into the little swing dress she'd arrived in, and much more comfortable heels, but she was still eye to eye with the ex-model as she faced him. "You guys did a great job with everything. Definitely one of the smoother shows I've been in."

"Right? It went off without a hitch!" Chase said happily, and Jaxson chuckled as he wrapped his arm around Chase.

"It helped that it wasn't a larger show. Our East Coast location can hold a lot more guests, and we have the space for a much larger event." Shrugging, Jaxson pointed to one side of the tent with the hand holding his champagne. "Over the summer we had a really nice show near the pool, and I think we had twice as many guests because we had more space."

"I think I saw pictures from that," Cassandra said, trying to remember the designer's name. "Who was it again?"

"Jiri Kalfar," Chase answered, but waved his hand quickly. "I don't want to talk about work though, I want to talk about *you*. How have you been? How's Roberta?"

"I've been great." Shrugging, she gestured around her with a laugh. "I've been doing *this* all over the place. I got booked for a Badgley Mischka campaign, which was amazing, and... it's been a lot this year. I feel like I've barely been home! Roberta is a freaking angel, and I love her so much. She's intent on getting me everywhere."

"Well, don't let her run you into the ground, Cassandra. She's good, but she also doesn't know the meaning of a break." Jaxson was being serious, and his concern for her made her smile. He'd always been prickly, more than a little standoffish, and she had a feeling that it was probably Chase and Emma's positive energy rubbing off on him.

Or fatherhood.

"I appreciate it, Jaxson." Reaching over to touch his arm, she gave him a little squeeze. "I mean it, and I promise I'm looking out for myself. My roommate would totally call me out on it if I wasn't, and if *she* didn't, my family would be all over me."

"That's good," Chase said, leaning into his husband's side. "But Jaxson is right. It's why we got out when we did. Emma was obviously a part of it too, but we were burning out, and neither of us want that for you."

"My God! You guys are almost as bad as my brothers. I swear, I'm fine. I'm twenty-two and still perfectly happy to end a call at one AM, only to be back up for another at four." Grinning, she glanced around the hectic tent with all the noise and the people, the designer clothes now securely stored in their hanging bags, the trashed makeup tables, and she shrugged a little. "It's what I love to do."

"Then I'm so fucking happy for you," Chase said, leaning forward to press a kiss to her cheek. When he stepped back, he rolled his eyes. "Now I think we have to head back in to make the rounds before all the guests leave."

"I saw you roll your eyes," Jaxson whispered, doing a little *tsk-tsk* under his breath. The blush on Chase's cheeks had Cassandra biting back another smile as Jaxson looked at her. "Unfortunately, we do need to head back inside. I'm glad we got to see you again."

"You guys too!" she called after them as Jaxson led Chase to the entrance of the tent.

"Holy shit, you know them?" Delilah asked as soon as they were out of earshot, and she turned to find a few models standing close.

"Yeah, we met years ago. I was still a kid, had *no* idea what I was doing traveling for runway shows, and I got lucky."

The questions tumbled out of the other girls — who, what, when, where, how — and Cassandra tried to answer them without sounding like she was bragging.

She knew her story wasn't everyone's. Many girls fought hard through hundreds of cattle calls before getting booked for the first time, and others were like her. Discovered at a beauty pageant her mom had dragged her to when she was only fifteen. Her first runway had been at sixteen, and a few months later she'd somehow ended up at the same event with Jaxson Davidson and Chase Cartwright.

It wasn't as if she hadn't worked hard too. Finishing high school on the road, dealing with the pressures of modeling as a career before most kids had their first job, but she'd done it. That didn't mean Chase and Jaxson weren't a major part of her success. Their influence, and getting connected to their agent, Roberta Price, had been one of the biggest blessings of her career. Doors had started opening, and in no time, she was booked practically year-round.

Most days, it didn't feel real, except she was exhausted enough to know for sure it was.

"Guys, I'm starving," Cassandra finally said with an apologetic grin, trying to change the topic from her to food. "What are you doing after this?"

"I'm in for food," Poppy immediately replied, clearly excited about the idea.

"I'm in too," Maritza added, glancing at Delilah, who rolled her eyes.

"Of course I'm in."

"I can go with you guys, too!" another girl said. "I just need to say bye to a friend that came to see the show."

Logan! Fuck.

"I actually need to say bye to someone before we go too!" Grabbing her bag from the floor, she started backing toward the entrance of the tent. "Meet in the parking lot in fifteen?"

"Sounds good!" Maritza called back as she hurried out of the tent and across the lawn to the stone stairs.

Guilt was tugging at her as she ran up the steps, digging in her bag for her phone so she could text him, and then she heard a low laugh.

"Took you long enough." The voice made her freeze one stair short of the patio, and she abandoned her search for her phone as she looked up to find Logan Chisholm leaning against the wall. He looked just as good as he had the night of Roulette, the winter sun turning his pale blond hair into a halo as he walked over to her with a wicked smirk. "I was starting to think you were going to ditch me for the little party going on down there."

Grinning, she took the last step onto the patio. "And what if I did?"

"Well..." Logan shrugged a shoulder, his perfectly tailored suit shifting with the movement. "I might have contemplated walking down to join the festivities just to drag you away."

"Drag me away?" She bit down on her lip for a second as she pictured that particular scenario before the grin took back over.

"I'm not sure that would have gone over well with all the security guards and, you know, the *vanilla* crowd in attendance."

"Doesn't mean I didn't think about it," he replied, moving close enough to be well within the bounds of her personal space. "Just like I've been thinking about you."

So. Damn. Smooth.

Laughing, she reached over to pluck at the lapel of his suit jacket. *Wool, finely woven, likely Italian.* Everything about Logan Chisholm screamed money at the top of its lungs — just like he had the night he'd bid on her. Tweaking his lapel, she leaned in closer to him. "If you've been thinking of me, why haven't you texted? Called?"

"You haven't reached out to me either," he challenged.

"Who says I wanted to?" she asked, keeping her voice light, but the flicker that passed over his face for a second was definitely *not* humor. "I'm kidding. I've been busy."

"I noticed," he said, a lot more stiffly than before. "I think the last time I tried to get you out on a date, you told me you were in Paris. Before that it was... Rome? And before that it was either New York or Rio de Janeiro or—"

"I get it," she cut him off with a chuckle, feeling the guilt trickle back in. "I tried to tell you the night of Roulette that I don't get to be in L.A. as much as I'd like."

"Well, you're in town now." Logan grinned, tilting his head toward the mansion as he closed the gap between them. "And I know a great place to spend an evening."

"Logan—" she started to explain just how tired she was, but then his lips were on hers, his hands finding the back of her neck and her waist at the same moment to pull her against him. The kiss seared her, bringing back every intense moment they'd had in Black Light together. Every sting of pain, every orgasm, and every explosive kiss that had earned her a free month at the club that she had yet to cash in.

God, this feels good.

It had been too long since anyone kissed her, too long since she felt *anything* like this, and even though it was the wrong thing to do, she leaned into it. Let him take control, claiming her mouth as heat spiraled through her in a way it hadn't in months. Nipping her lip, he turned them, pressing her back against the stone railing, and then his body was against hers as he reclaimed the kiss. The moan was uncontrollable, only made worse when she heard an echo of it rumbling in his chest, because she wanted more.

Dropping her bag to the ground, she caught his shirt in her hands to pull him closer, and his fingers tightened on her waist as he broke the kiss to trail more kisses down the side of her neck, nipping her skin.

"Say yes," he commanded, and all she could do was let out a little whine as he bit down a little harder on her shoulder. "I want to take you out to dinner, on a real date, and then I don't care what happens. We can come back here to Black Light, or I can take you to my place and show you my playroom. Just say yes, Cassandra."

It was the low growl in his voice, the dominant edge, that had her weakening — but it would be wrong to lead him on. To make him think this could be a thing, a *real* thing, because she was already booked out for London in January. New York after that. The list went on and on.

Logan lifted his head, his blue eyes searching hers as he reached up to cup her face in his hands. "Say yes."

You want him. You know you want him, and you know exactly how good it will be.

Swallowing, she wrapped her fingers around one of his wrists and did the only right thing. She said, "No."

CHAPTER 5

LOGAN

*I*t felt like the earth had spontaneously shifted to one side, and as he stared into her eyes the only word he could work past his lips was a confused, "What?"

Cassandra smiled, but it didn't reach her eyes as she pulled his hand away from her face and shifted out from between him and the railing. "I can't go on a date with you, Logan."

"Yes, you absolutely can," he argued, running a hand through his hair as she stepped back to put more space between them. "Just say yes, Cassandra!"

"Logan…" She sighed, shaking her head as she looked at him with what almost seemed to be pity. *That* was not a look he was used to seeing, and he wasn't sure if he'd ever seen it. Especially not on the face of a woman he wanted as much as he wanted her.

Had she really not felt that?

Kissing her had been like striking a match in a dark room. So much better than he remembered, and then *she* had pulled him closer. She'd wanted it just as much. Fuck, he'd heard that little moan slip past her perfect goddamn lips!

Shaking his head, he moved forward, catching her by the

waist to pull her close again. "Tell me you haven't thought about it. Tell me you haven't spent a single night since we played Roulette remembering our scenes, and I'll walk away right now. I won't ever bother you again."

"You don't want to date me," she whispered, staring directly into his eyes as she told a complete lie. It grated him, and if they weren't outside Runway in broad daylight, he'd have swatted her ass for it.

"Don't tell me what I want, Cassandra, because I think I've made it pretty damn clear that I want you."

"Logan, you—" A little frustrated screech escaped as she shoved his hands away from her, turning to pace a few steps one way, and then the other.

He wanted to grab her again, to shake her until she stopped denying the obvious fire between them, but this wasn't Black Light, and she definitely wasn't his submissive. *Yet.*

"I'm a persistent asshole when I want to be," Logan finally said, spreading his arms a bit. "If you want me to text you every day asking you out — fine. You want me to be your own personal stalker? Okay. I can do that."

That made her stop, her brow furrowing for a second as she stared at him, and then she laughed. At first he thought she was mocking him, but when it continued he found himself smiling despite the confusion and frustration whirling inside him.

"Did I say something funny?" he asked, fighting the urge to laugh himself.

"You're insane, you know that?" Cassandra's laugh wound down, and she reached up to delicately sweep under her eyes as she grinned at him. "Who on earth *offers* to stalk a girl?"

Shrugging, he tucked his hands into his pockets to keep himself from touching her. "Hey, I don't judge kinks. If you're into that, I can absolutely stalk you. Maybe wait until you're alone... take you to my secret lair."

She groaned, biting down on her lip for a second as she shook her head. "Don't tempt me."

Fuck.

He'd already been working toward a hard-on with her pressed against him, but that little bit of sass was about to make it impossible for him to walk back inside Runway with any shred of decorum.

"Jesus Christ, Cassandra." He had to swallow to erase the image of taking her, pinning her down, and making her come over and over. "Do you think I'm playing around? That I'd show up here if I didn't mean every word? I want you, Cassandra, and I'll do whatever it takes to have you. Stalk you, be your daddy, make you scream — whatever it takes."

"You don't even know me," she said, but a smile tugged at her lips, and he knew he was close to closing the deal. He had the same thrumming tingle running down his spine that he got at work before something big happened.

"I've already had my whole hand inside you, Cassandra, and you *liked* it. What more could I do on one date?" Logan felt the grin spreading across his face as she gawked at him for a moment before breaking out into another laugh.

"I cannot believe you just said that!"

"It's true." Taking a small step forward, he went for it. "Just say yes, Cassandra."

"Fucking hell," she groaned, crossing her arms under her breasts as she stared at him, that beautiful smile dancing on her perfect mouth. "No date. But... I'll meet you here at Black Light."

"Tonight?" he clarified, trying not to let the excitement show in his tone.

"Yeah, tonight. Eight o'clock?"

"I'll be here," he said, unable to take his eyes off her as she picked up her massive purse. "Wait, why don't I pick you up?"

Rolling her eyes, she took a few steps past him toward the doors. "Because this isn't a date, Logan."

"What is it then?" he asked, chuckling as she walked backward.

"Fun," she answered with a naughty little giggle that had him groaning.

"Oh, I'm definitely going to have fun," he called after her, and she laughed as she pulled open the door. "And you're going to pay for all those eye rolls!"

That got her to turn back around, catching the swinging door on her hip as she gawked at him for a moment before her grin came back — and then she stuck her tongue out.

Logan was too caught off guard by it to say a thing before she'd disappeared inside, her laugh cut off as the door closed, leaving him shaking his head as he stared at the reflection of the sun in the windows. Chuckling to himself, he wiped his hands down his face and turned to lean on the stone railing.

Cassandra wasn't just a masochist, she was a brat with a sassy mouth, and he was going to spend his afternoon planning out just how he wanted to tame her. And... he'd start planning as soon as his dick calmed down enough for him to walk through Runway without embarrassing himself.

Just one more thing you'll pay for tonight, beautiful.

CHAPTER 6

CASSANDRA

"W here are you going?" Abelita asked from the doorway, grinning as Cassandra glanced back at her.

"I'm just meeting up with a friend," she answered, trying to keep her voice light because Abelita might be one of her best friends, but she didn't know about Black Light — and talking about it was an absolute no-no.

"A friend," Abelita repeated, doubt tainting her tone as she crossed her arms. "Is this friend a *guy?*"

"Maybe." Flipping through the clothes in her closet, her hand paused on a beautiful Givenchy top, but then she remembered how Logan had treated her silver one during Roulette and she shoved it aside. Grabbing out a much less expensive item, she turned to hold it up against her in the mirror, and Abelita sighed dramatically.

"If this is a date then you should dress for it. Take that bra off and put on the push-up bra I got you for Christmas." Her room-mate was already digging in her closet, and Cassandra turned away as she started to swap her bras.

"It's not a date."

"Sure. You're back in town four days and already going out with a guy, a 'friend.' Let me guess, he saw you walking the runway today, and he's already in love with you? Wants to wine and dine you?" Abelita grinned over her shoulder at her because she knew exactly how Cassandra reacted to guys like that. "Why did you say yes?"

"I didn't say yes to a date, I said yes to meeting up."

"That's a date."

"It's *not* a date!" Cassandra laughed, walking back to the closet to bump her hip against Abelita's as she scanned the clothes. "It's just fun."

"Oooo, he must be hot as hell if you just want to get laid." Abelita lifted her eyebrows a few times before she chuckled and tugged out a little black dress. "If you're trying to keep it casual, then go with the old reliable."

"This is sleeveless," she answered as she took it from her.

"It's going to be sixty degrees, you won't freeze." Abelita smacked her hip and nudged her toward the mirror. "Go on, put it on."

"Why do you always act like a stylist around me?"

"Because you'd happily walk around L.A. in sweatpants if I didn't pester you," Abelita retorted, grinning at her in the mirror as Cassandra slid the dress on and smoothed it. She couldn't argue that fact, but sweatpants were in style sometimes. The whole cute, just-rolled-out-of-bed look, and she could pull that off.

Not that she wanted to do that tonight.

That fucking kiss had been... fire. It was all she'd been able to think about all afternoon. Well, *that* and every minute of their time at Roulette, because Logan had been right. She had thought of him, more than once. Alone in various hotel rooms with her hand between her thighs, remembering every sharp note of pain and every earth-shattering orgasm as he'd teased her with that damn Hitachi while he'd worked his fist inside her.

Logan fucking Chisholm.

Rich boy with a crush, used to getting everything he wanted without ever having to work for it... but he had a flair for dominance that made her knees weak.

"Wear these with it," Abelita said, holding up her thigh-high black boots, and Cassandra grinned.

"Those are perfect!"

"Of course they are." Rolling her eyes, Abelita went back to the closet to dig around again. She was in a pair of jeans that hugged her long legs, and a slashed gray top that showed off her ample cleavage. Abelita was a model too, and her curves meant she did a lot of commercial work for lingerie — although Abelita had done a few runway shows too, with her ultimate goal to walk for Victoria's Secret. For the past two years they'd crossed fingers and toes hoping for a call back, but VS hadn't even called her back for a catalog shoot yet.

It'll happen.

Cassandra believed that good things happened if you believed in them. Think positive thoughts and positive things happen, then you just let the rest roll off your back. Abelita had a similar mindset, it was why they'd ended up as roommates — and a part of Cassandra couldn't help but wonder if all the time she'd spent thinking about Logan Chisholm had made him seek her out. With his good looks, his money, and that air of asshole'ish dominance around him, he probably had women throwing themselves at him all the time.

So why me, Logan?

The thought rolled around in her head as she pulled on the boots and stood. They added a few inches to her height, which meant she was over six feet tall. Almost as tall as Logan. *Perfect.* Spinning around, she checked herself in the mirror, and Abelita thrust a multi-colored kimono cardigan at her.

"If you really think you're going to get cold, then wear this."

Cassandra reached over to run her fingers over the silk, but she pulled back and looked at herself in the mirror. With her hair still done from the show, and her makeup touched up, she looked fierce in just the black dress and boots. A reminder to Logan that she wasn't a meek, quiet submissive who would bow and grovel to his every whim. She'd never been into service submission, or humiliation, but under the right circumstances she loved being told what to do.

It was just that there were so few guys strong enough to face off with her personality, and she wasn't going to dim her light just to make them happy.

Logan didn't back down.

Sighing, she had to admit that her brain seemed a lot more confident in Logan than she did. It was her heart that had nervous energy tickling under her skin, because — while she definitely wanted another night with him — Logan Chisholm wanted more. She could sense it in him, even though it was already painstakingly obvious from the fact that he'd tracked her down at the show.

Men didn't do that for a booty call.

They did it for someone they really wanted, and Logan had been honest about that, which is why playing with him again, fucking him again, was probably a huge mistake.

In ten months they hadn't managed to meet up once, and this would only end tragically. For him.

"What's wrong?" Abelita asked, tucking the kimono back into the closet before she moved closer to rub her back. "You look super sad all of a sudden."

"Maybe I shouldn't meet up with him. I think he wants more than just something fun and—"

"Cassandra, seriously, you don't have to take care of everyone. He's a big boy, and if you made it clear what you're showing up for, and he agreed, then why fuck with it?" Pulling her into a hug, Abelita squeezed her tight. "You're allowed to just have fun, okay?"

"But—"

"No buts!" Abelita announced, leaning back to grab her by the shoulders. "You're going to go out, have some fun, and come back in the morning and tell me all about how big his dick was and how he rocked your world." She tilted her head, grinning. "Or how spectacularly disappointing he was, and if it's that one then we'll have mimosas for breakfast."

"And pancakes," Cassandra added, and Abelita groaned.

"Fine! But, my God, not everyone has your metabolism, Cass."

Grinning, Cassandra pecked her on the cheek and snagged her clutch from the bed. As she pulled out her phone to request a car, she was tempted to tell Abelita she didn't need to worry about pancakes in the morning. Cassandra already knew just how good Logan was, both during a scene *and* in bed, which was just one more reason tonight could be a total disaster.

The truth of it was, if things were really as good as she remembered… then it wasn't just Logan's heart she was worried about.

CHAPTER 7

LOGAN

*H*e'd been sitting at the bar for over half an hour, staring at his watch and then the door and then his empty glass. Rinse and repeat.

"Ready for another?" Susie asked, leaning on the bar so that her breasts almost popped out of her top. Any other night he'd have enjoyed the view, but right now she was just reminding him of the second drink he *shouldn't* have, and why.

Where are you, Cassandra?

"No thanks, I'm good." As his watched ticked to 8:02, he tried not to let his mind wander through the litany of what-ifs that were awaiting him. What if she doesn't show up? What if she changed her mind? Blahblahfuckingblah.

"You sure? You look tense as hell."

"I'm good. Just run it on my account," he answered curtly, standing to dig out his wallet and put a twenty down to tip. The cash was quickly swiped off the bar, and it meant she left him in peace.

Well, relative peace.

His head was still spinning in circles, which was *not* normal for him.

Snagging his duffel bag from the floor, Logan wandered past the other members who were socializing, laughing, and parked himself against the wall by the door. It was quieter near the entrance, less likely that anyone would talk to him, and he needed a fucking minute to center himself before Cassandra showed up — because she *was* going to show up.

He knew she would.

Kissing her like that had been a ballsy move, but he'd never been one to play it safe, and it had paid off. She'd felt the spark between them, the same one they'd both felt the night of Roulette. There was no way in hell she hadn't felt it. He could still remember the sensation of her hands fisting his shirt to pull him closer, the hungry way she'd kissed him back. There hadn't been any reticence there, and although she'd refused to call tonight a date… she was still coming.

She will be here.

Groaning, he knocked his head back against the wall and forced a deep, slow breath. All of this bullshit wasn't him — the nervousness, the begging her to say yes, the tracking her down four months after she'd even sent a text — this shit was what pathetic guys did. He was always in control, always the guy people turned to for guidance, for answers. He spent every damn day at work being one hundred percent on top of everything, running a multi-million-dollar company with confidence, but just thinking about Cassandra Moreira had his palms sweating like a goddamn pre-teen working up the balls to ask out the hottest girl in school.

He dropped the duffel bag at his side, nudging it with his shoe as he checked his watch again. 8:09. Almost ten minutes late. Clenching his jaw, he decided that was exactly how he planned to start things as soon as his bratty submissive showed up for the evening. One swat for every minute she was late, one for every eye roll, and if that meant they didn't start for another half an hour he was just fine with that. Her ass would be on fire before he even started with what he'd planned out that afternoon.

The door beside him opened, and he stood up straight, only to be disappointed as a couple walked in, the guy leading his sub with a firm grip on her wrist.

Someone's already in trouble.

Logan grinned to himself as he watched them grab a table, the woman sliding to her knees beside the man's chair as he leaned down to tell her something. The whole visual had his dick waking up in his pants, and he tore his eyes away from them to look at his watch again. 8:10. Oh, he was going to light her ass up. Not a single one of them would be warm-up spanks either. She liked to play hard, and he already knew what she could handle, so he'd give it to her right off the bat.

Naughty girl, where the fuck are you?

Just as his watch ticked to 8:11, the door opened... and he saw her. Cassandra took a few steps past him, her gaze sweeping across the room as she searched the bar and the tables, and he snuck up directly behind her.

Getting as close as he could without touching her, he leaned in and said, "Boo."

Cassandra jumped, spinning around to smack him in the chest as she laughed. "Logan! Christ, you scared me!"

"Good," he answered, reveling in the lingering panic that had her breathing faster and her pulse jumping at her throat. "You're late."

"Traffic," she said, rolling her eyes. *That's one, plus the two from earlier.* "I texted you from the Lyft."

"No phones inside the club, remember?"

"Shit." She bit down on her lip a little before she shrugged. "Well, I'm here now!"

"Eleven minutes late," he scolded, and she rolled her eyes again. *Four.*

"The hard-ass routine doesn't work on me, Logan," she

sassed, and he caught her by the arm and spun her around, backing her up until she collided with the wall. Her honey eyes were wide and only went wider as he slid his other hand up her throat to catch her jaw in a firm grip.

"I know it's been a while, Cassandra, so I'll remind you. In here, you refer to me as *sir*. You do whatever I tell you, or I'm going to make you very, very sorry." Leaning in close, he almost touched his lips to hers, but stopped short. "And the only thing that's going to stop me is your safe word, which is red, per house rules. Understand?"

Cassandra swallowed, the bump of it moving against his hand as her breathing picked up a bit. Then a smile slipped over her lips. "Not even going to buy me a drink first?"

"This isn't a date," he retorted, smirking. "You made that choice. *And* you forgot to address me as sir, so that's another swat already."

Laughing softly, she stared right into his eyes as she asked, "How many am I up to, *sir*?"

"Eleven minutes late, four eye rolls today, and one missed sir. That's sixteen before we even get to start the scene I have planned." Squeezing her jaw, he forced her head back just a bit, reveling in the way her eyes flickered closed for a second before meeting his gaze again. "Want to make it seventeen?"

"Maybe." Cassandra grinned. "Sir."

"Little brat," he growled and kissed her. When she tried to reach for him, he caught her wrists and pinned them to the wall, making sure she understood exactly who was in charge tonight — and it wasn't her and her smart mouth. Just like that afternoon, kissing her was like mainlining electricity, and he felt the buzz of her moan as he nipped her lip and went back for more. With his body pressed against hers, feeling every wiggle of her hips, it was an act of God to pull himself back and focus enough to follow protocol. "What's your safe word?"

"Red," she answered, panting a little. He tilted his head at her, letting his grin spread, and finally she laughed a little and added, "Sir."

"Good girl," he purred, keeping one hand on her wrist to tug her off the wall as he snatched his duffel bag from the floor. He didn't hesitate to drag her across the bar and through the curtain into the play area.

Only a few other couples were here this early, but that was fine with him. He didn't mind an audience, but he didn't need one either. This was about him and Cassandra. Scanning the space, he saw an empty couch and headed toward it, stopping about ten feet away.

"Kneel." The command came out easily, all of the nervous energy falling away as the familiar surroundings of Black Light let him slip into the controlled state of mind he needed. Turning away, he didn't keep his eyes on her, not wanting to reward any hesitation with recognition — or give her the opportunity to mouth off again.

Not yet anyway.

Walking away from Cassandra, he dropped the duffel bag by the couch and unbuttoned the cuffs of his shirt. He'd left his suit jacket with coat check just so he wouldn't have to keep track of it, and as he started to roll up his sleeves, he turned slightly to his side. Most of his back was still to where Cassandra *should* be kneeling, but that was on purpose. Brats liked their antics to be seen, they wanted the reaction, and he was going to make it clear he wouldn't tolerate it tonight. Not here.

Finally, Logan finished rolling his sleeves up his forearms and he turned to look at her, glancing up before he faked nonchalance as he adjusted his shirt, making sure each sleeve was even. But he'd seen her. How he'd missed that sexy black dress, or the thigh-high boots, he had no idea… because she was fucking delicious.

Pointing to the floor at his feet, he met her eyes. "Crawl to me."

The flash of fire in her gaze had the corner of his mouth twitching to smile, but he kept his face clear of it. She glanced around, shaking her head before she looked at him again. "I'm not into humiliation, Logan."

"You just got to seventeen. Want to make it eighteen for being disobedient?"

He was pretty sure she cursed under her breath as she leaned forward to crawl, but he wasn't going to count off for that. He liked her dirty mouth, and the brazen things she said, and she could curse all she wanted as long as she called him sir and did what he told her to.

Damn.

This had to be the best view in all of Black Light. Cassandra Moreira on all fours, her lean curves swaying with each movement, and as short as that dress was anyone walking through the curtain behind her was going to get an eyeful of her perfect ass. Not like his perspective wasn't incredible. The neckline of her dress scooped down, letting him see her cleavage every time she lifted her head to glare at him.

Feisty little brat.

When she finally settled at his feet, sitting back on her heels, he leaned down to pinch her chin. "Good girl."

Her slow smile showed just how much she wanted to smart off, but instead all that passed her lips was a sarcastic, "Thank you, sir."

Fake, sugary sweetness had tainted every word, and he chuckled as he lifted her chin, craning her neck back. "Stand up and take this dress off for me. You can leave the boots on for now."

Logan held out a hand to help her up, and she looked at it for a long second before she sighed and accepted it, letting him help her to her feet.

"You're so strange. *Sir.*"

He chuckled, moving back to enjoy the show as she bundled

the fabric to her hips, making her big hair bounce as she pulled it over her head in one sweeping motion. There wasn't even a tiny hint of hesitation to her undressing, but he imagined she spent a lot of time half-naked around people as a model. That thought sparked a flare of jealousy inside him, but he pushed it away because there were so many better things to focus on. Every inch of her warm brown skin made his fingers itch to touch her. He could be patient though, because that would happen soon enough. "How am I strange?"

"You can be such a pushy asshole, and then you do the gentleman thing like it's no big deal," she answered, laughing as she tossed the dress onto the arm of the couch behind him. "It's strange, but it makes you interesting."

Shrugging, he didn't argue the fact that he was a pushy asshole, or that he'd been raised to be a gentleman at all times — and, like a gentleman, he allowed almost a full thirty seconds before he grinned. "That's eighteen."

"God dammit," she muttered under her breath as she shook her head, but her smile was sunshine bright when she looked at him again.

"Been a while?" he asked, stepping closer to slide his hand along the curve of her waist, resting it on her hip to squeeze.

"About ten months," she replied, still smiling, but his thoughts stumbled as she quickly added, "Sir."

Wait, is she serious?

"You haven't played since Roulette?"

"Not a lot of time to track down the local BDSM club when I'm traveling for shoots or events, and the short times I've been back in town have kept me busy." Cassandra shrugged like it wasn't a big deal. "So, yeah, you could say I'm a little out of practice, sir."

Fuck. And he'd been playing the hard-ass on protocol.

"Well, then I guess you can be forgiven. We'll keep it at seventeen," he said, trying to play it off, but she scoffed.

"I don't need you to take it easy on me, *sir*. Or did you forget I'm not breakable?"

"You have such a mouth on you," he growled, catching her by the back of the neck to push her the last couple of feet to the couch. Sitting down, he hauled her across his lap in a single motion, yanking her ass into position to land the first hard spank. The sting burned *his* palm, so he knew she'd felt it, but all he got was a quick gasp. The next swat was firmer, making her ass shake, and he loved the way her body tensed. "Let me lay out the ground rules for tonight, my little brat."

"I am not—" she started to argue, and he cut her off with another hard smack of his palm, immediately adding a matching one to the other cheek.

"Every time you act like a brat, I'm going to make you suffer a little longer. Each time you forget to call me sir, you're going to wish you hadn't." *Smack.* "And whenever you think about being disobedient, remember that it was your choice to come to Black Light tonight. *You* chose this over dinner."

The next three spanks he added in quick succession, feeling the burn building in his hand as he focused each one on top of previous swats. Her hips wiggled over his lap, a sweet little sound slipping past her lips before she laughed. Propping herself up on her elbow, Cassandra twisted to look back at him. "Do you hear me complaining, sir?"

"I swear..." Logan landed the next one directly on her sit spot, concentrating there to punctuate each of his words with hard swats. "You. Are. Such. A. Brat."

She squirmed against him, waking his cock up all the way as she let out a satisfied little groan that almost sounded like a purr. "If this is how you treat brats, sir, then call me whatever you want."

Biting back his smile, he grabbed a handful of her ass and squeezed, reveling in the heat as he added up the spanks in his head. *Fourteen. Four more.* Cassandra felt way too good stretched over his thighs, and if he wanted to get to what he'd planned, he needed to get her off his lap.

Naughty girl.

"Oh, you're in so much trouble," he growled, landing another stinging swat.

CHAPTER 8

CASSANDRA

*H*er ass was on fire, but she loved it.
She loved *this.*

It was like she hadn't even let herself think about how much she craved the pain, the kink, the dominance and submission until Logan had pushed her up against the wall. Then it had all flooded back like a sinful tidal wave, and each fierce spank just sent another wave crashing over her.

How had she gone so long without this?

Smack! A fresh rush of fire spread out from his hand, and she bit back the moan as it blended in with the heat in her skin. It hurt in the best way. Logan wasn't playing around tonight, and she appreciated it. She didn't want to waste time reminding him of what she was capable of taking, and the fact that he remembered what she liked had her smiling into her arms as another hard spank landed right on her sit spot.

Hissing air between her teeth, she lifted one foot off the couch without thinking about it, but she slammed it back down when he chuckled above her.

"Aww, did that one sting?" he mocked, and she laughed.

"Maybe a little." Another crack of his hand seemed to echo

off the walls as he laid the swat directly over the same sensitive place, and she groaned with that intoxicating blend of pleasure and pain as the endorphins rushed through her system like delightful little soldiers. Her entire ass felt like it was glowing, and when he stroked his hand up her thighs to squeeze one cheek she bit down on her lip.

"How do you address me at Black Light?" he asked, his voice edged with a growl that went straight between her thighs.

"Sir," she answered, and he shifted under her, his cock pressing into her side, but she'd seen his restraint during Roulette, and she had no doubt it would be a while before he fucked her.

What scene have you come up with, Logan?

His hand moved slowly, stroking over her ass and down her thigh before gliding back up on the inside. It sent a shiver through her as he got so close to where she wanted his touch — but he reversed, sliding back down her opposite thigh. Then he repeated the movement again. Ass, thigh, and then up the path between her legs, only to stop short.

"Toying with me, sir?" she asked, leaning up so she could turn to see him. His gaze was focused on her ass for another minute as he continued his maddening strokes, but he eventually paused with his hand just inches from her underwear, looking over at her with a wicked grin.

"I'm just getting started," he replied, swatting her hard before completely lifting his hands from her. "Time to get up."

"What?" The surprise in her voice wasn't fake as she rolled to her side on his lap, staring at him.

He just stared back, lifting his eyebrows the tiniest fraction, and she groaned.

"Sir," she added, and he chuckled as he folded his hands behind his head.

"Go on. Get up."

Shaking her head, she laughed under her breath as she

climbed off his lap, planting her boots on the floor to stand. Logan Chisholm looked absolutely gorgeous reclining on the couch, his blond hair caught in that perpetual just-fucked state that made her want to run her hands through it. In that position, his button down stretched nicely across his muscular chest, and although she knew he was quite a bit older than her... he made it look good. Everything about him had her squeezing her thighs together in anticipation, but it was his blue eyes that had her attention for the moment.

That devious little glint in them held so many promises.

His gaze roamed over her curves, and it was almost like she could feel every place he looked. A tingling rush of memory from the last time he'd really touched her, up against the wall. *That wall*, she thought as her eyes flicked over to the space near the pool, remembering just how good it had felt to have him inside her, her legs wrapped around his hips as he made every thrust count.

Fuck.

Cassandra could feel the heat in her cheeks, and she just hoped that he couldn't tell she was blushing, but his grin as he stood told her he had an idea.

"No sass?" he asked, tilting his head.

"I've got plenty, sir."

He chuckled. "Oh, I know that. I've been aware of your brat side since Roulette."

"You keep calling me a brat, sir, but I'm not. I don't throw tantrums," she retorted, grinning at him.

"I didn't call you a little, Cassandra. Brats have many flavors, and your sassy mouth and attitude are one hundred percent brat."

"So, you don't want me to call you Daddy?" she asked, and a groan rumbled through his chest as he caught her by the waist and pulled her tightly against him.

His lips brushed against her ear, a warm rush of breath

sending a chill rushing over her skin just before he growled, "I've never really been into that... but if you get the urge when you're begging later, feel free to try it out."

Goddamn.

If her underwear wasn't soaked already, it was now. Cassandra's mouth felt dry as he dug his fingers into her hips and leaned back, skating his gaze over the meager cleavage Abelita's gift had managed to create.

"Ready?" he asked, grinning, and she tried to shake off the image he'd planted in her head as she nodded. "Good girl."

Logan turned away to grab his duffel bag from the floor, tossing her dress over his shoulder before he caught her by the back of the neck. Under any other circumstances she would have punched a guy in the throat for this kind of demeaning direction, but with Logan it felt natural.

Hell, it felt *good.*

She liked the way his fingers pinched in just enough for her to feel the strength in his hands, a public display of dominance and possession as he pushed her past the pool and up the steps into the dim hallway where all of the fantasy suites were tucked away. They didn't have to go far though, because the little screen outside the door in front of them read 'Reserved' and Logan walked her right to it.

"Inside," he commanded as he opened it, releasing her neck to swat her ass again.

"Yes, sir," she answered with a laugh, moving forward into the playroom that looked exactly like a doctor's office. The walls were stark white, and the ominous metal cabinets glinted in the bright, clinical light. But, the centerpiece of the room was the padded exam table, complete with a strip of paper running down its center. "So, do I call you doctor, now?"

"Sir is fine," Logan replied as he shut the door. Not that it mattered, since the huge window in the wall meant anyone wandering down the hall could see everything they did. It did make it a lot quieter though, muffling the music the club kept on as Logan put his duffel bag up on the counter next to the tiny sink.

Moving to the exam table, Cassandra turned and hopped up onto it. Listening to the paper crinkle as she leaned back to grin at him. "I don't know... dirty doctor sounds like a lot of fun."

Logan glanced at her from where he was gathering things from the drawers, a handful of shiny devices that he dropped onto a little metal tray with a clatter. "Did I say you could get on the table yet?"

"No, sir," she answered. Spreading her knees a little, she watched his eyes flicker down before coming back to hers with a hard expression.

"Up," he commanded, but she lingered, curious what Logan would do when she wasn't tied down to a spanking bench. It only took a second for him to close the gap between them, a hard grip finding the back of her neck as he yanked her off the table and immediately turned her around to bend her over it. Shoving her down with his hold on her neck, he spanked her again and again. Brilliant flashes of burning pain had the heat returning fast, accompanied by the sting with each crash of his palm, and she knew she was thoroughly soaked when he finally stopped.

Breathing harder, head spinning, Cassandra tried to find something clever to say, but then he was pressed against her. Leaning over her back with his hand still on her neck, controlling her, holding her down while he ground his dick against her ass.

Fuck.

It was the weight of him pinning her down, or the hard bulge she could feel trapped behind his slacks, or the combination of both that kept her tongue still. All she wanted was to feel him inside her again, and she squirmed under him to get it, rubbing against his erection until he smacked her hip.

"Naughty girl," he purred, nipping the skin over her ribs. "You're trying to push my buttons."

"Seems like I'm succeeding," she quipped, and he delivered a mock thrust as he landed another swat.

"Oh, my little brat, you *wish* I'd fuck you right now. I've got way more self-control than that." Chuckling, Logan released the back of her neck, leaning up to unhook her bra with a flick of his fingers. Then he stepped back, his fingers finding the edge of her underwear to drag them down her thighs, over her boots, and then he tapped each ankle to make her lift her feet free of the delicate lace.

"Not tearing my clothes this time, sir?" she asked, propped up on her elbows to turn and look at him. Logan stood up and shook his head, her underwear dangling from one of his fingers.

"Do you want these in your mouth, or do you want to be able to beg?" The words shot straight between her thighs, and she honestly couldn't decide which option sounded hotter, but he chose for her when he tucked them into his pocket. "Never mind. I definitely want to hear you begging."

"Confident, aren't you?" Cassandra grinned as she turned onto her side, laughing a little as his gaze trailed over her, a blaze of hunger in his pale blue eyes before he dragged them back up to her face.

"That you'll be begging?" He smirked and wrapped his hands around her thighs, flipping her onto her back in a smooth move that bent her knees and pushed her thighs wide — leaving him in an excellent position between them. "Absolutely."

"You're so cocky." Her eyes trailed down to the bulge in his slacks. "Sir. Especially since you didn't get me to beg during Roulette."

"Really? I seem to remember you saying a lot of '*please please please*' while I had my fist inside you." Logan had mocked her, adding a breathy tone to the words, and she couldn't help but laugh.

"Okay, you're right, I probably said please." She shrugged. "I still don't think that counts as begging, sir."

"Guess I'll just have to try harder tonight," he replied, not seeming to be even the smallest bit fazed by her comment. Sliding his hands up the backs up her thighs, and then down the slope of her calves, he set her heels down on the edge of the table. "Now it's time to take these incredibly sexy boots off for your exam."

"You like these, sir?" she asked, watching as Logan grabbed one of her boots to start pulling it off, and she twisted her foot inside it to help him. "My roommate picked them for the outfit."

"She has excellent taste." With one final tug he got the first boot off, walking to the wall to set it out of the way.

"Who says my roommate is a girl?" Cassandra loved the flicker in his expression before that mask of self-control descended again.

Was that jealousy?

"Whoever it is has excellent taste then," Logan corrected, and she laughed as he grabbed the second boot to repeat the process. This one took a little more effort, and he ended up stumbling back a step when her leg finally came free, grumbling under his breath.

"Her name is Abelita," she finally said, having some mercy on Mr. Serious, and Logan sighed, shaking his head as he went to set the boot next to its match.

"Do you fuck with everyone like this? Or are you just a brat with me?" he asked as he came back to the table, pulling one of her wrists above her head to loop a built-in cuff around it, tightening it with a sharp jerk.

"I don't take life too seriously, sir." Cassandra watched his face as he threaded the cuff back through, walking around the back of the table to tether her other wrist down as well. He looked so intense, but that seemed to be his default expression when she wasn't making him smile or laugh. "*You* might benefit from doing that more often."

"Doing what?" he asked, looking down at her as he finished cuffing her arms above her head.

"Not taking life so seriously."

"Right." Logan scoffed, reaching over her to place a hand on the table beside her ribs while the other trailed up her side, circling the outside of her breast. His gaze avoided hers, staring instead at her nipple as it slowly tightened into a peak without him ever touching it. It was the teasing touch that kept sweeping so close without ever actually reaching the sensitive bud that caused it, sending a shiver over her skin and bringing both nipples to attention.

"You don't believe me?" she asked, her voice a little breathier than before as the slow burn of arousal spread.

"I just don't think that mindset works for everyone. I'd get eaten alive in the boardroom if I was laid back, relaxed. People don't follow weak leaders. Shareholders wouldn't have faith. Stock prices would plummet." He switched sides, leaning his hip against the exam table so his other hand could repeat the teasing traces on her other breast.

"Do you think I'm weak?"

"What?" His eyes snapped up to hers, crystal clear blue, brow furrowed in brief confusion before it smoothed, replaced with irritation. "That's not what I meant, and you know it."

"Mmhmm," she murmured, grinning, and he suddenly pinched her nipple between his fingers and twisted. The sharp shock of pain had her back arching, a gasp ripped past her lips, but he just as quickly let go. Laughing, she looked down at her breast and then back up at him. "Sensitive, are we, sir?"

Clenching his jaw, Logan walked away from the table to dig in his bag. He wasn't answering her, and she knew it was because he didn't want to admit the bullshit he was spewing. Mr. Serious had to be serious or his job was on the line? *Please.*

If anything, he'd probably find work easier if he didn't let every little thing bother him.

"How old are you?" she asked, and he looked back at her with another flash of irritation. "Sir?" she added with a grin.

Sighing heavily, he dropped a few things on the metal tray beside him before he looked at her again. "Why does that matter?"

"Curiosity."

"I'm thirty-eight. I was thirty-seven when we played before and you seemed perfectly happy about it." There was a defensiveness in his tone that made her fight the smile that wanted to spread across her lips.

Why is he so easily riled? Age is nothing but a number.

"I'm still perfectly happy playing with you. I was just curious about how many years you've spent without knowing how to have fun in life."

Logan chuckled, shaking his head as he picked up the metal tray and set it on a tiny, wheeled table a little harder than necessary. Then he dragged the table and a short, rolling stool back over to the table, but he didn't sit down. Instead, he moved between her legs and leaned over her, planting his hands on either side of her. "I absolutely know how to have fun, and *that* is what tonight is supposed to be, isn't? Not a date and not a game of twenty questions?"

"You're right, sir. I'm sorry." There was no biting back the grin this time and he groaned as he stood back up.

"You are incorrigible." A loud *clunk* came from under the table just before he swung out one of the stirrups, unfolding it until he could place her foot in it. "Fortunately, I know how to deal with bratty submissives."

"Not a brat," she sing-songed, and he groaned as he started to strap her ankle into the conveniently attached cuff.

"Don't make me gag you, Cassandra. I really do want to hear you beg."

"We'll see, sir," she replied, and she could see him fighting a smile as he brought out the second stirrup and tethered her to it.

"Try and close your legs for me," he commanded, and she rotated her knees in, easily closing them.

"That's what I thought." Heading back to his duffel, he came back with two bundles of bright blue rope. Dropping one on her stomach, he unwound the other and started wrapping one thigh in a trio of pretty diamond shapes.

"Shibari?" she asked, more than a little impressed at his easy confidence with the rope as he finished and drew the rope tight, tying it off to the stirrup's metal arm.

"I've been taking classes here on different things, and the ones on rope have been some of my favorites." Starting on her other leg, he glanced up at her. "*Someone* said I wasn't very creative, and I've never been one to miss an opportunity to improve my skills."

Biting down on her lip, she felt a laugh threatening to bubble up. "Did I say that?"

"You did. During Roulette." The rope jerked sharply, spreading her thighs wide as he tied it off. The trio of diamond shapes on each thigh were beautiful, and there was no way in hell she was going to be able to close them now.

"Oops?" she offered, and he chuckled.

"Yeah. Oops covers it." Reaching over to the metal tray, he lifted a silver butt plug in the air, showing her the sparkly blue stone in the base. "Speaking of Roulette, I seem to remember how much you liked this last time, so I wanted to bring it back."

Groaning, she let her head drop back to the table. She had definitely *not* liked him working that plug in and out before he'd started paddling her, and he knew it.

"I brought a larger one too, just in case you felt like being extra sassy." Logan was wearing his grin with pride now, settling onto the doctor's stool as he wheeled it between her thighs. "Of course, we'll start your exam with this one just to see how you feel."

"So kind, sir," she mumbled. The sound of a rubber glove snapping on brought her head back up. "Sure you don't want me to call you doctor?"

"I think you'll call me a few different things before the exam is over." The cold plug slid over her clit and down through her folds, and she felt her fists clench as a chill ran over her skin. Then he pushed it into her pussy, and she jumped.

"That's cold!"

"I know, I'm warming it up first." There was definitely laughter in his voice as he spun it inside her, pumping it back and forth. "Look at this, you're already so wet. I'll definitely have to mark that in your chart."

"Ha. Ha."

"Hold onto this for me," he said, leaving the plug sitting inside her, and she instinctively clenched around it as he popped the top on a bottle of lube. The grin on his face turned him from cute to hot in an instant, and she groaned as he leaned in close, letting his warm breath brush over her most sensitive parts before he pulled at the plug. "I need this back now."

"And here I thought you didn't have a sense of humor, sir."

Logan just shook his head as he reached forward, and she felt the cool smear of lube across her ass, followed too quickly by the press of his gloved finger. She tensed instantly, and he laughed low. "Relax."

"Easy for you to say," she muttered, before quickly adding, "sir."

It was good advice though, and she took a deep breath and forced her muscles to relax, feeling that odd sensation of wrongness as his finger dipped inside.

"Not so bad," he said in a faux concerned voice and she leaned up to glare at him, prepared to make a smartass remark, but then he rested the butt plug on her lower stomach, and she stayed silent. Holding it in place with his fingers, he slid his thumb down over her clit and her hips lifted instinctively. "See?"

Chewing on her lower lip, Cassandra dropped back to the exam table with a sigh as he started slow, teasing circles over her clit, the rhythm matched perfectly by his finger in her ass. Pleasure was a slow spiral, nothing rushed about it, and she tried to just ride it, enjoy it. But just as she started to rock her hips, there was the click of the lube bottle and a second finger joined the first at her ass, pushing in until she felt her body stretching to accommodate. She swallowed the whine in her throat, knowing it was what he wanted, and — well — maybe she was a bit of a brat, because she didn't want to give him the pleasure of knowing he was getting to her.

"So quiet. Did I find your mute button?" He thrust his fingers deeper into her ass and she groaned, but his thumb picked up speed on her clit, balancing out the small discomfort. Still, she couldn't let that go without a comment.

"Isn't tonight supposed to be about fun, sir?" she asked, leaning up to look at him, and he arched an eyebrow at her.

"I'm having a lot of fun, aren't you?" His laugh as she lay back on the table was worth it. Mr. Serious was enjoying warming her ass up for that stupid, sparkly butt plug, and he looked positively sinful between her thighs.

And he definitely knows what he's doing.

Heat was spreading between her thighs, inching its way up her spine as pleasure built, and although she'd never admit it to him… the feeling of his fingers working back and forth in her ass was a naughty thrill. Then, as if he could read her mind, he pulled them out and grabbed the plug with a wicked chuckle.

"You do have a beautiful ass," he mused as he added more lube. Standing up from the stool, he placed the cool metal tip against her hole and met her gaze. His thumb rolling slow circles over her clit, he started to push it in, but too soon it was stretching her again and she bit down on her lip to keep the whine inside. "God, the expressions you make…"

"What?" she asked, clenching her teeth as he let the plug slide back a little and then pushed it forward more firmly.

"I wanted to make sure I could see you this time, and it's so worth it." Logan glanced back between her legs, working the plug back and forth before holding it at her limit. "You're going to take this plug, Cassandra. You're going to take it because I want you to, and even if you think it's going to hurt, I want you to take a deep breath and accept it."

She just stared at him as he eased back for a second, only to push harder when it returned.

"Say 'yes, sir.'" It was a command, said in that low, intense tone that had first caught her attention during Roulette, and all she could do was obey.

"Yes, sir," she said, and then he forced the plug forward, a whine slipping past clenched teeth as her body stretched around it, and then it was in. Breathing hard, Cassandra relaxed against the exam table, but he wasn't done. He tugged on it, pulling it back out as she gasped, and then he held it at the widest point as she tried to squirm. A sharp smack over her clit made her body jolt with the sudden sting, and she lifted her head to stare at him.

"Be still," he ordered her, but before she could smart off, he put his thumb back on her clit and started rubbing again. "It's not as bad as you think it is, Cassandra."

"Have *you* had one of these in your ass?" she asked the ceiling, and he chuckled.

"Not my kink."

"It's not mine either!" Immediately, another spank over her clit had her groaning, and he pushed the plug in and pulled it out a few times without any distracting pleasure.

"That wasn't very polite," he chastised, but she could hear the damn grin in his voice. "Want to apologize?"

"No, *sir*," she answered, knowing she'd pay for it, but it was almost worth it when she heard him chuckle again. Another swat over her clit made her thighs jerk at the ropes, the sting making her sensitive flesh tingle, but he finally seated the plug in her ass and let go of it.

"My little brat…" Logan was shaking his head as he stood up, taking the glove off as he walked over to the trash to drop it in. "I told you I'd have you regretting the sass tonight."

"Upgrading the butt plug already?" she asked, watching him move to the tray to lift two tiny clips into the air, waving them back and forth.

"Not yet, I've got other plans first."

OTHER PLANS.

Two nipple clamps, twenty clothespins, and twenty minutes of a goddamn Hitachi were not just 'other plans.' It was a fucking battle plan.

Twisting against the cuffs, pulling on the ropes, Cassandra couldn't do anything but whine and pant as Logan pressed the Hitachi to her clit again and pleasure exploded. Every muscle in her body was tight, her skin coated in sweat, and she could feel the orgasm coming. It was right there, *so fucking close*, but just as she started to buck her hips against the vibrator — Logan yanked it back.

"SIR!" she shouted, barely holding back the frustrated tears burning her eyes as she dropped to the exam table again. The paper was torn, sticking to her skin, but she couldn't care about that.

"Aww, do you want to come?" Logan asked, his voice full of laughter as he plunged three fingers inside her again. Her back arched, and she was sure she babbled something as he tapped her g-spot in an off-rhythm pattern that only made her more needy. "You know what you need to do."

Beg.

He'd told her exactly what he was going to do as he applied each clothespin, alternating between teasing her clit and applying each wooden torture device. Logan Chisholm had promised to edge her until she was begging to come. Of course, he'd also told her that every smartass comment earned her another clothespin that would have to come off eventually.

Cassandra had earned twenty.

Really, she'd only earned nineteen. The last one she'd done on purpose to make it an even number... *and* because he'd told her it would be a bad idea to keep going.

"Okay then," Logan said, removing his fingers to bring the Hitachi back. It was impossible not to cry out, some garbled version of *ohmyfuckinggod* as she clenched her fists and tried to come before he took it away again. But Logan was watching her, devious fucking dom that he was, and just as that perfect horizon got close enough to taste... it was gone.

Bucking against the restraints, Cassandra worked her hips uselessly into empty air before going limp once more, fighting the urge to give in and beg.

"You're making a mess of the floor." He was chuckling, tracing his fingers through the flood between her thighs, teasing her oversensitive flesh. "Come on, Cassandra. Don't you want me to fuck you? Make you come again and again?"

"Yes, sir," she managed to say through clenched teeth.

"So polite," he praised, kissing the inside of her thigh. "You know you want to beg for it, my little brat."

"No, sir." She shook her head, taking deep breaths to try and calm down. It was stupid, but now she just wanted to win. Edged to hell and back, and maybe not allowed to come, but she would have won.

"You sure?" This time he pressed the Hitachi to the butt plug, sending vibrations echoing up through her body that were so good, but nowhere near enough to come. She could have handled that, could have held out, but then he leaned forward and slid his tongue through her folds until he reached her clit.

Oh God.

Logan only teased her for a second before he went for it, sucking and licking until she was pretty sure her ears were ringing from how hard her heart was racing. It was raw pleasure, so close to oblivion that she stopped breathing in anticipation of the climax — and then he laughed.

"You're going to kill me!" she whined, quickly adding, "Sir! Fuck! Sir!"

"Good catch. Here's the thing though... I'm not doing anything, Cassandra. This is all you." Rising from the stool, Logan kissed the inside of her knee as he moved the Hitachi to her thigh, slowly sliding it down, moving it closer and closer to where she so desperately needed it. "You're the one in control right now. Trust me, I want to watch you come apart. I want to watch you come until your eyes roll back in your head and you're begging me to *stop*."

All she could do was whine, because if she opened her mouth, she was going to give in.

"You decide when this ends, beautiful," he added, more light-hearted than she'd ever heard him as he circled her clit with that damn vibrator. He waited, giving her time to be smart, but then the Hitachi was back.

Everything in her focused down to the rising promise of bliss, the heat rushing in her veins, pooling between her thighs, so ready to explode, and over all of the chaos inside she could hear him.

"Beg me for it, Cassandra."

A command.

Tears brimmed in her eyes as he brought her to the very edge again and lifted the Hitachi away just as she almost made it. For a split second she thought she might still come, her body so tense that she was teetering on the verge of a stellar orgasm… but then it slipped away. Faded back just enough that she knew it was impossible. It was the final straw. Without even realizing it, she was crying. Pure frustration, but crying nonetheless, and as her breath shuddered with the first pathetic sounds of breaking, she felt him rubbing her knee. Soothing her.

Logan didn't say a word, because he knew he didn't have to. He'd won, and now he was just waiting for her to admit defeat. And as much as she wanted to win, she needed to come more.

"Please," she whimpered, and his thumb stilled on her knee. "Please, sir, please let me come?"

"God, you're so fucking hot," he growled, and then the Hitachi was back. Pressed firmly to her clit, yanking her back to the edge of bliss so fast that it tore the air from her lungs. Pleasure burned like wildfire through her veins, but her body was hesitant. A hundred near-misses of orgasm had twisted up all the signals, and for the longest moment of her life she hung in torturous near-ecstasy.

"Please, please, please, please!" Begging wasn't even a choice anymore, she needed to come more than she needed her next breath.

"Come for me, Cassandra," he commanded, gripping her knee tight as he pushed her leg just a little wider — and then the universe inverted. Everything went black for a second, her body overloading on pure light before it exploded, and she was pretty sure she screamed his name as pleasure set every cell inside her on fire. It was crippling ecstasy, so powerful that she couldn't get her eyes open again as she arched off the table, but Logan kept the Hitachi in place.

Too much, Jesus Christ, too much!

"Sir, please!" she managed to choke out, just before he ripped one of the clothespins off and the brilliant strike of pain sent her into another orgasm. Writhing, Cassandra shook her head back and forth, needing just one second to breathe, but it was like the floodgates had been opened. The merciless buzz of the Hitachi, combined with every pinch of pain as he removed another clothespin, had the orgasms piling on top of each other until she couldn't tell one from another.

Finally, the Hitachi lifted, and she gasped for breath, eyes opening to find Logan working at his shirt, his pants already undone. Her muscles were shaking, practically vibrating in an echo of the Hitachi, but she kept her head up just so she could watch. The button down was thrown to one side, and then he ripped the undershirt over his head, and she couldn't help but stare. He was firm muscle, no insane eight-pack, but she could see the definition in his stomach and the strength in his chest and arms.

"Such a good girl," he purred as he shoved his clothes out of the way so he could fist his cock. She pulled against the cuffs, trying to reach for him, and he moved closer. Tearing the foil of a condom wrapper with his teeth, he rolled it on just before he pressed against her. "Beg me."

As if she could argue right now.

"Please, sir," she whispered.

"Please what?" He grinned, leaning over her, but he still wasn't inside. Teasing, still fucking teasing after everything.

"Please fuck me, si—" The word didn't even finish before it was swallowed by a moan as he thrust deep on the first stroke, his groan practically feral. Then Logan kissed her, possessive and fierce. Sparks lit up the darkness behind her eyes, and she would have laughed at the visual if she could have managed a breath. Instead there was only him, above her, inside her, everywhere, and every touch was overwhelming. Still too sensitive, too close to the edge.

"You're incredible," he whispered against her lips, leaving her dazed as he started fucking her.

There was no warm-up, not like she needed one, but every stroke was dizzying. Every brush against her clit like the shock from a live wire, winding her up until she came again, crying out.

"Fuck, Cassandra…" His groan had her smiling as another wave of catastrophic bliss rolled through her nerves, amplified when he ripped another clothespin free.

It would have been pointless to try and bite back the moan, even if she'd had enough brain power left to try. Another clothespin *snick'd* as it gave one last bite to her skin and she clenched him tight.

Logan growled above her, pausing his thrusts to take another off, and then another, and somewhere her nerves got confused because the next one crossed wires in her brain and she came like he'd turned the goddamn Hitachi back on.

"Please, please," she babbled, unable to form any other words as he groaned and started thrusting again. Hard. Brilliant light wound through her, turning the world into a hazy glow as he filled her over and over.

"One more time, baby. One more," he urged, and she could feel how close he was, hear the way his breathing caught, and so she let go, letting the rush take her under again as he took off one of the nipple clamps. Pain clashed with bliss, another orgasm rocking her as she felt his cock jerk inside her, his low growl changing into a groan of pleasure right beside her ear. "Fuck…"

There was nothing she could say that would be any better than that, and she wasn't entirely sure her tongue would work at the moment anyway. Her muscles were a shivering mess, still shaking as he pressed her into the table, but she didn't care. His weight felt comforting in the chaos of her nerves, because after-shocks were still rolling through her. Involuntary tremors that had her tense one moment and boneless the next.

Logan lifted up enough to kiss her, but it was slow. Cool

water after the raging inferno that she was pretty sure had hollowed her out completely while easily taking the number one spot for best scene ever.

Probably best sex ever as well.

If she'd had the energy, she would have laughed, because it would have stroked his ego too much to know that he'd just beaten himself out for the number one spot.

Logan fucking Chisholm... what the hell am I going to do about you?

CHAPTER 9

LOGAN

*a*s soon as he'd been able to stand up, he'd removed the last clothespins as gently as possible. Shushing her and apologizing as he'd taken off the last nipple clamp — but goddamn, the sounds she'd made. Every sweet little whine ran like a buzz over his skin.

Cassandra wasn't exactly conscious, caught in that hazy middle ground where she groaned when he removed the buttplug and ran a warm cloth between her thighs, but she never even opened her eyes. Throwing everything into his duffel bag, he put the strap over his head so it wouldn't slip off while he was carrying her, and then he heard a very light series of taps at the door.

Walking over, he cracked the door to find Weston on the other side of it. The tall dungeon monitor had taught almost every rope class he'd attended, and he eased the door further open to accept the blanket the man was holding.

"Thanks," Logan said quietly, keeping his voice down. Weston smiled at him, glancing past him to where Cassandra was curled on her side, away from the windows where quite the crowd had gathered during their scene. It hadn't taken long to get her out of the rope and the cuffs, but even from here he could still see the lines embedded in her skin from her struggles.

"That was impressive," Weston whispered, slapping him lightly on the shoulder. "Well done."

"I had enough time to plan for it."

"Either way, you guys were the crowd favorite tonight." Chuckling softly, Weston nudged him toward her. "There's a bunch of chaos going on in the pool right now, so just be careful if you go that way. Slippery when wet and all that."

"Red light district any better?" Logan asked, and Weston rolled his eyes.

"Hell no." They both laughed under their breath, keeping their voices quiet, and then Weston offered his hand to shake. "I saw your rope work. Looking good, Logan."

"Thanks, Wes." Getting a compliment from a DM at Black Light could be like pulling teeth sometimes, and so Logan gladly shook the man's hand.

"We'll get the room cleaned up as soon as you're out, just take care of your girl." Weston leaned out into the hallway, looking down the row of rooms as he sighed. "I gotta handle something. Have a good night, man."

"You too." Heading back to Cassandra, he draped the blanket over her before he scooped her off the table. It took a bit of shifting, but he managed to get her covered without setting her back down. She was mumbling as he carried her into the hall, and he was relieved that their audience had dissipated, blending back into the club. As soon as he got to the steps down to the main play area, he heard the splashing. Then loud giggles, a scream, and he clenched his jaw, glancing at Cassandra to see if they were bothering her.

Blissfully unaware. *Good.*

She needed aftercare and quiet, and he hoped that one of the cool-down rooms was empty as he carried her across the main floor of Black Light. It was prime time for kink. After ten on a

Friday night was always busy, but it seemed more full than usual as he slipped past someone getting caned on a spanking bench and then had to sidestep a rough blowjob.

Finally, he got to the curtained rooms set aside for aftercare, and movement caught his eye. It was Elijah, the Dungeon Master for Black Light West — and he was headed straight for him at a quick pace. Groaning under his breath, Logan prepared to thwart a lecture on whatever the man thought he'd done wrong, because while Cassandra was light, he was also exhausted, and the last thing he wanted to do was make her stand up before she was ready.

"Hey, Logan—" Elijah started and Logan cut him off.

"Can this wait until I get her in a cool-down room?"

"That's what I'm over here for. Give me a minute to clear one." Elijah stepped past him to peek behind one curtain and then the other. He seemed to debate for a second before going back to the first curtain and speaking softly through it. After a moment, Elijah smiled. "Thanks, man."

"I appreciate it," Logan said, feeling like more than the usual level of asshole as Elijah grinned at him.

"Don't worry about it. I heard about your scene with her." Elijah laughed as he crossed his arms. "You're a mean sonuvabitch."

"I didn't—"

"Relax, it was a compliment." Another too-loud laugh escaped him and then he cut it short. "Shit, sorry. She totally out?"

Glancing down at Cassandra, he shifted her in his arms, and she made a soft noise. "Not totally, but it'll be a bit."

"I'll tell the DMs that cool-down one is occupied for now. Can you just leave the curtain open when you guys head out?" Elijah asked, moving out of the way as the previous couple exited the room. It was a pair of guys, one in a leather harness and nothing else, the other in just jeans, juggling a backpack, a bundle of clothes, and a blanket as he tried to wrap his boyfriend up in it.

"Sorry, one second," the guy said, halting his boyfriend who yawned sleepily, managing to grab onto the blanket as the one in jeans threw the strap over his shoulder and hurried back into the room for their shoes. "He fell asleep."

"No worries, brother," Elijah replied. "We appreciate you letting someone else use the room."

The dom smiled, glancing at Cassandra before he turned to Logan. "We wore them out early tonight."

"Yeah," Logan answered, offering a smile in return as the dom guided his boyfriend to a nearby couch to get him dressed.

"All yours! Thanks for waiting," Elijah said, giving a quick two-fingered salute before he turned back to the main floor.

Logan didn't hesitate, moving into the cool-down room to lay Cassandra on the deep chaise and close the curtain back. Dropping the heavy duffel bag, he unzipped it to take out their clothes, doing his best to shake out the wrinkles as he draped them over the chair against the back wall. He was about to take off his shoes when he saw the curtains move and then a hand reached in to set two bottles of water on the floor.

Weston.

Had to be the DM, because Elijah was probably already busy with something else. The next time he saw the guy off-duty, he needed to buy him a drink. For the shibari lessons, and the help tonight.

It took about thirty minutes for Cassandra to stir, but Logan would have been fine if she'd stayed exactly where she was. Her cheek pressed to his chest, curled up in his lap as he leaned against the back of the chaise.

Everything about it felt right.

More right than he had any right to feel, because it was only their second time playing. Ever. But he hadn't been able to get her out of his head for ten months, so it shouldn't have been a surprise that the connection was still there. He didn't have words for it, didn't know what to call it... All he knew was that Cassandra Moreira was something special, and there was no way in hell he was letting her walk away again.

She shifted against him, yawning and stretching, and he felt a smile tugging at his lips as he watched her. The rope marks on her thighs were fading, but he could see tiny bruises from the clamps in the dark brown of her nipples. All he wanted to do was take them into his mouth, soothe them with his tongue... but he was supposed to be letting her cool down right now.

"Logan?" she asked sleepily, looking up at him with a sweet little smile. "Hey."

"Hey," he said back, helping her sit up when she tried to on her own. "How are you feeling?"

"I'm fine." Rubbing her face, she looked around the tiny room, her brows pulling together.

"I brought you in here to rest. We're in one of the cool-down rooms, but there's no rush." Leaning over, he brushed his thumb across her cheek, smiling when she leaned into his palm. "You can lay back down for a bit longer, or we can head back to my place to sleep."

Her nose wrinkled for a second, and she turned to place a kiss on his palm before taking his hand into hers. "Logan..."

"I know, it's not a date. But I'm not putting you in a Lyft as dazed as you are. So, your options are that I either drive you to your place, or mine."

"You're doing it again," she said, her beautiful brown eyes meeting his gaze.

"Doing what?"

"The whole asshole but a gentleman thing," she answered,

but the end of it turned into a yawn that could have cracked her jaw.

Chuckling, Logan shrugged. "Well, as an asshole gentleman, I'm going to have to insist that you decide which house I'm driving you to, because I want you to eat something and get some sleep."

Cassandra groaned, but it ended with a smile. "Fine. My place. But you have to leave by ten."

"Any particular reason?" he asked, not wanting to push his luck, but curious all the same.

"I'm meeting friends for lunch." Cassandra swung her legs off the end of the chaise, then stretched again, and he took in every curve as she laughed softly. Glancing back at him, she sounded incredulous as she said, "I cannot *believe* you edged me like that."

"Believe it," he answered with a grin, standing up to grab her bra for her. Then he dug her underwear out of his pocket, and she rolled her eyes. "We *are* still inside Black Light, Cassandra."

"Yeah?" she replied, clearly not catching on as she put on her bra.

"I can still spank you for rolling your eyes."

Grinning, Cassandra stood up and moved in close, trailing her fingers over his ribs before catching the waist of his pants and pulling him against her. "You don't scare me, Logan."

"Good." The kiss was some combination of the two of them, both reaching for the other, but he moved his hand to the back of her neck to take control. Tasting her lips, her tongue, until all he wanted to do was drag her out of the room for round two — but she needed rest.

Although if he got her home fast enough, he *might* be able to squeeze in a second round before they both passed out.

That was all the incentive he needed to break the kiss, smiling at the soft sound she made as he looked into her eyes. "So, you've got plans tomorrow, but what about Sunday?"

Cassandra looked down, snagging her underwear from his hand, and then she stepped back to slip them on without answering. Irritated, Logan grabbed her arm gently, but he didn't let go when she pulled back. "Come on, Logan. Let go."

"Answer me," he demanded, and she just stared at him for a long moment. "What is going on in that head of yours, Cassandra? You had fun tonight, didn't you?"

"Obviously," she said, rolling her eyes again, and this time he turned her to the side and landed a hard spank on her ass without hesitation. Her mouth was open in surprise as she turned back to him, a laugh slipping out as she gawked at him. "I can't believe you did that!"

"You've really got to start believing me when I tell you something." Blowing out a breath, he tugged her closer. "And I already told you that I'd do whatever it takes for you to give this a chance, so why do you keep trying to walk away?"

"I'm not trying to walk away, it's—" Groaning, she shook her head. "Can we just talk about this in the morning? I'm fucking exhausted because *someone* made me come until I basically blacked out."

He knew it was a distraction, a stroke to his ego to get him to shut up, but it wasn't a no.

That's progress.

"Okay, fine. I want to get you home anyway, but we will talk about it in the morning." Once he let go of her arm, he passed her the dress and then gathered his clothes. Cassandra wasn't looking at him, and he couldn't figure out why.

Tonight had been amazing. Incredible.

There was no way in hell she didn't feel it too, and no matter what was holding her back, he was going to figure it out and overcome it.

CHAPTER 10

CASSANDRA

"Oh my God, it's so good to see you!" Vanessa cheered, hugging Cassandra tight.

"It is," Wyatt confirmed with a smile as they all took their seats, his eyes immediately dropping to the menu in front of him.

"I know, it's been months. Life has just been so crazy." Glancing at the menu, Cassandra skimmed it before looking up at Vanessa again. "How have *you* been? Last time I was in town I got to see you in *A Midsummer Night's Dream*, and that part was a big deal, right?"

"She was Hippolyta, and she out-danced Titania easily," Wyatt spoke up, looking at Vanessa like she hung the moon as the woman blushed.

"Wyatt," Vanessa groaned.

"You did leap around the stage like crazy. I was impressed," Cassandra confirmed.

"Yes, it was a big part, and I was very lucky to get it." Vanessa waved a hand in the air before smiling warmly at Cassandra. "The more *important* thing is that you were able to come into town for it! I can't tell you what that meant to me. I just wish we'd had more time hang out. I feel like I only got to see you for like an hour at the party and we haven't been able to meet up since."

"It's been a busy year, but I'm going to be here in L.A. for *The Nutcracker* this month, so I'm totally coming to that," she promised, and it made her feel good to see the excited smile on Vanessa's face. The girl was a good friend, willing to text long distance, and she understood all the pressure of having to be perfect every single time you did your job. Mess up once and you didn't get the next call-back, the next role. It was intense, and not everyone got it.

"You're so sweet to take time out of your schedule to come to the show, and I'd love you for you to be there, but if you have other stuff to do while you're home, I totally understand."

"She said she wants to go," Wyatt admonished under his breath, and Vanessa snapped her mouth shut. Glancing up at Cassandra, he gave her a kind smile. "She meant to say thank you and that she'd love for you to come see her perform."

"I'll be there," Cassandra replied, grinning as Vanessa's cheeks turned bright red.

"Can we *please* talk about something other than me for a minute?" Propping her elbows on the table, Vanessa leaned forward. "Tell me what you've been up to! You were just in London, right? For that shoot? I bet it was amazing."

"It was fun, but fucking freezing. We did the shoot near the Thames, and I was in a gown, barefoot, trying to look haute couture without damaging the dress while the photographer kept telling me to extend my neck." Laughing, Cassandra leaned forward dramatically. "Like I'm some kind of giraffe. I wanted to yell at him '*my neck only goes so far!*' but that would have got me in so much trouble."

"I bet the photos are beautiful though!" Vanessa sighed dreamily. "You get to go to the coolest places, Cass. When will the photos be out?"

All she could do was shrug. "No one tells me that stuff. I'm just a model."

"I don't think 'just a model' is any more accurate than Vanessa is 'just a ballerina.'" There was a dominant, chastising edge to Wyatt's quiet tone, and for a guy who was usually pretty reserved, she was impressed by the stare he leveled at her across the table.

"Sorry?" she offered with an apologetic smile, and he sighed.

"Anyway, I'm sure you looked beautiful. I think Vanessa found every picture of you from that Baggage Mishka lady," Wyatt added, and Cassandra fought the urge to laugh.

"It was Badgley Mischka, and they're actually two male designers. Mark Badgley and James Mischka, but seriously, no one knows that stuff unless they're obsessed with fashion or work in the industry." Reaching over to squeeze Vanessa's arm, she winked. "No more work talk. Tell me about you two. All moved in?"

"Yeah," Vanessa answered, leaning into Wyatt's shoulder, and he immediately slid his arm around her, pressing a kiss to her hair. "It's been... four months?"

"One week shy of four months," Wyatt filled in quickly before he sighed to himself. "Not that it matters."

"He's detail-oriented," Vanessa explained, smiling as she lifted herself up to kiss him. The sight of it had Cassandra thinking back to that morning as she'd tried to shove Logan out the door before Abelita saw him. He'd stepped out the front door, only to pull her out after him, pressing her to the wall to claim her mouth again.

You shouldn't have fucked him again this morning.

Bad decision.

Vanessa's cheeks were bright red when she faced forward again, and Cassandra shifted her gaze back to the menu. Everything in the trendy café was organic and super healthy, which was fine, but today she really wanted comfort food. Settling on the Asian salad, she was about to ask them what they were getting when she caught the mischievous look on Vanessa's face.

"What?" Cassandra asked, growing more wary as Vanessa grinned.

"Welllll, are you seeing anyone? Some sexy model? A bad boy from Italy?"

Rolling her eyes, Cassandra laughed. "Oh my God, no. I'd never date another model, and my single one-night stand on my travels was in Paris, not Italy."

"Was he hot?" Vanessa leaned closer, and Wyatt groaned.

"He was definitely hot, but so boring." She shrugged, adding quietly, "Vanilla as hell."

Wrinkling her nose, Vanessa sat back in her chair, snuggling back into Wyatt's arm. "Well, that's disappointing. I was kind of hoping for some juicy stories of the gorgeous men abroad, but— Ow!"

"Gorgeous men abroad?" Wyatt repeated, lifting his eyebrows a bit as she turned to look at him.

"I only want you, baby." Smiling, she pressed a kiss to his lips. "But Cass deserves to find someone too, abroad… or maybe local?" Vanessa turned back to her, and she could see the woman's gears turning as she lowered her voice. "Maybe we need to take you to Black Light while you're in town, see if we can find a dom for you."

"Sure," Wyatt agreed, and Cassandra could feel the heat in her cheeks as he continued. "If you've got time for it, that is. We don't want to monopolize all your time back home."

"Yeah… I was sort of already at the club. Last night."

Vanessa smacked her hand to her forehead, groaning. "Oh my God! That's right! You had that show yesterday, and I totally forgot about it. I'm such a shitty friend. Here you came into town for me, and I couldn't even get my ass to Runway to see you!"

"No, no, no!" Cassandra waved her hand, shaking her head.

"Seriously, it was fine. The show was super short, and it wasn't a big deal."

"Did you at least have someone there to support you? Did your roommate go?" Vanessa asked, and Cassandra could see the guilt written all over her face.

"Abelita was busy, but someone did come by... and I might have gone to Black Light with them last night?" Her voice was a whisper, but Vanessa's excited gasp was full volume.

"What? Who! You have to tell me who it is, Cass. Come on," she begged, and Cassandra groaned under her breath as she debated whether telling them about Logan was a good idea — not like she'd been making stellar choices during the past twenty-four hours.

In for a penny, in for a pound.

"Well, you remember the special event where you guys met?"

Vanessa's eyes widened. "Oh my God, you mean the guy you got paired with? Shit, what was his name..."

"Logan," Cassandra filled in, defeated, and Vanessa sat up straight.

"Yes! That's freaking awesome! I mean it is, right?" Her eyebrows pulled together as she stared across the table. "Why don't you look like this is awesome? I thought you guys hit it off that night."

"We did," Cassandra admitted, waving her hands in front of her as she tried to find the right words to explain all of the shit in her head. "It's just... we tried to find time to see if there was more to our thing, but I kept having to leave town, and then whenever I was back in town our schedules were all screwed up. I mean, I thought it was just the universe telling me it wasn't meant to be, but then he just shows up at the show yesterday. Just, *poof!* out of nowhere. No text, no call — hell, we hadn't texted in months! He just showed up, being all sexy and domly and gorgeous, and he kept asking me out and he kissed me and... fuck." Dropping her hands into her lap, she shook her head. "I agreed to meet him at the club last night."

"I'm still confused as to why this isn't a good thing?" Vanessa propped her elbows on the table. "Sure, it sucks that you guys weren't able to connect before now, but it sounds kind of romantic. Logan surprising you at an important event like that just to ask you out... That's a pretty big deal."

"I know." Groaning, Cassandra wiped her hands down her face.

"What's the problem?" Wyatt asked, leaning forward to keep his voice hushed. "Is he not a good guy? Did he cross a line?"

"No, nothing like that, it's just—" Cassandra stopped short as the waiter appeared beside them.

"Sorry about the wait, we're busy today. What can I get you guys?" he asked, giving them that polite service smile that made it clear he needed to be a hundred other places at that moment. Everyone leaned back from the table, quickly scanning the menus to put in their orders, and she could see the appreciation in his face as he scribbled them down and nodded. "Got it! I'll bring you some waters, and we'll get that out to you as soon as we can."

"Thanks," Vanessa replied, waiting for him to rush away before she swung her gaze back to Cassandra. "Okay, spill, what's going on with you and Logan."

Sighing, she rolled her eyes. "That's the problem. I have no fucking clue what's going on with us."

"Well, what did you guys do last night?" Vanessa asked, and Cassandra laughed.

"Not sure I can discuss *that* here."

"Did you at least enjoy it?" Vanessa was trying to be a good friend, and she appreciated it, but Cassandra hadn't expected an interrogation over lunch. But it wasn't like the thoughts weren't already spinning through her head on repeat, so she might as well talk to the only people she could actually mention Black Light around.

"Yeah," Cassandra finally said, trying not to remember the torturous edging and the mind-blowing orgasms that had followed. Shaking her head, she continued, "It was pretty amazing actually, but that was never the issue with Logan. The chemistry has always been there, he's just..."

"What?" Vanessa prompted when she didn't keep talking, but all she could think about was how nice it had felt to wake up next to him. To turn into his body heat and feel him wrap his arms around her without a word, like they hadn't even needed them. Everything with Logan just seemed to flow. Easy, natural, while at the same time being explosively passionate. The intensity she felt every time he kissed her was proof enough of that, but...

"But that's the problem," Cassandra said, and she could hear the hint of a whine in her voice as her frustration came through. "It's good, it's fucking amazing, but in January all my shit starts up again. Roberta is already booking me out for next year, and I need her to! I'm getting better contracts, better runway shows, people are starting to recognize my name, and that's how you succeed in this business. You put yourself out there and say yes to everything, which is only going to mean traveling *more*, not less."

"And having a boyfriend in L.A. doesn't exactly fit into that life," Vanessa finished for her, nailing the issue Cassandra hadn't even managed to say inside her head yet. Logan Chisholm was pursuing her, and if she were any other girl, she'd be exhilarated to have a hot, rich, successful man who *also* happened to be incredible in bed tracking her down and insisting she be with him. But she wasn't any other girl, and she'd spent too long building her career to drop it now just because he could make her come hard enough to see stars.

"What does he say about it?" Wyatt asked, and Cassandra

looked up at him as he chuckled. "You haven't talked to him about this yet, have you."

Not a question.

Wyatt had turned on dom voice with the flick of a switch, and she could hear the chastising edge in it, which — if she were honest — she deserved. Cassandra had avoided the discussion completely, and when Logan had pushed for a date that morning, she'd agreed just to avoid it again. Of course, she'd bargained him down from dinner to coffee on Sunday afternoon, and she'd refused to call it a date, but she knew she wasn't being fair.

"You've got to talk to him about it, Cass," Vanessa said softly.

"I know," she conceded, blowing out a breath as the waiter swept by the table to drop off their water. Grabbing hers, she took a sip just to keep from talking, but Wyatt wasn't letting it slide.

"Do we know Logan, baby?" he asked, looking at Vanessa.

"I'm sure you've seen him around. He's been at a few of the classes we've gone to... tall, blond, usually partners with one of the volunteers for Weston's shibari classes." Vanessa shrugged. "He doesn't talk to anyone really."

He doesn't?

"Well, that explains why I don't remember him. When we're at the club my attention is pretty focused on you, not other men." Wyatt chuckled as Vanessa rolled her eyes. "But I'm not the most talkative guy either, so it's not like I'd have started up a conversation with him spontaneously. Still, the right thing to do is talk with him, Cassandra."

"I get it!" Throwing up her hands, she leaned back in the chair and laughed to herself. *The universe was definitely not being subtle today.* "I promise I'll talk to him. Okay?"

"All right, I'm going to have Vanessa follow up with you on that," Wyatt replied sternly, still in dom-mode, and Cassandra sighed. She'd gone from zero doms in her life to feeling surrounded by them in less than a day, and there were really just two problems with that. First, she liked the dominance a lot more than she was ready to admit out loud, and second... she liked Logan Chisholm way more than she should.

Hell, she wouldn't even let him call it a date, and she was going to talk to him about their future? A future that he might not even be thinking about? How the hell was she supposed to bring that up over coffee?

He said he'd do anything for you to give it a chance.

Sighing, she twirled her water glass on the table, staring at the shiny circle it formed as she shook her head. She'd always prided herself on rolling with the punches life threw at her, always looking on the bright side... but the deeper she got into things with Logan, the worse the fall-out would be if things didn't work out.

CHAPTER 11

LOGAN

*H*e'd arrived too early, again, but he'd been taught that being on time was being late, and it was a hard habit to break. It didn't make the waiting any easier, and while the board at work knew he always started on time, he had a feeling Cassandra would just laugh at the idea.

Of course, hearing her laugh wasn't exactly a hardship, and this wasn't a board meeting... It was just coffee.

Not a date, not even lunch, just coffee. He'd accepted it because it was all he could get out of her without bending her over his knee in full view of anyone who happened to walk by her apartment — which could have been entertaining, even though it likely wouldn't have changed anything. But today he was going to figure out what was going on inside Cassandra's head, even if they sat at the damn coffee shop all evening.

Shifting in his seat, he glanced at the time on the dash again and sighed. He could either wait in his car like a patient man or be an asshole and knock on her door ten minutes early.

'You're always an asshole,' he thought to himself and turned off the car.

Heading up the steps to her door, Logan adjusted his suit

jacket, running his fingers through his hair before he rapped his knuckles just to the side of the wreath hanging over the peep-hole — *not safe*. A woman's voice came from within, and then he heard Cassandra yell, "Coming!"

The door flew open a half-second later, and he found himself smiling. She was in form-fitting jeans, a black sweater, and her hair was wrapped up in a colorful scarf as she stepped to the side to wave him in. "Sorry, I'm not ready quite yet."

"You look great," he replied, and she rolled her eyes. His palm itched to spank her, but movement caught his eye, and he turned to find another woman at the little kitchen table.

Cassandra leaned in to hug him, whispering against his ear, "She doesn't know anything about Black Light, so behave."

Behave?

He raised his eyebrows as she stepped back from him, and she rolled her eyes again.

"Please," she whispered, before turning toward her room-mate. "Try not to eat him alive while I finish getting ready."

"No promises," the woman responded, laughing brightly as he closed the door behind him and wandered into their living room. Cassandra disappeared into her room without another word and he let his eyes wander. She'd rushed him out the morning before, so he never had the chance to look around. There were pictures on the end tables of the couch. A mix of both Cassandra and her roommate, sometimes together, some-times with other people who could have been family or friends. A cute little Christmas tree in the corner, and fake garland over the wide window. Their coffee table was a cluttered mess of magazines and mail, and he was pretty sure that not a single piece of furniture in the room matched. It was a riotous mix of colors and textures, capped off by a huge splatter-painted canvas that hung above the couch.

"We made that last year," her roommate said, and he turned toward her with a smile.

"It's good. I'm Logan, by the way." Walking over, he offered his hand, and she leaned forward to shake it without getting up. "I apologize, I should have introduced myself when I came in."

"Don't worry about it. I'm Abelita, Cass's roommate."

"Nice to meet you, Abelita," he replied, tucking his hands into his pockets.

"Well, you're cute, that's for sure, but..." Her eyes raked him from head to toe before she laughed under her breath. "You obviously don't know Cass very well."

Taken aback, Logan tilted his head and tried to come up with a more polite response than *how the fuck do you know*. It took a second, but he settled on, "And why would you say that?"

"You showed up to take her out for coffee in what I'm pretty confident is a Brioni bespoke suit, which is at least ten grand. That means you're already way overdressed for Cass before I even add on whatever the rest of that outfit costs." Abelita grinned, crossing her arms as she leaned back in the chair. "You're wearing more money than some people make in a year, and she would have been happy going out in sweatpants."

Clenching his jaw, Logan did his best to not let the girl's remarks get under his skin, but they were already bothering him. It wasn't like he could change, and why should he? This is how he dressed every day, unless he was at the gym, and even if Cassandra was comfortable going out for coffee in sweats, there was no way in hell he would.

Meeting the young woman's gaze, he kept his face blank. "Cassandra is well aware of how I dress."

"Riiiiight." Shrugging, Abelita turned back to the laptop on the table. "I just thought you should know that money isn't going to impress her."

Don't ask, don't ask, don't ask.

"And what would impress her?" Logan asked anyway, ignoring the way his brain groaned at him internally. "Since you know her so well."

"Be spontaneous. Interesting. Don't take life so seriously," she answered, running her eyes over him again. "Sometimes coffee is just coffee."

"And if I want more than coffee?" *Jesus Christ, his mouth just kept going.*

Abelita stared up at him for a moment, appraising him before she finally spoke. "I already told you what would impress her. It's up to you to be worth her time. Or not."

"Well, thank you for the advice," he replied, keeping his tone quiet and civil, because the last barrier he needed with Cassandra was her roommate hating him for more than his clothes. All he wanted was for her to give this a chance, to give them a chance to see if the heat between them was a flash in the pan... or something else.

"Sorry!" Cassandra shouted from her room. "Almost done!"

"No rush," he called back. "Just getting to know your roommate."

"Fuck." The curse made him chuckle as he heard a drawer slam in her bathroom.

"Oh yeah, we're becoming good friends," Abelita added, raising her voice so that it carried through the small apartment.

Looking over at her again, he tried to shake off the comments she'd made. "So, are you a model as well?"

"I am. Mostly lingerie, because"—she grabbed her breasts through her top—"these."

Logan almost choked, but it came out as a laugh. "That's... good to know."

Abelita grinned, leaning to the side in her chair to peek into Cassandra's room before she met his gaze. "Look, Cass obviously likes you enough to see you again. If you want some real advice, don't try so hard. Nothing has to be perfect. Sometimes it's better when it's messy, disorganized, unplanned."

"Spontaneous," he added, repeating her word from before, and Abelita winked at him.

"You might just have some hope after all, rich boy."

A crash came from the room behind him, followed by a string of curses that would have impressed him on his worst day, and then Cassandra was in the doorway with her hair in a halo of tight, shiny curls around her head. "Sorry that took so long."

"You looked beautiful before," he replied, and she laughed, pointing at him.

"So smooth." Cassandra glanced over at Abelita and then back at him. "Do I even want to know what the hell you two talked about?"

"Probably not," Abelita answered, grinning mischievously, and he fought the urge to roll his eyes. Cassandra's roommate might not know about Black Light, but she was a bit of a mouthy brat too.

"Well? What do you have to say?" Cassandra asked him, and he raised his hands.

"I plead the fifth."

"Oh my God, I should have never left you two alone." Grabbing his arm, she dragged him toward the door, snagging her purse from a chair on the way.

"Have a good afternoon, Abelita," Logan called back over his shoulder.

"We'll talk again soon!" she returned, and Cassandra groaned, yanking the front door open.

"Out, out, out!" She shoved him out the door as he laughed, and before the door closed again, he could hear Abelita laughing as well. Sighing, Cassandra shook her head. "I swear, you can only believe half of what she says about me."

"Noted," he replied, walking down the steps to the sidewalk as he tilted his head toward the car. "I'm parked over here."

As soon as they were buckled in, she turned toward him. "You've got to tell me what she said."

"Why?" he asked, studying the amused, but slightly

concerned expression on her face. "Afraid she spilled your dark roommate secrets?"

"Ha. Ha. Seriously, Logan, what did you guys talk about?"

"You," he answered, grinning as he started the car. "And she grabbed her chest and told me she was a lingerie model."

"She did not!"

"Oh, she did," he confirmed. Cassandra's open mouth had him laughing as he pulled out of the parking lot, and soon enough she was laughing too.

"I'm going to kill her."

"Let's hold off on that. I'd prefer if you weren't in jail." Reaching forward, he grabbed his phone and unlocked it, handing it to her. "Pick where we're going."

"Me?" she asked, taking the phone to look down at it. "Don't you already have somewhere picked out?"

Not anymore.

"You said you wanted coffee, so find us somewhere to have coffee."

"Okaaay…" she said as she started tapping at his phone. He couldn't resist the urge to glance at her, and when he saw the smile lingering on her lips, he knew this had been the right choice. Spontaneity.

Thank you, Abelita.

THERE WERE PROBABLY a thousand coffee shops in L.A., or more, but Cassandra had chosen Dinosaur Coffee. The shop was a good size with the usual overly trendy design typical of an L.A. place, but it wasn't like Logan cared where they drank coffee.

"This is the cutest thing," Cassandra cooed, turning her cup to show him the dinosaur emblazoned on the side of the sleeve as they grabbed an open table. "I've got to post this! I've been wanting to come here for forever. Do you mind?"

"Go ahead." Taking a sip of the latte he'd ordered, he watched her dig out her phone and pose for a few selfies, holding the cup beside her bright smile. Then she suddenly turned in the chair and snapped another with him in the background.

Laughing, she faced forward and showed him the picture. "You look cute when you're surprised."

"Please don't post that," he said, sighing when she rolled her eyes. "You know, I'm keeping track of all the eye rolls, Cassandra."

"Why don't you want me to post it? It's a good picture of you." She was staring down at her phone now, tapping away at something, and he leaned forward to peek at it. The photo on the screen wasn't the one of him, which was all he cared about.

"I'm not sure my shareholders, or the board, would be excited about me showing up on Instagram."

Her honey brown eyes flicked up to scrutinize him, her mouth tilting to the side in a naughty little smirk that spoke volumes of the mischief she was thinking up.

"I mean it, Cassandra."

"Okay, I promise." Laughing under her breath, she set the phone down and turned it so he could read the post. It was just her and her beautiful smile beside the dinosaur-emblazoned cup with the shop in the background. She'd tagged the coffee shop and included a warm review of her latte and how much she loved the little dinosaurs hidden around the interior. No mention of him, or even that she'd come with anyone, just a few dinosaur emojis to end the post.

"Thank you," he replied, nudging the phone back toward her. "Do you post on there a lot?"

Cassandra shrugged as she tucked her cell in her purse. "I sort of have to. A lot of the bigger brands will look into your social media, and the size of your following, when making decisions on models. Luckily, it's not that much work to keep posts going up. I like it, and it's fun, but I'm not trying to be an influencer, you know?"

Not really.

"Do you have a big following?" he asked, taking a sip of the coffee.

"No, not really. I mean, I think I'm at eighteen thousand? But that's nothing compared to some of the more popular ones, and I've only got that many because I got tagged at this show in London by Terése Rendarre. She's super popular and has over five million followers." The words she was saying barely made any sense to him, but he didn't care. He liked how animated she got as she talked about her job, hands flying, eyes rolling, smile bright. She was beautiful. "Anyway, I don't think your company would care if I showed you in a post about coffee."

Logan chuckled, glancing out the window for a moment to watch traffic rolling down Sunset. "I'm not so sure. If clients saw the CEO of their finance firm hanging out at Dinosaur Coffee with a model sixteen years younger than him..." He shrugged. "They might have an issue, and then my ass would be on the line with the shareholders and my team."

"Do *you* have a problem with the age gap?" she asked, eyes sparkling with humor as she leaned forward on the table.

"Not at all." Smiling a little, he reached over to take her hand in his. "I'm just not sure if rubbing their noses in it would earn me any grace with our clients."

"You know, you don't look thirty-eight."

"What does thirty-eight look like?" he asked, raising an eyebrow, and she laughed again, pulling her hand back to lift them in an animated shrug.

"I don't know! You're the one that brought the whole age thing up."

"Actually, *you* brought it up on Friday night," he corrected, but he smiled to ease the serious tone in his voice. "Either way, I don't have any issues with it, and I'm not on social media, so maybe I'm wrong. Maybe they wouldn't care."

"Then let me post a picture of you," she challenged, and even though it made a shiver of anxiety roll down his spine, he knew just how to use her sassy comment to get to the conversation he really wanted to have.

"Okay, deal." He raised his hand when she started to excitedly dig for her phone again. "But you can only post the picture if we go on a date. A real one. Not the club, not coffee — dinner."

Cassandra's shoulders dipped, her hands sliding back onto the edge of the table, and he knew she was preparing to decline. Again.

Fuck no.

"Cassandra, I don't know what's going on in that head of yours, mostly because you won't talk about it... but I'm not being subtle here. I want to give this a chance, a *real* chance, and I'm pretty confident that you do too."

"You're always confident," she muttered, her eyes flicking up to his before returning to the dinosaur on her cup again.

"Well, am I wrong?" he asked, and she sighed.

"No."

"Then what the hell, Cassandra? Are you trying to play hard to get, because I'm not really into games." His frustration was showing through, and he leaned back in the chair to take a breath and calm the fuck down.

"I'm not trying to play games with you, Logan," she answered, and he watched as a sad smile slid across her lips. "That's actually what I'm trying to avoid."

"I have no fucking idea what that means."

Groaning, she braced her elbows on the table and shifted the cup back and forth between her hands, sliding it over the table as she seemed to debate her next words. Finally, she caught the cup and looked at him. "What if this is great?"

"What—"

"No, Logan, listen to me. What if we do this whole dating thing for the next few weeks... and it's great? What if it's fucking amazing? What if all this *stuff* between us actually means something?" She threw her hands up again, laughing harshly. "And then I leave again! Bam! I'm already scheduled to be in London again the second week in January. I've got New York after that, and then—"

"Stop." He held up his hand, needing her to stop talking long enough for his head to stop spinning. "Are you telling me that all this hesitation bullshit, this refusing to call any of this a date... it's all been because you were worried it would be *good?*"

Cassandra shrugged one shoulder. "Well... yeah."

"Fucking hell... I am going to stripe your ass for this," he growled under his breath, keeping it quiet enough that none of the other customers could hear — but Cassandra did. Her eyes widened, and her hands stilled around the coffee as he met her gaze. "We're going on a date. This week. You pick whatever night works with your schedule, and I'll adjust mine."

"But what if—"

"No," he cut her off like the asshole he was, leaning closer to wrap his hand around her wrist and squeeze. "We are going to give this a chance. We're going to see if it's as good as I think it is, and if it turns out to be terrible... then we'll know. And if it turns out fucking amazing? Then we'll figure it out."

"How are we going to figure it out?" she asked, and he chuckled, letting her go as he leaned back.

"Weren't you the one that said we shouldn't take life so seriously? Enjoy it? Carpe diem and all that shit?"

"Oh, so now you're all about having fun and trusting the universe?" she quipped, the sarcasm heavy in her tone, and all he wanted to do was bend her over the end of a bed and belt her ass until her inner brat was tamed and begging for him to make her come again.

Later.

"I can do that," he replied, and she laughed.

"Really."

More sarcasm, more doubt… but he didn't feel any of those things when he looked at her.

When it came to Cassandra Moreira, for the first time in his life he thought the universe might actually be speaking to him. Opening that random email from Runway to see her name had been random chance. It could have just as easily been swept into the trash with all of the other junk in his inbox, but he'd opened it, and he'd known he had to go. Had to try one more time before he gave up on ever seeing her again — and then he'd found her, felt that same ineffable pull, and he wasn't giving up now.

"For you… I think I can wait and see what the universe has in store."

Cassandra laughed, her bright smile flashing again as she leaned forward. "You are so smooth… but I think you're a little too controlling to do the whole 'wait and see' thing."

"Oh, I never said I was going to play fair with the universe." Grinning, he reached forward to trace his fingers over her palm, up to her wrist, before grabbing on to pin her hand to the table. "In fact, I plan on playing very dirty."

"Okay," she whispered, nodding. "We can go on a date."

"Good girl."

CHAPTER 12

CASSANDRA

She'd made Logan wait until Thursday for their official date, but they'd talked every day. Practically all day. He'd been texting her during meetings, claiming he was pretending to respond to emails when he was really just flirting with her, and it kept going until they were falling asleep each night.

They'd swapped photos too. It had started with the photo shoots she'd done on Tuesday and Wednesday, and he'd responded with hilariously boring pictures of him in his office with the L.A. skyline at his back.

Well, most of them were boring. The one he'd sent of him mimicking one of her poses was now his official photo in her phone.

Logan had *not* found that amusing, which had only made her love it more.

And through it all he'd teased her. Made promises of all the things he'd do to her when he got her alone again, and she'd taunted him just to get more. Maybe she was a bit of a brat, but Logan was absolutely playing dirty, and she liked it.

However, when he'd told her to wear a nice dress for

Thursday night, she'd expected him to take her to some over-priced restaurant with twenty courses and food topped with foam. She had not expected The Cicada Club.

Located downtown in a historic art deco building, the club looked like it had been pulled from the roaring 20s and dropped almost a hundred years later in the exact same place. Guests were showing up in a mix of flapper outfits and gorgeous gowns, and Cassandra couldn't stop turning to look at more people as they waited in line.

"This place is wild," she said, leaning close to his ear so he could hear her over the already loud music.

"I thought you might like it," Logan replied, pulling her tighter to his side with his arm draped around her waist.

The couple ahead of them moved off to take their seats, and they stepped forward to the hostess. "Name?" she asked.

"Chisholm."

"Two?" The woman lifted her eyes to him, and Cassandra watched as her gaze lingered just a little too long on Logan before flicking over to her.

"Yes, two," Logan confirmed, and Cassandra couldn't help but grin as the hostess looked back at him once more before studying the table map in front of her.

"Of course, sir. Thank you for joining us tonight for this special event, and we hope you enjoy your evening." The blare of trumpets almost drowned out her final words as a waitress arrived to lead them to their table. Every inch of the restaurant was beautiful, and people were already dancing as the band played, dressed in era-appropriate suits. But they didn't stay near the dance floor — their waitress led them up a gorgeous staircase behind the dance-floor and onto the narrow second floor that overlooked it all.

"What is this party for? And how the hell did you get us in?" Scanning the room, she couldn't help but laugh as they took their seats at a small table where both their chairs were tucked together against the wall. The balcony barely had enough room for the waitstaff to walk in front of the tables, but it was worth it to see everyone dancing below.

"A friend of a friend's company is putting it on. It's their holiday party before the vacations start."

"So, we're crashing?" she asked, laughing at the absurdity of it.

"My name was on the list, wasn't it?" His grin was wicked as he leaned over to whisper directly into her ear, "So be a good girl and enjoy the evening."

"And if I'm not a good girl?"

Logan's hand slid up her thigh, pushing the dress up with it, and she squeaked as she scrambled to catch his hand, but then he squeezed tight, and she froze. A light touch to her chin turned her until she could only see him in the dim light. He was sinfully gorgeous, dangerously tempting as his eyes roved over her, and then his tongue teased his bottom lip before he pulled it between his teeth. "If you're not a good girl… then I won't show you my surprise."

"Surprise?" she breathed, and his hand slid about half an inch higher.

"Mmhmm." Logan nodded slowly, that grin teasing her almost as much as his touch. "And trust me, you want this surprise."

"Yes, sir," she whispered, and he leaned forward to kiss her. By 1920s standards it would have been risqué, but for a dimly lit corner in 2019 it wasn't even close to what she craved. Just as her lips parted to let him take control, he pulled back, removing his hands from her at the same time.

"Good girl. Now, look at your menu so we're ready before the waitress comes back." Tilting his head toward the menu, she tried to focus on the appetizer salads, but her eyes kept drifting back to him. Eventually though, she had to read it so she could order, and just as she'd picked options, a loud cheer from below preceded a man stepping up to the microphone.

"Is that your friend?"

"Friend of a friend," he answered, and she laughed under her breath.

"So, it's true all you rich assholes know each other?"

The deadpan look Logan sent her was all threat, and all she could do was smile until he finally sighed. "No, that's *not* true. And from what I know of David Thornton, he's not anywhere near the asshole I am. After all, he's bringing his leadership team here, and I'm just giving my employees bonuses and wishing them a merry whatever-the-fuck-you-celebrate."

"Nice," she retorted on a laugh, rolling her eyes on reflex, and then she groaned. "You saw that didn't you?"

"Yep."

"Fuck," she muttered, but they were both grinning as the man below talked about getting ready for 2020 with jazz and drinks and dancing. Then he wished everyone happy holidays and a happy new year, and everyone cheered. Cassandra applauded too, but Logan was just watching her.

"Tell me what got you into modeling," he said, leaning back from the table. "Other than the fact that you're gorgeous."

Cassandra almost rolled her eyes, but she caught herself in time. "You're actually not far off from the truth. I'm the only girl in my family, and my mom used to drag me to pageants when I was growing up. When I was fifteen, I was at one in Miami, and I got the runner-up spot, but after it was over there was this guy talking to my mom about modeling. He wanted us to come see him, my parents looked into it and they were a legit agency, so… we went."

"And then you were a model?" he asked.

"Yeah. It happened so fast that I don't think any of us were ready. Mom traveled with me the first year, and then it was just me going all over the country, and then the world." Cassandra shrugged. "It was really cool, obviously, but sometimes I wish I'd finished high school the normal way. You know, parties, prom, the whole thing."

"Did the modeling agency hire tutors for you to finish?"

She almost laughed at the idea. "No. I finished high school online. The nice part was I got to finish a year early."

"That doesn't surprise me at all."

"What about it?" she asked, studying his serious expression.

"That you finished early. You're quick-witted, which is always a sign of intelligence." The raw honesty of the compliment stunned her for a second, because she couldn't remember the last time a guy had said something nice about her that didn't involve her looks or her clothes.

"Thank you, Logan."

He shrugged like it meant nothing while he scanned the dancers and the band below. "Okay, your turn."

"My turn for what?"

"We're on a date, right?" he clarified, a smirk sneaking over his lips. "That means we try to get to know one another *outside* of the kink."

"Okay... well, how did you get into your career?"

"Family business." The answer was short, abrupt, and the pause lengthened as he avoided her gaze, but then he finally glanced at her and she gestured for him to continue. Sighing, Logan pushed a hand back through his hair, leaving it tousled as he started to speak. "It's boring, but fine. My grandfather started the company on the East Coast. Wall Street and all that. Came out here to be closer to all the new money in California, and it was a smart move. The company did well, my father took over when my grandfather retired, and then I took over when my father died. All inherited, and you can feel free to call me out on that as you like."

Dead?

There was no quick-witted response to that. All she felt was sorry for him, and before she could even come up with the appropriate thing to say, the waitress appeared to take their orders. Sitting up straight, Cassandra managed to get through her order, adding a martini to go along with his old fashioned.

As soon as the waitress walked away, Logan turned to her and grinned. "My turn."

"Wait, Logan, I'm so sorry about your dad. When did he die?"

"Seven years ago," he answered stiffly, his body language matching his tone, and she leaned over to grab his hand, forcing him to let her fingers intertwine with his.

"I'm really sorry. Is your mom still around?"

He tugged at her grip on his hand as he said, "No."

"What about your grandparents?" she pressed, holding his hand tighter as she leaned forward to try and catch his gaze again, but his eyes were glued to the party going on below. "Logan?"

"It's my turn." It was a clear end to her questions, but it left her with so many more. Still, she didn't want to ruin the evening by dredging up his bad memories, so she relented.

"All right, what's your question?" Cassandra made sure she was smiling when he looked at her, and she felt him relax a little beside her.

"What was your talent?" he asked, his grin returning slowly. "When you were in the pageants."

"You are such an asshole." Laughing, she leaned back in the chair, feeling her cheeks burning with a blush.

"Come on, tell me." He squeezed her hand. "I promise it'll be our secret."

"I hate you so much for this…" Groaning, she closed her eyes so she didn't have to see his face as she said, "Baton twirling."

His chuckle made her open them, and she reached over to smack his shoulder.

"Don't laugh!"

"No, no, that's great. Honestly, I'm just glad to know you've always had a talent with handling batons," he replied, laughing more, and she couldn't help but groan before she started laughing too.

"God, you're such a dick."

"I never claimed to be otherwise," he retorted.

"Whatever. My turn," she said, smiling up at the waitress as she dropped off their drinks before hurrying back down the row of tables. Grabbing her martini, she saw Logan holding his glass out and she tapped it with hers before taking a sip. Cassandra waited for him to put his drink down, but he wouldn't look at her.

"Go on. Ask," he said, a little sharply, and she grinned.

"What's your favorite color?"

"What?" Logan turned toward her, obviously confused, and she shrugged.

"I want to know."

"It's blue. Actually, more of a dark blue. Like that second dress you wore in the show." His eyes slipped down her body before coming back to her face. "I would definitely buy that dress just to see you in it again."

"What did you think of the show?"

"I thought you were gorgeous," he replied, taking another drink before he shrugged. "The rest of it is kind of a blur, honestly. Definitely not how I normally spend my time."

"How *do* you normally spend your time?" she asked, sincerely curious, but he shook his head at her.

"Oh no, it's my turn."

"Come on!" she encouraged, quickly switching tactics when she could tell he was going to refuse. "Please, sir?"

Logan's mouth was already open to argue, but it snapped shut as he turned to stare at her. "That's not fair."

"You know you like it when I beg," she whispered, and the groan that rumbled in his chest made her grin. "Pretty please?"

"Brat," he said on a laugh. "Fine, I pretty much work all the time. If I have to go out to dinner with prospective high-end clients, I do, but those are always miserable. I go to the club for classes, or to try and find someone to play with — which has been difficult this past year — or I'm at home. Working. Usually with a movie on in the background."

Seriously?

Cassandra didn't know what she'd expected, but it wasn't something so... reserved. Solitary.

"Now it is my turn, no arguments or pleading will be accepted." Logan picked up his glass, taking another sip as he narrowed his eyes on her in a faux serious stare. "What's your favorite movie?"

"*Spaceballs*," she replied quickly, and he chuckled. "What? It's an awesome movie!"

"It definitely is. You just continue to surprise me." Leaning over, he pressed a gentle kiss to her lips. "Mine is *Die Hard*. All of them, actually. I've seen them an embarrassing number of times."

Smiling, Cassandra grabbed his shirt to pull him in for another kiss. "They're good movies."

"I knew you had good taste," he replied in between kisses.

They continued to ask each other stupid questions as they ate dinner, but the answers were actually good. She found out he'd played lacrosse in school and later at Yale. His comfort food was gelato, which she whole-heartedly supported, and there were a dozen other little details that made Logan someone real. There was still that nagging concern for how they could make things work, but in the haze of laughter and good food and well-poured drinks... she didn't care as much.

"You done?" he asked, and she could tell he was because he moved his chair back to stand.

"What about dessert?"

Grinning, Logan held out his hand for her and leaned his

head toward the stairs. "We can have dessert after we enjoy the band a bit."

"Promise?"

"Get up, Cassandra," he commanded, and she stood with a grin, taking his hand so he could lead her back down the beautiful staircase. There were other people standing around the perimeter of the dance floor, watching the couples as the songs alternated between instrumental only and ones where the singer took the mic.

"This is so cool," she said, leaning close to Logan's ear, and he moved behind her to wrap his arms around her waist.

"I'm really glad you like it." He pulled her back against his chest, swaying with her to the music, and she was mesmerized by the couples who were moving quickly around the floor to the beat. "Think you can stow your brat for a little while?"

"Why?" she asked on a laugh.

"Because I need you to trust me for a minute."

Leaning to the side, she met his gaze. "I do trust you, Logan."

She had never seen him smile as brightly as he did right then, and a second later he caught her hand and pulled her tight before turning them onto the dancefloor. The next moment he spun her away, catching her just as their arms fully extended to tug her back against him, forcing her to sway with him as they whirled through the other couples.

Holy shit, he can dance.

There was no time to react, or speak, all she could do was laugh as he dipped her on a downbeat, lifting her upright only to twirl her. With a smooth sidestep, he moved behind her, catching her under the arms, only to take a huge step back so that she almost fell — but she didn't. Logan was there, tossing her back to her feet in perfect rhythm to the song, and then her head spun again.

"Logan!" she half-shouted, still laughing as he caught her by the hand again. Facing him now, she saw him shuffling back with the kind of footwork she'd only seen in movies, before tugging her against him again for another fluid move around the dancefloor. Breathless, she heard the music change, a faster rhythm, and Logan matched it perfectly.

"Hold on," he whispered against her ear just before he spun her away, but this time when he pulled her back toward him, he caught both of her hands and swung her under his legs and back upright.

There was no break, and she tried to just follow his lead without screwing him up. Dance had never been her thing, but maybe she'd just never had the right partner, because *this* was way more fun than any dance class she'd been forced to attend. Logan twirled her, lifted her, tossed her over his shoulder, and spun her around the dancefloor until her cheeks ached from all the laughing.

Finally, with one last blast of the trumpet, the music died down and Logan spun her back into his arms, dipping her to place a rather chaste kiss to her lips. Over the blood rushing in her ears and the sounds of their frantic breathing, she heard applause as he lifted her upright. People were whistling, cheering, and she could feel the heat in her cheeks as they nodded at the other dancers and the small crowd. Squeezing his hand tight, she tugged him toward the edge of the dancefloor, and he went with her.

As soon as they snuck through the crowd, stopped by several people complimenting them — complimenting *him* — they reached a more open space by the stairs and all she could do was stare at him and try to catch her breath. He was breathing hard too, and she wasn't surprised.

"Why the hell didn't you warn me you could dance like that!"

"It was a surprise," he answered, grinning broadly. "Honestly, I'm just glad I remembered as much as I did."

Smacking his arm, she laughed. "Are you kidding? That was

fucking incredible! I— I don't even know where I've seen something like that!"

"Cassandra..." He caught her hand again, yanking her hard against his front, and then she felt the burn of the swat as his palm landed on her ass. "You're going to have to stop hitting me, or we're going to have a very different evening."

"Like what?" she asked, struggling to breathe evenly as he shifted her back against the little piece of wall beside the steps. Blocking her in.

"I'm not opposed to a little take-down play if you feel like being feisty," he purred against her ear, tightening his grip on her wrist as he stroked over her hip, pushing her more firmly into the wall.

"That sounds fun, sir," she whispered, heat pooling between her thighs.

"Fuck," he groaned, his blue eyes ablaze, and she nodded.

"Yeah, exactly."

"We're going to my place." It was a command, a cocky assumption, but it was one she was definitely not going to argue.

There was only one thing she wanted to ask.

"How soon can we get out of here?"

CHAPTER 13

LOGAN

The car ride home took an infuriatingly long time, but Cassandra kept their fingers entwined almost the whole time — at least until he left the highway and her hand moved to his thigh... and then to his dick. He'd almost slammed on the breaks to fuck her in the first dark spot he could find, but logic managed to override need, and he made her sit on her hands, testing the speed limit on the way home.

Pulling into his garage, Logan started to close it before he even turned off the car. "Out," he growled, and she flashed a naughty little smile as she obeyed.

They collided as he was opening the door into the house, her lips just as hungry as his, and then they were stumbling together down the hall. He grabbed the dress and ripped it over her head, immediately reaching for her again as he dropped the fabric to the floor.

"Feel like fighting me?" he asked between kisses, tracing the line of her throat as she made a soft sound and reached for his pants, fumbling at the belt.

"Don't think I can play hard to get at the moment," she

answered, and he nipped her shoulder hard, earning a delicious squeak and a breathy sigh.

"Next time then." Taking her hand, he practically dragged her up the stairs, but he'd been patient enough. He'd waited days to touch her again, and the little brat had taunted him all night with her sass, and then teased him in the car. All he wanted was to hear her whimper and moan, to feel her come again.

"Jesus Christ, your house is huge," she said with a laugh, and he caught her just outside his bedroom, pinning her to the wall.

"I'll give you the tour in the morning. Right now I have other ideas."

"I'm good with that," she purred, kissing him again, and he took control. Running his hands over her curves, needing more, and he couldn't do that in the damn hall. Grabbing her under the thighs, he lifted her, shifting his hold to her ass when she wrapped her legs around his hips. Kissing her was better than any drug he'd tried in his misspent youth, and he took his fill while he carried her into his bedroom.

"You've been such a naughty brat tonight," he whispered against her lips just before he dropped her onto the bed, catching one thigh to flip her to her stomach. She laughed as he yanked her back to the edge by her hips.

"I thought I'd been a good girl?"

"Did you think I forgot the eyerolls? The sass?" he asked, ripping his belt free, and he loved the way her thighs snapped together, her toes digging into the rug under his bed. She'd lost her heels somewhere in his house, but he'd worry about that in the morning. Cassandra was ready, lifting her ass because she knew exactly what was coming, and his little masochist wanted it.

The first snap of the dress belt was stiff, wrong, and he groaned and threw it at the wall. Stomping over to his closet, he grabbed a better one, wider, softer, and then knelt down to take his shoes off as quickly as he could.

Abandoning them in his closet, he returned to the bedroom to find her on her side, staring at him, and he shook his head. "Did I say you could move?"

Cassandra laughed, moving back into position fast, but that wasn't good enough. Landing the belt hard, he watched her arch, a sweet groan leaving her lips before he leaned down to wrap his hand gently around her throat.

"Did I say you could move?" Logan repeated, tone much harsher, and he felt the way she swallowed against his palm.

"No, sir," she whispered, and he squeezed just enough to have her squirming before he let go and stood up again.

"That's right. And naughty little brats get punished, don't they?" he asked.

The question was obviously rhetorical as he brought the belt down again, but she still shouted her answer with a perfect, "Yes, sir!"

"Good girl," he praised, adding another stripe to her ass. "Eventually you're going to learn that rolling your eyes around me isn't a smart idea, and we both know how smart you are."

"Apparently not that smart," she sassed, and he aimed the belt at her sit spot, immediately repeating it, which made her hands clench in the bedding as she hissed air through her teeth. "Fuck!"

"Not yet," he replied, grinning behind her as he fulfilled his promise to light her ass up for refusing date after date on the fragile premise that dealing with her schedule would be a challenge. Thinking of their conversation made him bring the belt down with a zipping smack, and she whined into the bed, her hips wiggling. "So, did you enjoy our date?"

"I'm still waiting to see how it ends." There was laughter in her voice, and he had to bite back his own laugh as he shook his head behind her.

"You have no sense of self-preservation, you know that?"

"Are we still warming up?" she asked, and he bit down on the urge to go and grab the cane he had in his playroom. They'd need to talk about that first, because *those* marks wouldn't go away in a day, and he didn't want to fuck up a photoshoot for her... but someday he'd find time for it. In the meantime, he brought the belt down in a rapid series of swats that he knew would build on top of each other, and her keening whine was music to his ears.

"Foot down," he growled, catching her ankle where she'd tried to block him to deliver a quick, stinging strike to her arch.

"Fuck!" Cassandra whined, twisting in his grip, and he let her put it back on the floor.

"Be a good girl and that won't happen again." Looking over the welts, he added another few where the skin was already raised, and she wiggled and groaned but kept her feet down and out of his way. "Still think we're warming up?"

"I'm warm!" she answered loudly, and he let the chuckle roll out as he dropped the belt and flipped her onto her back. Her eyes were sparkling, possibly with tears, and it made her look even hotter with the way her lips pouted.

"You sure?" he taunted. "I can get something a little more hardcore if you'd like. Maybe a dragon's tail, or a cane?"

"I'd rather just have you." Sitting up, she tried to reach for him, but he caught her wrists and pushed her back to the bed, pinning her.

"I'm not done with you yet." Smiling down at her, he loved the way she arched off the bed, spreading her thighs for him, all desperate need... but he could push her further. "Stay still."

"Logan," she whined as he let go of her, standing up to take his shirt off. When she propped herself up on her elbows he stopped, snapping his fingers before he pointed at the bed.

"Down."

Groaning, Cassandra dropped back, and he continued unbuttoning his shirt, reveling in the way her eyes followed every movement.

"Forget something?"

"Yes, *sir*," she said, fighting her smile, and he debated whether her tone negated it as he tossed his shirt onto the chair then sent his undershirt after it.

"You've got such a mouth on you."

"Then let me use it," she offered, and this time when she sat up, he didn't stop her. Cassandra shifted to her knees on the floor, and he had to admit that the real-life visual was infinitely better than the fantasy. Her honey brown eyes tilted up at him, the victorious little smirk on her lips as she freed his erection — it was perfect.

"This doesn't get you out of all that sass," he advised, biting back a groan as she wrapped her hand around his shaft and stroked.

"We'll see." More sass just before her mouth closed around the head of his cock, and his breath caught. Watching her lips stretch as she teased him with her tongue was more than perfect, it was heaven. Every sinful sweep sent electric pulses rushing under his skin, and he let her take the lead for now, enjoying it. Her other hand moved up his thigh, teasing his balls before she cupped them and squeezed. The thrust toward the back of her throat was instinctive, but the sharp gag it earned had him grinning.

"Come on, you can take it," he growled, cupping the side of her face to wrap his fingers at the back of her neck. Another shallow, testing thrust resulted in another soft gag, but Cassandra didn't pull back. Instead, he felt the buzz of her moan run up the length of his cock, and he groaned and thrust harder, the warm, wet seal of her mouth dragging a low moan out of him as he eased into her throat.

Fuck.

A shiver rushed through him, and he slid back just enough to let her breathe before repeating it, pushing further, feeling the tight stroke of her throat working around him. Cassandra choked again, and he pulled out, leaning down to meet her tearstained gaze. *Beautiful.*

"You want more?" he asked, and she licked her lips before she nodded.

"Yes, sir."

"Goddamn you're perfect. Move back." Guiding her until her back was braced against the bed, he slid his hand behind her neck again, forcing her to look up at him. "Three taps if you want me to stop. Got it?"

"Yes, sir," she replied, her breathing still fast, with that delicious hint of nervous panic in her eyes that had his dick throbbing.

"Good girl, open."

As soon as she obeyed, he slid in, working slow for the first few strokes, teasing the back of her throat, testing, and then he tightened his grip on the back of her neck to warn her. The next rough thrust sent a rush up his spine, a spiral of lust that was only compounded by the sweet, desperate sounds she made when he pulled back to do it again. He tried to take his time, to pace himself, but when she didn't tap out as she gagged again, he let go. Fucking her face, completely absorbed in the incredible feeling of her as she slurped and whined around his cock. When her hands gripped his thighs, he paused, barely able to stop from another thrust, but she didn't push him away. Cassandra's fingers just dug in, a garbled sound coming from her that he was sure would have been something smartass if she'd been able to talk.

Little brat.

Closing his eyes, he returned to the deep thrusts, taking her throat until the friction of her tongue and the feeling of her swallowing around the head of his dick forced him to pull back. He almost stumbled, wavering on his feet as he kicked his pants off and pointed at the bed.

"Get up. Now," he growled, and she scrambled to obey.

Seeing her move, still in her goddamn underwear, with the tears on her cheeks and her mouth shiny, had him teetering on the edge of playing much rougher than he wanted to on her first night in his house. "Bra off."

Cassandra sat up to unclasp it, and through some miracle he managed to wait for her to toss it off the bed before he ripped her underwear down her thighs, forcing her back onto the bed as she slid toward him. Pushing her legs apart he leaned forward to taste her, dragging his tongue through her folds as she whined and bucked her hips against his hold.

"Be still," he snapped, swatting her side, but she kept wiggling as he returned to licking her, focusing on her clit until the moan she released changed into a desperate little screech.

"Logan! Please!" It was the begging that stopped him, the raw need in her voice, and he felt it too. Climbing onto the bed, he shoved her thighs farther apart and captured her mouth in a fierce kiss as he lined up, but just as his cock brushed through the wet mess between her thighs, he yanked himself back.

"Fuck!"

Condom, goddamn fucking condom. Idiot!

Turning, he ripped open the drawer beside him and growled as he slammed it shut. Stomping around the end of the bed he hauled open the other one and ended up grabbing three in his haste. Dropping the other two to the bed, he tore the foil open and snapped his fingers.

"Come here," he growled, impatient as she shifted, and he met her halfway across the bed. Logan dragged her under him as he spread her thighs again.

"You didn't need to—"

"We can talk about that in the morning," he cut her off, lining up again to press against her. "Right now, I just want to hear you come."

He didn't have the patience to tease her anymore, he thrust deep on the first stroke of his hips, and Cassandra arched, her mouth open in a silent cry that he wanted to memorize. There was no waiting, and he fucked her hard, lifting himself up so he could reach between them and rub her clit.

"Fuck, fuck, fuck!" she whined, writhing under him, squeezing his cock inside her as he dragged her back to the edge and forced her over it. Her cry was loud, completely uninhibited, and so fucking sexy as her body clenched him in delirious waves that tested him to his limits.

"Again," he demanded, and she bit down on her lip, eyes clenched tight as he rocked her against the bedding with every hard thrust. The electric buzz of pleasure wasn't something he could ignore. Being in her mouth had worn down all his self-control, but there was no way in hell he was coming before he felt her come again. "One more time. Come for me, Cassandra."

He focused on her clit, entranced by the way her brows pulled together in a false mask of pain as she fisted the covers on either side of her. She whined, babbling something under her breath as her hips lifted to meet every surge of his own, and then she went tense under him, gripping his cock tight in her heat, and she came with a shout.

"God! Logan!" she cried, and he braced his elbows beside her to drive in, thrusting hard, but he was lost already. The world went bright as fire shot down his spine, leaving cataclysmic ecstasy in its wake as he held himself deep and groaned, coming hard.

For a moment all he could hear was his own breathing, his ears buzzing, and then he felt her arms around his neck, pulling him into a kiss that he accepted gladly. They were both hot, sticky with sweat, but he didn't care as he pressed her into the bed. A shiver rolled through her muscles, and she squeezed him again, dragging a buzzing groan from him.

Too much.

"Fuck, you are amazing," he breathed as he pulled out, grinning when she whined at him and tried to bring him back. "One second."

Ripping the condom off, he debated getting up to walk to the bathroom, but he wasn't completely sure his legs would hold him, so he dropped it off the side and decided he'd deal with it in the morning. Turning back to grab her, they managed to find their way under the covers, her curled against his front, and then she wiggled.

"What is it?" he asked, and she sighed.

"Nothing."

Leaning back, he grabbed a palmful of her ass and squeezed hard before he spanked her. "Want to try that again?"

"It's not like we can fix it, so—"

"Answer me," he demanded.

"Fine. I don't have anything to wrap my hair up for bed, so it's going to be a wreck in the morning *and* I'm going to be rubbing my face and yours in all the oils." She sighed and he could practically hear her rolling her eyes. "Like I said, nothing we can fix."

It took him a second in his orgasm-rattled brain to process what she was saying and then he sat up and climbed out of bed. Grabbing the condom from the floor, he swung by the bathroom to toss it in the trash before heading to his closet to flip the light on.

"Logan, just come back to bed," she called, but he kept searching until he grabbed what he was looking for and returned.

"Will either of these scarves work? This one is cashmere. This one is silk." He held them out and Cassandra sat up in bed with an odd look on her face.

"Seriously?"

He tried to think back to what she'd worn the night after Black Light, his mind spinning to think of what was different other than the colorful pattern. "What kind of fabric do you need?"

"Logan, you are... fantastic." She crawled over to him, sitting up on her knees to catch his face in her hands. "Thank you."

The kiss wasn't fevered and intense like their earlier ones. No, this one was softer, deeper, powerful in a completely different way. He leaned into it, wrapping his arms around her back as she took her time tasting his lips and tongue, occasionally tracing her teeth over his lower lip before returning for more. Then she hugged him, her face buried in the crook of his neck, and all he could do was hold her.

"Did I do something right, or something stupid?" he asked quietly, and she laughed softly, pressing another kiss to his shoulder.

"You did something very right." Sitting back on her heels, she held out her hand with a smile. "Can I have the silk scarf?"

"Of course," he answered, handing it over to her. As he went back to the closet to return the other one and turn off the light, he spoke over his shoulder. "Just tell me what you need, and I'll get it."

"You don't need to do that," she said, and he stared at her from the doorway of the closet as she pushed her curls on top of her head and started to wrap them.

"Since I absolutely plan on fucking you here again, I consider it a smart investment." Searching the floor, he found his pants and dug out his phone to set his alarm. "Do you have anything going on tomorrow?"

Cassandra glanced over, still giving him an absolutely delicious visual as she knelt on his bed. "My schedule is clear tomorrow. You?"

"I have a mid-day meeting I can't skip, but that gives us the morning together." Plugging his phone in, he sat down on the edge of the bed to watch her. "You know I'm going to make you give me that list of what you need here, don't you?"

She laughed to herself as she tucked the scarf in place, shaking her head. "There you go, being an asshole and a gentleman at the same time."

"That didn't sound like a 'yes, sir' to me," he replied, pulling her back down to the bed before he yanked the covers over them.

"Yes, sir," she answered with a sarcastic sigh, settling against him, and he wrapped his arm around her to pull her tight to his chest.

"I knew you'd see it my way." Grinning, he placed a kiss on her shoulder before he settled in.

"Asshole," she muttered under her breath, but he heard the smile in her voice as she got comfortable, and he let the comment slide. Mostly because he was tired, but also because it was true. He'd never been one to back down once he had his mind set on something, and tonight had only confirmed what he'd been thinking for days.

He didn't just want to have fun with Cassandra Moreira, he wanted *her*. He wanted *this*. Her in his arms, sleeping in his bed, making him laugh at dinner, squealing with joy as he spun her on the dancefloor, and whimpering and crying and coming underneath him.

In fact… he was pretty sure he'd never wanted anything more.

CHAPTER 14

CASSANDRA

*S*he woke to an empty bed, reaching blindly for him before sitting up to search the room.

"Logan?" she called out, shifting to the edge of the mattress as she recognized the soft sound of music coming from somewhere in the house. Getting up, she found her dress and purse laid out on a big chair, underwear and bra on top, with her heels tucked under it.

How long have you been up, Logan?

Digging out her phone, she woke it up to find that it was just after 8:30 in the morning. He was an early bird, apparently, and the thought made her smile as she tucked her phone back into her purse and got dressed. Wandering into the bathroom to see if her hair was salvageable, she found it frizzy as hell, but not as bad as she'd expected for not brushing it.

Leaving the scarf on the counter, she couldn't help but smile to herself as she remembered how thoughtful he'd been. Plenty of guys had never cared one way or another, but he hadn't just cared... he'd done what he could to help. Even though he *was* bossy about it.

An asshole and a gentleman for sure.

Cassandra grabbed her purse and followed the music out of his bedroom and toward the stairs. In the daylight, it was easier to see the house. The top floor was all tastefully decorated, minimalistic, and when she headed downstairs into the huge living room she found more of the same. Beautifully designed, but no pictures, no souvenirs, nothing personal — and no Christmas decorations. Not even a tree.

It almost looked staged. Like it could be for sale tomorrow.

Turning another corner, she found Logan sitting at the island in the kitchen with the music pouring out of a tiny speaker in front of him. He was already dressed in a suit with his jacket draped over the chair beside him, staring at his laptop with a coffee cup at his side. The morning sun poured in through all the windows, turning his hair into a golden halo as he smiled at her. "Hey, did the music wake you?"

"I don't think so, but I like it," she answered, moving to the edge of the island to lean on it. She'd been listening to the music as she'd wandered, a mix of different indie songs, some darker and closer to rock, others softer. This one was more instrumental, but he reached over to the little dark blue speaker to turn it down anyway.

"How did you sleep?"

"Very well," she replied, grinning. "Did you have trouble, or are you always up this early?"

"I woke up at seven, which is pretty late for me."

"Oh," she said with a laugh. "If I don't have to be up for a call, I'm happy to sleep in. I've always been more of a night owl."

"I wish I could sleep in. Too many years of being told not to waste the day, get up with the sun, all that." He shrugged, getting up to move toward the coffee pot. "Want coffee?"

"Sure." Glancing around the kitchen, she went to the fridge and opened it to find it relatively empty. Some glass containers were stacked on the shelves, and she slid one out. The top of it had a label with his last name on it and 'Mediterranean chicken and couscous with seasonal vegetables.' Looking at a few more of the containers she saw they were all prepared, ready-to-eat meals by the same person. "Who is Chef Russo?"

"Oh, that's a meal service I pay for. Chef Russo does catering and meal plans for one of my VPs, and he got me hooked last year," he answered. "It makes dinner easy."

"I see." Tucking the glass container back in its stack, she was amazed by how barren the rest of his fridge was. It barely looked like it'd been used at all. "Are any of these breakfast?"

"Shit. No." Walking over to her with a cup of coffee, he pointed to the half-and-half sitting lonely in the door. "Are you hungry?"

"Well, yeah... do you not eat breakfast?" she asked, grinning as she took the cup of coffee from him to set it on the island so she could make it the way she liked.

"Not usually. I just grab a protein shake and about a gallon of coffee." Shrugging apologetically, he turned to look around his kitchen. "You can have any of the meals, or we can go out and get something."

Laughing, she shook her head and took a sip of the coffee. *Bitter, blech.* "It's fine. I can eat later."

"I don't want you to be hungry. Maybe I can have something delivered? Let me—"

"Logan, it's fine," she said, cutting him off as she stepped closer to give him a quick kiss. "Anyway, you promised me a tour of this massive place."

"If you're sure." Stealing another kiss, he moved back to his laptop. "Just let me finish this email," he added, typing while she walked over to the little container of sugar beside the coffee, grateful he at least had that.

Taking a much more satisfying sip, she set down her purse and leaned back against the counter to watch him. He was clearly focused, but not stressed. This wasn't some emergency situation he'd got out of bed to handle... it was just his normal routine.

The life of a CEO?

When he finally closed the laptop, he flashed a smile at her. "Ready?"

"I am! I want the grand tour." Raising her coffee cup, she moved toward the doorway. "Come on, show me around your mansion."

"It's not a mansion, Cassandra," he replied with a sigh, leaving his coffee behind as he led her back into the living room. "It's just a big house. Yeah, it's got more space around it than others, but I like the privacy."

"That makes sense. I can hear everything my neighbors say when they get into an argument." She laughed a little. "Although, Abelita and I say it's kind of like listening to a soap opera, because they are dramatic as *hell*."

"Maybe I'll get lucky and catch an episode," he said with a grin, turning to look at the massive living room, and she had to admire his confidence. Last night he'd said he wanted her back in his house, and now he was talking like he'd be at her apartment often enough to listen to the neighbors get into it again. One thing was definitely true about Logan — he wasn't shy, and she liked that.

"Maybe you will," she replied, smiling at him over her coffee mug, but he just shook his head at her as he chuckled.

"All right, so you want a tour..." Waving his arm dramatically at the living room, he put on a ridiculous movie announcer voice. "This is the center of the house, a spacious living room that — as you can see — extends up to the second floor, leaving vaulted ceilings and plenty of sunlight. The built-in wet bar has its own fridge, and the fireplace is made of a stone... that I can't remember the fucking name of, but I'm sure it was expensive. The last owners installed it."

"Oooo, ahhh," she replied, exaggerating her awe before she laughed.

"Hey, you're the one who wanted a *grand* tour, brat," he answered, returning to his normal voice as he swatted her ass and turned her slightly. "Over there is the dining room and the exit to the garage, and behind you is the pool."

Turning around, she looked out the floor-to-ceiling windows to see the pool in a well-landscaped yard bordered by tall, bushy trees on one side. The other side looked out over Los Angeles — the sprawling city spread out under a haze that did nothing to lessen how impressive it was. "You really do live a charmed life, Logan. That's a very nice view."

"It's okay," he replied, and when she realized he was being serious, she was a little surprised.

"You're kidding, right? It's awesome, and I bet it's beautiful at night. All we can see from our apartment is the parking lot, so *this* is amazing." Tilting her head, she watched his face as it went placid. "You recognize that, don't you?"

Logan shrugged. "There's plenty of much larger houses in L.A. with better views."

"Does that make yours any less fancy?" she asked, and he sighed at her. "If you don't like it, then why did you buy it? It's not like you couldn't afford something else, Mr. Moneybags."

"Do you want to see the house, or do you just want to mock my skills in house hunting?" he asked, and she grinned.

"Can't I do both?"

"Such a brat... I cannot wait to show you the playroom upstairs," he replied, a low, threatening tease before he tilted his head toward the living room. "But let me show you this stuff first."

"Wait, where's your Christmas tree?" Cassandra circled her finger in the air. "Or *any* holiday decorations. Whatever you celebrate."

"I don't really do that. Not my thing." Logan pointed across the living room. "May I show you the next stop on our tour?"

"Okay, lead the way, Grinch," she said, laughing quietly because Logan was hating this as much as she was enjoying it.

"I am not a Grinch," he muttered, turning to guide her down a side hall as he pointed into different rooms. "Gym, guest room, there's a wine room at the end of the hall." Taking a few steps forward, he opened a door on the left. "And this is my study."

Approaching him, she peeked through the doorways. Every room was perfectly maintained, spotless, and the equipment in his gym looked better than the stuff at her local one. But the room that instantly pulled her inside was his study. Unlike the rest of the house that was all cool tones, designer chic, with clean lines, his office was almost cluttered. Floor-to-ceiling book-shelves lined one wall, filled with random books — mostly fiction based on the colorful spines — and, finally, there were pictures.

A handful were of him in different places around the world, alone, and from what she could tell he was younger in most of them. Moving down the wall of shelves, she searched for any pictures of him with friends or family, but there were none. Some were completely void of people, just photos of scenery. Beautiful… but empty.

Like his house.

Crossing behind his desk, she found one frame perched on the corner. The photo was of a kid who looked enough like him for her to be sure the smiling woman at his side was his mom. The urge to ask him about her was strong, but she bit her tongue. She didn't need to ask to know his mom had passed when he was young. It was the only reason he'd have such an outdated picture on his desk, and the idea made her chest hurt.

Shit. I don't know what I'd do without my mom… or my dad.

Turning away from his desk, she found herself facing a large portrait hanging on the wall. It was another photograph, and this one had an older man sitting in a high-backed leather chair with Logan standing at his right, and she had no doubt this was his dad. Their faces were similar, their hair light, and even the way their shoulders filled out their suit jackets seemed to match, but it wasn't like any portrait her family had ever taken. The whole image seemed cold, forced, from the wan smile on his father's face to the stiff way Logan rested his hand on the back of the chair, barely smiling at all.

"You can ask." Logan leaned against the wall on the other side of a small bar filled with crystal decanters. "I know you want to, so just go ahead."

"We don't have to talk about it," she said, shaking her head. "I was just looking."

His gaze hovered somewhere near the floor, hands in his pockets, and she thought about just walking out of the study, but then he looked up at the portrait in front of her. "He died of a heart attack. Not sure if he knew it was an issue or not, he wouldn't have told me or anyone else if he had known… but he dropped dead at the Los Angeles Country Club, out on the golf course."

"Logan, I'm sorry," she replied softly, wanting to hug him, comfort him, but he was stiff. Tense.

"You don't need to be. I inherited all of my asshole genes from him." Smiling bitterly, Logan shrugged a shoulder. "Of course, he made damn sure I'd be enough of a gentleman to represent the family well. So, I guess you have him to thank for that."

No, I don't.

Everything about the way Logan talked about the man told her she wouldn't have the urge to thank his father anytime soon. Or ever. There was so much anger and pain brimming just under the surface, and she wanted to ask questions, to help somehow, but she couldn't find the words to broach a topic that intense.

"She died when I was ten." He tilted his chin at the picture on his desk, his eyes staying on the frame as he continued, "Well, I was almost eleven. Three weeks shy."

"How?" she whispered, immediately cringing at herself for asking.

"Accidental overdose. Vicodin." Logan stared at the ground again, running a hand through his hair in a fierce swipe as he laughed harshly. "Guess she was ahead of her time with the whole opioid crisis."

It was a dark joke, and she knew he was just saying it as a defense, but she had no clue what to say in response. 'Sorry' seemed such a hollow, meaningless word in the face of that kind of loss. Taking a deep breath, she set her coffee cup on the edge of his desk and walked over to wrap her arms around his middle, hugging him tight.

"It's okay," he said, running a hand down her back as if he were comforting *her* instead of the other way around. "It's all in the past."

"Doesn't matter," she replied, hugging him harder, and after a minute she felt him relax a little as he wrapped his arms around her.

"Okay, let's move on." He gave her a squeeze, then tried to pull back, but she held on.

"Not yet."

"Are you really going to argue with me right now?"

"Yep," she answered with a pop of her lips, keeping them right where they were. Cassandra had never been great at heavy conversations. Things like death and tragedy always just made her stomach squirm, but she could hug him. She could show him she cared about his losses, because she was pretty sure that he didn't have many people in his life — if any — who had done this for him. And even if his father was an asshole, which she believed, the man had still been his dad.

"I'm only letting you do this because I like how it feels having your chest pressed against me."

Groaning, she rolled her eyes and leaned back to look at him. "Asshole."

"Yep," he replied, mimicking the sarcastic emphasis she'd given to it as he grinned at her, but the smile didn't reach his eyes. Sadness and pain still lurked underneath all that cocky bravado... she just couldn't figure out how to reach it. Taking a deep breath, he gently pulled her arms from around him, squeezing them before he let go. "Ready to see the upstairs?"

"Sure," she conceded, knowing that he was done talking about his past for now, but her head was spinning as he moved away from her. Logan picked up her coffee off the desk, wiping at the wood with his hand before he brought it over to her and she cringed. "Did I leave a ring?"

"No, but I kind of wish you had. It would have given me an excuse to light your ass up this morning."

"I haven't earned that yet?" she quipped, laughing when he groaned and headed toward the door.

"You are an absolute brat." Jerking his head into the hall, he ordered, "Out."

"Yes, sir!" Cassandra gave a quick salute, which made him sigh as he disappeared through the doorway. She could hear his shoes on the tile, but she turned to look at the picture of his father one more time. If anyone was to blame for the darkness hiding behind Logan's eyes, it was that man.

"Cassandra?" Logan called out, and she followed quickly, her heels echoing in the spacious house as she tracked his voice to the base of the stairs. "Come on, there's more to see."

There were several other guest rooms on the second floor that could have been upscale hotel rooms for all the personal details they held. There was no dust anywhere, but she had a feeling no one had stayed there in a long time — if ever. Every ounce of her intuition was buzzing, creating a whirlwind of thoughts that wouldn't be silenced as he walked her around the top floor and into the playroom.

"Well, this is definitely impressive," she said, looking at all of the well-made equipment. A St. Andrew's Cross was bolted to one wall, a spanking bench tucked in one corner, hard points in the ceiling, and a small bed with only a black fitted sheet. Various toys and devious implements were laid out on a narrow table beside a tall cabinet she assumed held even more. It was a dream playroom, and it all matched. Every piece of wood in the room was stained to the same color, all of the leather a rich, matte black. Each restraint looked like they were made by the same person.

It was neat, ordered, and also the only room in the house with a thin sheen of dust.

"How long since you've had the chance to use this stuff?" she asked, and Logan shrugged as he leaned against the wall by the door.

"A while."

"And how long is that?"

Logan slowly crossed his arms, his eyes narrowing slightly. "Does it matter?"

"I guess not. It's just clear you invested a lot of money to make this what you wanted it to be," she replied, and he huffed.

"What is it with you and money?"

"Come on, Logan," she said as she walked over and hopped up onto the edge of the bed, waving a hand around her. "There's only one reason you bought this house, had it decorated by someone who *clearly* wasn't you, and then spent money to make your playroom look like this."

"And what reason is that?"

"To make sure anyone who comes here sees that you have money and—"

"That's not—" Logan tried to interrupt, but she let out a groan and he stopped himself, clenching his jaw for a moment. "Fine, since you seem to know me so well, why did I do all this?"

"Because you're trying to distract people from how empty this place is," she finished, meeting his serious gaze with her own. Silence reigned for a long minute, and she shook her head. "Where are the pictures of your friends, Logan? Why were you by yourself in every picture of you traveling the world?"

"I don't take a lot of pictures, Cassandra. Neither do the people I know." He shoved a hand through his hair, pushing it off his forehead for a moment before his arms were crossed again. "I don't do Instagram and all that social media stuff, remember?"

"So, you went on those trips with people?" she pressed, feeling like a bitch, but she knew she was right.

"I like to travel alone."

"Okay, well, who's your best friend?" she asked, wrapping her fingers over the edge of the mattress as she leaned forward. Logan's brows pulled together for a moment, his eyes flicking across the floor before they came back to her.

"Guys don't have best friends, Cassandra, that's—"

"That's bullshit, but fine," she interrupted, waving off his excuse. "Name five of your friends then."

"Paul Browning."

"And who is that?"

"He's the VP of marketing at work, and we eat lunch together several times a week," he replied, shoulders stiff, his jaw tense the second he stopped speaking.

Seriously?

"Do you talk about life or work?"

"We talk about work, and sometimes his kids, and—"

"He doesn't count," she said.

"Why not?" Logan snapped, dropping his arms to his sides as he took a step forward.

"Have you ever gone out with him outside of work? Ever had him here to hang out?" Cassandra asked, and she knew the answer without him even speaking. His shoulders dipped as he turned away from her to walk across the playroom. Pacing one way, and then the other. "What about at Black Light? Do you meet up with any of the other doms there?"

"Weston. I take a lot of his classes. And Miles does some cool shit with edge play and whips and—"

"Not classes, Logan. *Friends.* Who are your friends at Black Light? Or, hell, anywhere! Who do you spend your time with?" she asked, hearing the tension in her own voice as he continued to pace, shaking his head at the floor.

Wyatt said he never talks to anyone.

Jesus, is he really this alone?

"Logan, come here." Holding out her hand, she reached for him, beckoning him closer with a wave of her fingers when his eyes came up to seek hers. "Please?"

"I don't see why any of this matters," he said, still stiff as hell, but he came over to her. When he was close enough, she grabbed his hand, shifting her knees apart to pull him between them.

"Because." Cassandra squeezed his hand, looking up at him even though he wouldn't quite meet her gaze. "I like you, Logan"

That got his eyes to meet hers, the wrinkle appearing between his brows again as he stared down at her.

"I like you, and other people will too if you'll give them a chance," she continued, but he tried to pull back so she hooked her heels behind his thighs to keep him there. "Nuh-uh. You may not think it's important, or that it matters, but you need friends. Everyone does."

"Is that a pre-requisite to dating you?" he asked, his tone heavily laced with exhausted sarcasm, and she let a smile sneak across her lips.

"For the sake of this conversation, let's say that *yes*, it is."

"You can't be serious."

"I am." Grinning, she pulled him closer, appreciating that the bed was the perfect height to have him pressed against her in a very nice way. He seemed to notice too, because Logan leaned forward, his free hand tracing her neck before sliding to the back to cradle her head.

"This is bullshit," he muttered, but she could see the moment he relented. The tension was fading, and she knew exactly what they needed to do.

"Humor me," she answered, watching the way his eyes dipped to the neckline of her dress before coming back to her face. "My friend Vanessa invited me to go to Black Light with her and her boyfriend, Wyatt. I think we should take them up on it."

"Are you trying to set me up with this guy?"

"Absolutely. It's a friend date, but the bonus is that you get a date out of me at the same time." She couldn't bite back the wide grin of victory as he chuckled and leaned down to brush his lips over hers.

"And you're going to call it a date?" he asked, teasing her with another too-light kiss.

"Yes, sir. And you're going to make a friend."

Another low chuckle as he leaned up enough to meet her gaze. "What if I hate this guy?"

"I don't think anyone hates Wyatt, but if you hate him... we'll find you another future bestie."

Logan groaned, but there was a hint of a smile on his lips as he said, "Guys don't have *besties*, Cassandra."

"I'm going to greatly enjoy proving you wrong."

Laughing, Logan tightened his grip on her neck a moment before he leaned her back on the bed, lips hovering above hers. "Oh, my little brat, I'm going to drop you off at your apartment with a *very* sore ass."

"Sounds fantastic," she replied, biting down on her lip as he pressed her into the mattress, the growing hard-on behind his slacks rubbing her in just the right way. "But... I'm still right."

"That's it," Logan said, leaning up and flipping her onto her stomach in a fluid movement that left her bent over the side of the bed. "Time to give you a taste of what you'll get on our *next* date."

CHAPTER 15

LOGAN

*I*t had been two days since he'd seen Cassandra. They'd met up to watch a movie — his favorite Christmas flick, *Die Hard*. Tucked together on her couch, with her legs draped over his lap, it had been so simple, so easy. She'd cracked jokes through the whole thing, which would have annoyed him had it been anyone else, but with Cassandra he'd found himself laughing along with her. Her vibrant smile had let him relax, and he'd started quoting the movie to her in time with the characters, which only made her laugh more. They'd started making out as Hans Gruber fell from Nakatomi Plaza and ended the night in her bed for another round of mind-blowing sex. It hadn't been a fancy date, hadn't been spontaneous or adventurous, but it had been so damn good.

Everything was just… better around Cassandra Moreira.

He was better around her.

Which was why he'd tried to see her again, even for lunch, but other than the selfies she'd sent him via text he hadn't laid eyes on her smile in two miserable days. He knew he couldn't spend every night with her, and it wasn't like he could expect it. They were just starting to test the waters on this dating thing…

and she had a life. She had other people who wanted to see her, catch up with her since she was finally in town for a few weeks.

She had *friends.*

Growling under his breath, Logan turned away from the shitstorm on his computer screen to stare out the window at the bustle of downtown L.A. The conversation they'd had in his playroom had been playing in his head on repeat, like a low hum in the back of his mind that wouldn't shut up and leave him the fuck alone.

At first, he'd pushed the whole bullshit idea aside. He wasn't like Cassandra. He wasn't warm and outgoing. He was serious, an introvert, and he'd never needed another person — *a friend* — to make his life feel complete. People took time, and for the majority of the human population he wasn't willing to invest the time or energy in them that a friendship required. Corporate dinners and events were always miserable and draining, so why should he volunteer to do that shit in his free time? It was stupid.

Yet, her words kept coming back to haunt him.

Every time he entered his study, he saw the photos she'd mentioned. His solo trips to Dubai, China, Cape Town, Hawaii, Costa Rica, Thailand, and more… They'd always been nice memories. Now they were like an echo chamber, repeating her words, asking him why he hadn't gone with someone. *Anyone.*

But it wasn't like he'd had a lot of options.

He'd hated the pompous assholes at Yale, and when he'd started working for his father, everyone steered clear of him. Warren Chisholm had not been well liked within his own company, and the stain of his harsh demeanor had followed Logan for years, keeping everyone at arm's length.

And then he'd died, and Logan had taken over the company — which hadn't helped things. It just meant longer hours, more meetings, and more pressure to not fuck up his family's name.

How the hell was he supposed to fit *friends* into that?

The ding of another email made him turn back around, and it was more bad news. *Fucking bastards.* He wanted to kill someone, or break something, but instead of throwing his monitor across the room, Logan pushed up from his desk and walked to the bar against the wall. Ripping the lid off the ice bucket, he found it a third of the way full of water instead of ice.

"Laura!" he shouted, waiting for his assistant to come in as he slammed the lid back down and resorted to pouring the whiskey into a glass neat.

"Yes, Mr. Chisholm?" Laura hovered in the doorway as he took a sip of the liquor, feeling it burn down his throat, but it did nothing to soothe him.

"There's no ice," he snapped, leaving the bar to go back to his desk and deal with the nightmare that had started the day before and seemed to just be getting worse.

"I'll take care of it." His assistant moved quickly to take the bucket, rushing back to the door where she paused. "Is there anything else—"

"No, just the ice. I have to handle the Preline account." He paused to take another drink. "Actually, reschedule my next meeting and have Edwards come up here. Now."

"Yes, sir," she answered, shutting the door quietly, and he finished the glass as soon as she was gone. He knew he needed to figure out what their next steps would be — probably another miserable dinner to soothe the fucking client and make them feel special and appreciated, which he'd had to do last quarter as well.

But he had a feeling it wouldn't work this time.

Clicking the email so it opened full screen, he scanned the lines over and over. *Dip in the market. Preline executives are concerned.*

"Goddammit," he growled, standing back up to refill his glass. With or without ice, he needed to be steady in this next meeting, and the whiskey would make that possible.

~

THE DAY HADN'T IMPROVED, and by six o'clock he had to pull away from his computer feeling no better than he had at ten that morning. He'd started the coffee pot so it would be ready while he packed his play bag and changed. If he'd been smart, he would have stopped drinking earlier, but the hits just kept coming.

All damn day.

Like the universe that Cassandra trusted so much was trying to kick him in the fucking balls over and over.

Sitting down at his kitchen island, Logan drank the first cup of coffee black, the heat of it singeing his tongue while the bitter taste helped clear his head. All he'd wanted for days was to see Cassandra again, and he wasn't going to fuck it up. Not tonight in front of her friends.

Pouring another cup of coffee, he had some mercy on himself and added the half-and-half. He just needed to compartmentalize. Put all the shit from work away in a box that he could pick up tomorrow morning, because it *would* be there waiting for him. Tonight was about Cassandra, about making a good impression on her friends, and he wasn't going to accomplish that if he showed up tipsy and still pissed off.

Reaching for his phone, he opened up their text messages and scrolled through the pictures she'd sent, the sassy little comments, and the ones asking about his day. He hadn't told her anything about what was going on at work, because it would be too complicated to explain anyway, and all it would do was bring her down... and Cassandra didn't deserve that. She was inherently positive, *happy*, and Logan would do anything to keep her that way.

She doesn't deserve your bullshit, Logan. Let it go. Focus on tonight.

That's what he needed to do. Let it go and enjoy their night at Black Light. Show her that he could be creative, interesting, spontaneous, friendly — all of the things she wanted — because she didn't deserve his darkness.

Logan finished his second cup of coffee and poured another hefty serving into a travel mug for the drive over to her house. He could use the drive to brush off all the bullshit of the day and get his mind focused on her. At least Cassandra would be happy to see him today, which would be nice because he knew damn well no one else had been.

And if he'd ever wondered why he didn't have friends, that thought answered it for him. No one wanted to be friends with an asshole, much less the asshole who could fire them for their stupid mistakes and black ball them in the industry, and nothing was going to change that.

Not even a 'friend date' setup by a girl he probably didn't deserve.

~

BLACK LIGHT WEST

Cassandra had talked the entire way to Black Light, laughing as she recounted some mix-up that had happened at her shoot that day. Her agent was updating her portfolio, and several other girls, with more high-fashion shots, and somehow two photographers had been booked. Apparently, the two men had got into quite the pissing contest when Roberta suggested they split the models to get the work done faster.

He didn't really understand how it was so funny, but he did love listening to her.

It was her broad smile and the pure joy in her laughter when she couldn't get the next sentence out that had him laughing with her. Her laugh was contagious, and he didn't know if it was that or something else about her that actually managed to make his day fade into the background — but he didn't care. She was with him, on another date, wearing a skin-tight black dress that he couldn't wait to peel off.

Just as he turned off the car in the club's private lot, Cassandra shoved his shoulder. "Okay, spit it out."

"Spit what out?" he asked, glancing over at her in surprise as he adjusted his suit jacket.

"Whatever has you distracted! I don't think you've said more than ten words since we got in the car."

"It's nothing." He forced a casual smile on his face, leaning over to run his hand up her thigh, shoving her dress up until he could trace her underwear. "Long day at work, but I've been looking forward to this all week."

"Oh really..." Cassandra grinned, spreading her legs a little wider for him. "Excited to meet your new bestie?"

Logan pinched the inside of her thigh, eliciting a little yelp from her. "Trust me, I haven't been thinking about anyone but you."

"What a liiiine!" She laughed again, pushing his hand away before she leaned across the gearshift to kiss him. It was quick, too quick, but she leaned back smiling. "You're lucky that you're cute enough to pull that off."

"Oh, so I'm *cute* now?" he taunted, and she rolled her eyes.

"Let's go in!"

"I saw you roll your eyes, brat," he said, putting the edge in his tone that always got her attention. "That's one."

"Lucky me," she replied, winking at him before she climbed out of the car. With a sigh, he followed her, locking it as he took her arm to head inside.

It was only a little after eight when they entered Black Light, early for a club like this, but Brian had been ready at the security desk in the locker room, and a few other members were already milling around the bar.

Logan watched Cassandra for any hint that she saw her

friends, but it seemed they weren't here yet. Oddly, he felt a sense of relief at that.

Maybe they wouldn't come?

If they did skip out with some excuse, it meant he'd get his hands on Cassandra that much faster. So, even though it made him feel like an asshole, he was secretly rooting for a no-show from the couple she was so excited for him to meet.

"Let's just grab a table, I'm sure they'll be here soon," Cassandra said, tugging him toward the bar, and even though he was tempted to remind her of exactly where they were... he decided to just add the missing 'sir' to her running tally. "Can I have a glass of the Cakebread Chardonnay?"

"Sure thing," Susie replied with a smile, sporting a very uplifting corset for the night, and then she glanced at him for his order. He'd had more than enough to drink today, but he *had* sobered up with the pot of coffee and the idea of this awkward double-date actually happening had him on edge, so he tugged out his wallet to get his Black Light membership card.

"I'll take an old fashioned with the High West Double Rye if you've got it," he said, tapping the card on the bar top as Susie nodded at him and turned to get their drinks.

"I promise that Vanessa and Wyatt are nice, Logan. You're going to like them."

"Right," he said, letting all of his doubt stain the word, and she rolled her eyes. "That's four."

"Four!" Cassandra laughed, looking at him like she didn't believe it. "No way am I up to four already."

"Well..." Logan ticked them on off his fingers. "You rolled your eyes in the car, didn't use sir *twice*, and you just rolled your eyes again."

"That's bullshit, *sir*," she said, but she was still smiling. It wasn't like his masochistic brat was worried about the swats, she loved them, and he loved the way she reveled in the pain. It was why he was willing to do just about anything to prove to her that dating him wasn't a bad idea.

Even if it meant being set up on a 'friend date' with another dom like he was some kind of newbie in the lifestyle.

"Here you go!" Susie cheered, setting their drinks down before snagging the card from his fingers to run it. A few seconds later she handed it back, and he set a twenty on the bar. "Thanks, enjoy yourselves tonight."

"Okay, Cassandra, why don't you remind me of who exactly these two are before they get here." Sliding a hand across her back, he guided her over to a table with four chairs where they could clearly see the door.

Logan took his time with the drink in front of him while Cassandra told him all about Vanessa Novak's ballet career, how Vanessa had met Wyatt during Roulette on the same night they had. Except, Wyatt and Vanessa had stayed together, were *living together* now. It was like hearing about an alternate timeline that he could have had with Cassandra if he hadn't let her modeling schedule keep him from pursuing her more seriously.

Idiot.

"Anyway, Wyatt is a corporate business guy too. I think Vanessa said he's a CEO— wait, no, not that one. But another one like that," Cassandra added, casually waving her hand before she checked the door again. "It's why I think you two will get along just fine. You're both into BDSM, and you can talk business together."

"Does he work in finance as well?" he asked, tensing with concern that he might be one of the assholes at Berringer Holdings that had spent the last week fucking his life up.

"No, something with computers." Cassandra suddenly stood up from the table, waving with a cheerful little squeak. "Vanessa!"

"Cass!" A beautiful young woman with dark hair ran toward their table, followed at a much more leisurely pace by a man in a suit. He stood, watching as the girls exploded into excited babbling, hugging each other several times, before Vanessa finally looked over at him. "Logan! I do remember you from Roulette!"

"Nice to meet you again, Vanessa," he said, accepting her handshake over the table, without mentioning that while she seemed sort of familiar, he didn't remember her from the night of Roulette at all.

"And I'm Wyatt, also dragged here by my submissive." Chuckling, Wyatt came over to shake his hand, offering a firm grip. "I have a feeling you're in as much trouble as I am."

"What do you mean?" Logan asked, glancing at Cassandra to see if he was missing some inside joke.

"Dealing with an independent, successful masochist for a sub, which means we are often playing catch-up on *their* decisions." He was still chuckling as he released Logan's hand. "Like tonight, for example. Vanessa completely sprung it on me *yesterday.*"

The woman blushed a little, smiling sheepishly. "I sort of forgot I'd agreed to it when Cass called me."

"Right," Wyatt said, and Logan couldn't help but smirk at the tone he'd used. He knew that meant she'd likely already been punished for that, or was going to be tonight.

"Let's all sit down and talk! Wyatt, will you sit by Logan?" Cassandra asked, and when Logan arched an eyebrow she grinned. "Please, sirs?"

"Marginally better," Logan chastised, but he winked at her as he took his seat beside Wyatt.

"What would you like to drink, sir?" Vanessa asked. "Cass and I are going to go grab drinks from the bar."

"Rittenhouse Rye. Thanks, baby." Wyatt was smiling as the girls went to the bar, and then the man leaned back in his chair to give him an appraising stare. "So, apparently we're supposed to be friends."

Logan found himself chuckling, appreciating the blunt way the other man addressed the situation they'd been put in. "Yes, apparently we are."

"Well, like I said, we're both in trouble with them." Shaking his head, Wyatt looked past him to where the two women were standing at the bar. Cassandra's long legs had him shifting in his seat, thinking about bending her over a spanking bench again, but he distracted himself by looking at Vanessa. She was in a light pink skirt that barely covered her ass, pale tights... and ballet shoes.

"Did she come straight from the ballet?" he asked, turning to look at Wyatt who grinned slowly.

"No, actually, she wore that for me tonight." Wyatt shrugged. "Since we're all going to play later, she thought it would be fun to revisit the outfit I put her in for Roulette."

"Nice choice," Logan acknowledged, and Wyatt laughed softly.

"Cassandra looks very nice as well. They may be trouble, but you have to admit... we're both very lucky."

"You're right about that," Logan answered, keeping his voice quiet as the girls headed back to the table with glasses. Pointing at the wine in Cassandra's hand, he reminded her, "That's your last drink for the night."

"I know," she said, rolling her eyes, and he lifted his hand, showing all five fingers. Cassandra groaned, sliding his glass across the table. "Dammit. *Sir.*"

"Already up to five tonight?" Vanessa asked, grinning at Cassandra as she took her seat.

"Yep. *Apparently* I'm a brat."

"Makes sense," Vanessa replied, laughing when Cassandra shoved her playfully.

"Bitch," Cassandra retorted, but they were both laughing as Vanessa stuck her tongue out at her. The two women seemed close, but Logan wasn't surprised that Cassandra had managed to make a friend so easily. It was just who she was.

As the evening progressed, what did surprise him was how comfortable he felt around Wyatt. When the girls got wrapped up in a conversation about some show that neither of them knew anything about, Wyatt had started asking him about what he did for a living. He'd given the high-level of it and been relieved to find out that Wyatt was a CFO at an IT infrastructure company called Pytheas, named after some Greek explorer. While Logan wasn't remotely familiar with the field, he was very glad to know the man had nothing to do with his rival.

That would have been a nightmare.

The other dom also had good taste in liquor. They were both drinking rye and were busy chatting about the different brands they enjoyed when Cassandra suddenly reached over and touched his arm, a big smile on her radiant face.

"Sir! You have to tell Vanessa about where you learned to dance!"

"You can dance?" Wyatt asked, and Logan felt a hint of heat rising up his chest.

"Kind of," he answered, giving Cassandra a look that promised punishment if she kept going, but it didn't faze her at all.

"Bullshit! He was *amazing*, Vanessa. Seriously, he took me to this place that looks like it fell out of the 1920s, and then started swing dancing with me!" Cassandra laughed, leaning back in her chair to clap her hands together. "I swear, I've never been so shocked in my life, and I was getting plenty of death glares from some of the other ladies there."

"I don't think—"

"That's awesome!" Vanessa said, cutting him off as she leaned an elbow on the table. "So, where did you learn to dance? Cassandra said she didn't know."

"My father put me in classes when I was a kid," he answered, not seeing why it was important as he took another small sip of his second old-fashioned. He didn't want to finish it, he wanted a clear head when they started playing, but with this line of questioning he might just down it.

"Dance classes? That's pretty forward thinking," Wyatt said. "My mom was a ballerina when she was younger, but she never suggested it to me."

A bitter laugh slipped past Logan's lips. "Yeah, it definitely wasn't forward thinking. He put me in ballroom dance classes because he didn't want me embarrassing the family at social functions."

"Ouch," Vanessa replied, a wince passing over her face. "I'm guessing you hated it?"

"The ballroom dance? Absolutely. I think I was ten when he made me start going, and I didn't know how to talk to girls, or want to, and most of the girls that had to be there weren't exactly excited either." He shrugged, stealing another sip of his drink as he remembered too many awkward moments of placing his hand on a girl's hip he didn't even know before he'd even had his first kiss. "I only liked going there after the teachers let me switch to the swing classes two or three years in."

"Well, it paid off, because holy *shit* was it sexy!" Cassandra winked at him, and he couldn't suppress the urge to smile.

"I'm glad you enjoyed the date."

"I'm sorry he forced you into it though," Vanessa said, sighing as she leaned back with her wine. "As talented as Cassandra says you are, who knows? You could have been at the ballet with me!"

Logan shook his head, chuckling a little. "Yeah, I don't think that was ever in the cards. I didn't exactly have a choice about my future." His laughter faded as he looked around the table and saw that they all had vaguely concerned expressions, something dangerously close to pity. *Shit.* "Enough about me though. Cassandra said you're performing in *The Nutcracker* at the Dudorov Ballet right now?"

"She is," Wyatt spoke up, saving him from the awkward silence at the table, and the man was looking at Vanessa like she hung the moon. "And she's breathtaking as the Sugar Plum Fairy, which is the role she was born to perform."

"Sir…" Vanessa groaned, blushing brightly.

"It's true! It's a *Grand pas de deux*, and it's her first year as a principal dancer, and she got it."

"I only got the part because Tori moved to New York to join a different company, and— OW!" Vanessa gasped, looking over at Wyatt with a half-shocked, half-laughing look, and Logan was pretty sure he'd just pinched his sub's thigh.

"Want to correct that?" Wyatt asked, voice hard.

Sighing, Vanessa leaned back in her chair with a look of sass he recognized well, and her tone spoke volumes of how little she believed her next words. "I earned the role of the Sugar Plum Fairy through hard work and dedication."

"Oh, I'm going to make you pay for that, little whore," Wyatt whispered across the table, and the blush spread rapidly across Vanessa's face.

"Yes, sir," she answered quietly, but Logan could tell she was excited by the idea as her dom sat back with a huff.

"For the record, she actually *did* earn it through hard work and dedication, even if she doesn't believe it, and while I don't appreciate watching Michael put his hands all over my girl-friend… it's worth it to watch Vanessa turn her body into music."

"Michael is *married*!" Vanessa said through a laugh, but one hard look from Wyatt had her silent again.

"Well, I wish I knew more about the ballet, because all of that sounds very impressive," Logan interjected, ending the pair's staring contest.

"We should go see her then!" Cassandra piped up, a broad smile on her face again. "I already told Vanessa I plan on seeing the show, and if you'll go with me, sir, we can make it another *date*."

"Is that you trying to bribe me into going?" Logan chuckled, shaking his head at Cassandra's obvious ploy. "There's no need. I think it's been years since I saw *The Nutcracker*, and I'd be happy to go with you and see Vanessa work her magic, even if you refuse to call it a date."

"Why wouldn't you call it a date?" Vanessa asked, grinning at Cassandra as she leaned over to nudge her. "Sounds like a date to me."

"Cassandra seems to think that I'm incapable of problem solving around her travel schedule, which we would need to do if she decided to actually 'date' me." Logan smirked as Cassandra's mouth dropped open.

"That is *not* what—"

"Lying is most definitely a punishable offense," he interrupted, staring at her as he toyed with the half-full glass in front of him. *Not drinking any more tonight. I want to be present for each and every cry she's earned.*

"It absolutely is," Wyatt confirmed, raising an eyebrow as he crossed his arms over his chest. "And I seem to remember that when you mentioned this to Vanessa over lunch that you promised me you would discuss those concerns with Logan."

Interesting.

"Oh, she discussed it with me," he confirmed, glancing over at Wyatt with a smirk. "And she agreed to call our night out a date, but it's clear she still doesn't think I'm capable of problem solving the situation with her traveling for work."

"Vanessa! A little help here?" Cassandra asked on a laugh. "I'm getting ganged up on by two doms, and it's nowhere *near* as hot as I thought it would be."

Raising her hands in the air, Vanessa shook her head. "Oh, no, I'm not getting involved in this."

"Traitor," Cassandra muttered, sighing as she looked back at him. "If I made you feel that way, sir, I didn't mean to."

"How else would you describe it?" he asked, even though he already regretted starting this conversation in front of her friends. This should have been had in private, but it seemed like she'd already mentioned it to them… before she'd even discussed it with him… so maybe it was fair game.

"Me being overly cautious," she answered, flashing her broad smile as she waved a hand dismissively. "It's not like we need to worry about it tonight anyway, sir. The important thing tonight was proving that you could have a bestie in Wyatt, and it seems like you two have hit it off!"

"A bestie?" Wyatt echoed, glancing over at him like he'd had something to do with the term.

"Don't ask me," Logan replied, raising his hands. "This is all Cassandra."

"Come on! You guys would be perfect friends. You're both business guys, both doms in the lifestyle, *and* Vanessa and I are already friends." Cassandra shrugged. "It only makes sense."

"Please?" Vanessa added on, and Wyatt spoke first.

"I think Logan and I could have managed swapping contact info without either of you meddling, but fine. We'll do it right now so you can drop it." Digging out his wallet, he plucked a business card from it to slap on the table. "Go get me a pen from the bar, Vanessa."

"Yes, sir!" she chimed, jumping out of her seat to obey.

"I agree with Wyatt." Pulling out his wallet, Logan grabbed one of his business cards as well. "I appreciate the intention behind it, but it seems you two forget who's in charge when we're here."

"Good point," Wyatt replied, chuckling as Vanessa slipped back into her seat and offered him the pen.

"What's a good point?" she asked, looking around the table.

"That you two have been quite bossy about this entire little evening, and that you both might benefit from a reminder of just who is in charge when we're at Black Light." Wyatt scribbled on the back of his business card, sliding it over with the pen. He'd written down his cellphone number.

"We didn't mean anything by it," Vanessa said, sounding more than a little defensive. "We were trying to help."

"And you *did* need the help. Sir," Cassandra tacked the title on the end as an afterthought to her smartass comment, and Logan just chuckled as he added his cell to the back of his business card and passed it to Wyatt.

"*That* just earned you a whole lot of edging, brat." Tilting his head, Logan tapped the pen against his chin, pretending to think very hard. "Or, maybe, I won't let you come at all tonight. I'll just light your ass up and then put you on your knees. Finish in your throat, since I didn't get to last time."

For once, Cassandra's eyes widened. "You wouldn't."

Grinning, Logan leaned back in his chair to tuck away Wyatt's info and slide his wallet back into his pocket. "I guess we'll have to see just how well you can behave the rest of the night."

"Sir, come on, I was joking!" Cassandra looked around the table, glancing at Wyatt and Vanessa as if they might offer any kind of salvation from whatever he decided for the evening. Eventually, she just looked back at him and sighed, a smile creeping over her lips. "Well, it looks like I have to be a good girl, sir."

"Think you can handle that?" he asked, chuckling, and soon enough Vanessa and Wyatt joined in. Apparently, he wasn't the only one who knew Cassandra's brat side.

"Probably not," Cassandra admitted, bursting into laughter herself, and as he watched her joyous self-deprecation, he realized he hadn't thought about the bullshit at work in almost an hour. He actually felt... good. Relaxed. Maybe even a little happy?

And Wyatt wasn't a bad guy. He was someone Logan could actually see himself talking to at the club, or maybe even meeting for drinks... which meant Cassandra had been right about the man.

Although Logan would never admit *that* out loud.

No, it was better to keep her guessing, to keep her on her toes before the scene, and he had so many ideas for just how he could punish his brat for all those eyerolls, her sass, and her scheming.

"Why don't we go see what equipment is available for handling naughty, bossy submissives?" Wyatt suggested, pushing back his chair to stand and Logan followed suit with a grin.

"That sounds like a great idea."

"Told you they'd be friends," Cassandra whispered to Vanessa, grinning.

Bad girl.

Logan laughed darkly as he moved around the table, stopping just behind Cassandra to grip the back of her neck and lift her out of her seat with a firm hold. The little sound she made as her chair slid back was perfection. Cassandra was independent, damn good at what she did, but in Black Light she was *his*, and he needed to remind her of that. Leaning in close, Logan put his lips close to her ear, breathing in the incredible scent of her. "Oh, my naughty little brat, I'm going to greatly enjoy making you scream and beg tonight."

"Don't you always?" she whispered, her voice breathy with arousal, and he felt his cock twitch in response as he chuckled.

"Absolutely."

CHAPTER 16

CASSANDRA

"I like this one," Roberta Price said, tapping one of the photos on the screen, then she tapped another. "And this one."

"You don't think my neck has a weird angle in that one?" Cassandra asked, narrowing her eyes at the computer monitor.

"I think it shows off how long your neck is, and how you can pull off those more artsy poses that the high fashion people adore." Checking the picture in question, Roberta added the first one as well. "I'm not saying it'll be in your final portfolio, but I want to see full prints of these."

"Okay," Cassandra conceded. Roberta Price was known for her skill in the industry, and she trusted her eye. After all, Jaxson and Chase had put their careers in her hands, and they'd been at the top of a hundred designers' lists when they retired. Skimming the photos as Roberta scrolled, she reached out and tapped one. "Oh, that one, definitely."

"Nice eye! Yes, that angle you've got at your waist here is great. Which designer was that?" Roberta mumbled, flipping through the shoot notes at her side.

"Oscar de la Renta," she answered, and then she sighed as

more images scrolled by. "A lot of these are amazing. I loved that dress."

"It comes through in the photos," Roberta replied, winking at her as she clicked a few more photos to move to the next round of decision making. "Maybe he'll book you for a show!"

Cassandra couldn't stifle the eyeroll as the excitement bubbled up inside her. "Right, he's going to want *me.*"

"Shush," her agent snapped, elbowing her. "Having an attitude like that isn't going to bring you any luck from the universe."

"You're right," Cassandra sighed, leaning back from the computer to rub her eyes. She was getting a headache from looking at the thousands of photos from the shoot the day before, and they'd been at it for hours.

Hours? Fuck!

"What time is it?" Cassandra asked, standing up to look for her purse.

"Twelve-thirty, why?" Roberta answered, turning in her chair.

"Shit, shit, shit!"

"Have a date or something?" her agent asked, laughing slightly, but when Cassandra just gave her a guilty look Roberta burst into a smile. "You do! You do have a date!"

"Yes, a lunch date, and I'm going to be late." Groaning, Cassandra dug out her phone and pulled up Lyft. *Thirty-one minutes. Double-fuck.* "Definitely late."

"Well, go on! We have plenty chosen to move forward. I'll finish reviewing the last photos and we'll meet again to review the final choices before the dinner with Elite, okay?"

"You're a life saver," Cassandra replied, leaning down to press a kiss to Roberta's cheek before she rushed out the door, firing off a text to Logan as she took the stairs down.

Running late, so sorry! I'll be there in thirty.

Just as she made it out into the mid-day sun, she felt her

phone buzz in her hand. Logan had already replied, but he didn't seem upset at all based on the short text.

See you soon.

THIRTY-FOUR MINUTES LATER, Cassandra's Lyft driver pulled up outside the towering office building that held Whitney Asset Management. Logan had told her the company existed over several of the floors, but he was on forty-one, and her name would be with security at the front desk.

As soon as she entered the lobby she felt out of place in her comfy sweater and skinny jeans. The massive space was eerily quiet, with a ceiling that had to be several stories up. There were a few groupings of black chairs around steel-and-glass tables, but no one was sitting at them. It was just the guard at the large security desk centered between two elevator banks, with simple garland and a neutral holiday wreath decorating the front. The heels on her boots sounded too loud as she approached, echoing off the walls, but at least the man behind the desk knew she was coming.

"Are you here for an appointment?" he asked, tone way colder than necessary.

"Um, kind of? I'm here to see Logan Chisholm."

"Cassandra Moreira?" The guard said her name in the same deadpan tone he'd asked about the appointment.

"That's me! He's with—"

"Whitney Asset Management, right. I have your name here." He pointed to his left. "Take that elevator. I'll unlock floor forty-one for you."

"Thank you!" Cassandra said cheerily, offering him a smile that he pointedly didn't return as he stared back at the wide desk in front of him. Rolling her eyes as soon as the elevator doors shut, she laughed under her breath at the awkward interaction. If she ever had a job she hated that much, she'd just leave. Whatever the man was making couldn't be worth being *that* unhappy all day, every day.

It took almost no time at all to fly up the building, and she could feel the pressure of gravity tugging at her, and then the almost light-headed sensation as the elevator slowed.

Weird.

The doors opened into a very nice waiting area, and a much friendlier face greeted her behind the massive desk that had 'Whitney Asset Management' on the front in large silver letters and a little Christmas tree tucked in the corner beside it.

"Hello! You're Ms. Moreira, right?" the young woman asked, stepping out from behind the desk to meet her at the elevator doors.

"I am! I'm here to see—"

"Mr. Chisholm," the woman finished for her, still smiling as she tilted her head toward one of the hallways and started walking. "This way! He told us you were coming."

"Oh, great!" Cassandra replied, keeping pace with the woman's quick strides. She was in a pencil skirt with a white blouse, the shiny stilettos on her feet clicking over the tile until they met a carpet runner. "So, what's your name?"

"Me?" the girl slowed, turning to look at Cassandra as she caught up to walk beside her. "I'm Aubrey, but I'm just the front-desk secretary for the executive floor."

Cassandra laughed a little. "So? I just wanted to know who was helping me out. You're way nicer than the asshole downstairs."

Aubrey bit down on a laugh, her cheeks turning pink as her rapid pace slowed to something closer to a walk than a march. "That's Mr. Dover, and he's not exactly great at customer service. Takes the whole security job a little *too* seriously."

"Apparently. I think I've seen more personality in a potato,"

Cassandra said quietly, and Aubrey laughed, hushing herself quickly.

"Oh my God, I'm going to have to use that one."

"It's yours." She smiled as the young woman followed a bend in the hall, and the space opened up. Warm, dark wood doors appeared at random intervals, and in front of each was a large desk occupied by another professionally dressed employee. "Who are they?" she whispered.

"Executive assistants," Aubrey whispered back. "You want to see Laura, she's in the center on that wall. That's Mr. Chisholm's office. Well… it looks like she had to step away, but just grab a seat, and I'm sure she'll be back soon."

"Thank you so much for your help!" Cassandra said, smiling at the woman. "You're really sweet."

"Seriously? You are too! It's hard to get a smile out of people up here sometimes," she whispered, laughing a little as she made a face that said 'yikes' pretty well. "I hope you have a great day!"

"You too!" Cassandra waved as Aubrey headed back down the hall, and then she walked as quietly as she could over to the desk the woman had pointed out. The soft ring of the phone was constant, but the little headset was on the desk beside it.

Pulling out her phone, she sent off a quick text to Logan: *I'm here! Waiting outside your office… I think. ;p*

It was probably some corporate faux pas to snoop around the woman's desk, but she was curious about this side of Logan's life. Leaning over the large counter bordering the L-shaped desk, she peeked around. The woman had a few photos on display, one of her, her husband, her son, and a tiny dog. Another of her and her son in front of a creek, and another of her and her husband with their faces close together, smiling broadly. Those were the only personal items besides a pack of gum. Everything else looked too important to mess with. Stacks of papers, post-it notes, and of course, her computer.

Cassandra was about to sit down when she heard Logan's

voice through the door. It was muffled, but it definitely sounded like he was yelling. Glancing around at the few other executive assistant desks, she couldn't tell if anyone was watching her, but it wasn't like she shouldn't be there. Logan had invited her, put her name on the security list, and they were already over half an hour late. Feeling a little braver, she moved close to the large double doors and leaned in.

"How are we supposed to keep these clients if people don't do their fucking job?" Logan was definitely shouting, and she could hear the rage in his voice even though the thick wood. *"I want the entire team in a meeting this afternoon. Every fucking one of them."*

Something was not going well today.

The door clicked in front of her and Cassandra jumped back, but Logan's next shouted words came through the crack in the door crystal clear. "Didn't I ask you to keep me in the loop on this?"

"Yes, Mr. Chisholm," a quiet, feminine voice replied, and Cassandra could tell the girl was scared. There was a slight tremor to the way she'd said Logan's last name.

"Then do your fucking job!" Logan roared, and Cassandra felt a rush of heat flood her face as she pushed the door open, careful not to hit the woman just on the other side of it as she stepped into his office. It was massive. Close to the size of her entire apartment. And Logan was standing in front of a huge desk, red-faced, and frozen still.

"Hey, Logan," she said, keeping her voice pointedly chipper while he just stared at her for a moment, mouth slightly open.

"Cassandra. Right, we're going to lunch. Laura, I want this—"

"Oh, no," Cassandra raised her hand, interrupting him as she laughed a little, but there wasn't much humor in it. *"We* aren't going anywhere until you apologize to this woman." Turning toward her, she recognized her from the photos. A sweet looking brunette wearing a black skirt with a green blouse. "Laura, right?"

"Yes?" Laura said, clearly confused and still very nervous after Logan yelled at her like a Grade-A asshole.

"Lovely to meet you, Laura. I saw your pictures — you have a beautiful family." Flashing her a smile, she turned toward Logan and crossed her arms. "I'm waiting."

"You want me to apologize?" he repeated, and she was sure he was about to argue with her when she dropped the smile, and he stopped short. "It's been a bad day, okay? I'm just frustrated with some people here who aren't doing their job."

"And does that give you the right to speak to Laura that way?" she asked, glancing over at the wide-eyed woman once more.

"Cassandra…" Logan sighed. "Let's have this conversation over lunch."

"No."

"What?" he snapped, and she saw the dom in him wanting to respond, but she didn't give a shit about their dynamic at the moment.

"Either you apologize to Laura for how you just spoke to her, or you can have lunch by yourself." Cassandra waited for a beat, but when he didn't show any sign of speaking, she continued, feeling the heat rushing up her chest. "You're better than this, Logan. You can be a gentleman *and* an asshole as much as you want, but you don't get to claim the gentleman card if you treat people like this who literally come to work every day to try and make your life easier."

"I'm sorry," he said, jaw clenched tight, and she gestured over to Laura with a flick of her wrist.

"Oh no, don't apologize to me. You need to apologize to *her*."

Logan met her gaze for a long moment, his blue eyes blazing, but then it finally simmered. He worked his jaw for a moment, taking a deep breath, and then he finally turned toward Laura. "I'm sorry, Laura. Cassandra is right, I shouldn't have taken my frustration out on you. I would appreciate if you could gather the idiots who *did* piss me off for a meeting this afternoon."

"Thank you, Mr. Chisholm," she replied quietly, taking a step closer to the open door. "I'll be sure everyone is in attendance. Will you be back by three o'clock?"

"Yes, that will work. Thank you." Logan sounded more civil, but she could tell by the edge in his tone that she'd be in for it at lunch.

Worth it.

As Laura moved to pass her, she leaned back and gave the woman a warm smile. "I promise, he's really not as much of an asshole as he pretends to be. If he ever talks to you like that again, just call me."

Laura's eyes were wide, but Cassandra saw the edge of her mouth lift as she fought a smile.

"I'll call you later and make sure you have my number."

"Cassandra!" Logan snapped, but she just rolled her eyes.

"For now, I'll do you a favor and drag him out to lunch." She grinned, and Laura hid her smile as she turned to leave the office, closing the door behind her. Turning, she faced the wrath of Logan still smiling. "Is this where you tell me I'm in trouble for expecting you to treat other people with a base level of human decency?"

"I—" Growling, Logan walked around his desk, ripping open the door on a large cabinet to pull out his suit jacket. "I cannot believe you—"

Watching him fume, struggling to come up with a reasonable response, made her walk over to him, sliding her arms around his waist as he shoved his arms into the jacket. "So... it's been a bad day?"

"You have no fucking idea."

"I think I have *some* idea based on the performance you just put on." Smiling, she leaned forward to press a kiss to his cheek. "Do you want to talk about it?"

"Not really."

"Want a distraction?" she offered, and he seemed to lose some of the tension in his back, eyes narrowing on her.

"Like what?" Logan hadn't put his arms around her yet, but he also hadn't tried to pull away from her, and she counted that as a victory.

"There's a pretty cool spot maybe fifteen minutes from here that does all-day karaoke, and decent food, and I'm pretty sure that absolutely *no one* can feel angry after listening to day-drunk people butcher the billboard top 40."

"That sounds terrible."

"Exactly!" Cassandra said, grinning wide before she smacked his ass through his slacks, dancing back from him as an entirely different blaze caught behind his eyes.

"You're asking for it, Cassandra."

"Asking for what?" she teased, pulling her bottom lip between her teeth before she broke into another grin.

"Mmhmm," he hummed, tilting his chin toward the door. "I've had my car waiting for us, and the company driver is very discreet."

She felt a rush of tingles run over her skin, remembering just how many welts he'd put on her ass the night before last at Black Light. A few small bruises lingered on her backside, and just thinking of his hands on her made her grin.

"You won't be smiling in a few minutes," he threatened, and she laughed.

"Promises, promises, Logan." With her retreating backward to the door, he stalked her, attention completely focused exactly where she wanted it. On her. Not his job, whatever shit was happening, or the people he was mad at.

She may not be able to fix whatever was happening here, but

she could improve his day a little, and hopefully make everyone else's day a little better in the process.

"SAY IT," Logan growled, bringing his palm down over her ass again with a dull *pop*.

"No, sir." She smiled against the leather seat, still surprised that he'd actually dragged her over his lap in the back of the luxury car. The windows were tinted extremely dark, but the driver was nowhere near far enough away to miss what was happening in the backseat.

"Dammit, Cassandra." Suddenly, he reached under her, popping the button on her jeans, and he grabbed the waistband in both hands, getting it halfway down her ass in the first yank.

"LOGAN!" she shouted, but she dissolved into laughs as he tugged the jeans to just below her ass. All she could picture was the very stoic driver getting an eyeful of her ass in the rearview mirror, but the man didn't seem fazed at all. Of course, her laughter was cut short by the first skin-to-skin swat of his hand, the sting lighting up her skin in a blaze.

"Say it, Cassandra," he demanded, swatting her again, hard enough to leave the outline of his hand as he adjusted her across his thighs.

"I will absolutely *not* apologize for making you treat people humanely. We can spend your entire lunch driving around in circles giving Jeeves a show if that's what your plan is."

Crack! Crack! Crack! Crack!

Logan rained down spanks, hard, and the burn built until she couldn't bite back the whine as she squirmed on his lap, but there was no way in hell she was apologizing for defending Laura. If anything, she wanted to clarify if he usually treated her like that, and then demand he give the poor girl a raise. Hazard pay for dealing with his bad attitude.

CRACK!

She yelped, and he paused the onslaught, breathing harder. With a grunt, he tried to pull her jeans back into place, but he gave up and nudged her hip. "God dammit... sit up."

"Giving up already?" she teased, but the look on his face as she sat up wiped the smile off her face.

"No, but I'm not going to punish you when I'm angry." Logan blew out a breath slowly, drawing it back in even slower. "Look, it's just..."

Leaning back on the seat, Cassandra pulled her underwear and jeans back into position, buttoning them before she sat down in L.A.'s slow-moving traffic. She waited for Logan to continue, but when he didn't, she reached over to grab his hand. "Tell me what's going on."

"It doesn't matter," he muttered, looking out the window.

"Clearly it matters a lot. You wouldn't be this upset if it was nothing." She tugged at his hand, trying to get him to look at her. "Come on, talk to me."

"Things just aren't going well at work, and..." He sighed again. "I really don't want to talk about it. I'd much rather be distracted from it. Didn't you say that's what this lunch place would do for me?"

"If this won't work, the only thing that *would* is a trip to the club, and they're unfortunately not open for lunch." Cassandra laughed a little at her joke, but it faded quickly when Logan just stared out the window again.

She wanted to be able to help him, but she didn't even know the right questions to ask. Mostly because he'd given her absolutely nothing to go on. But pushing him for more information was only going to make him sulk longer, so she abandoned that tactic and dug in her purse for her phone.

"Hey, so... you remember when you said you wanted to catch an episode of the soap opera my next door neighbors are always involved in?"

Logan actually glanced at her, and she grinned as she unlocked her phone to find the video.

"Well, they had a crazy one last night, and Abelita and I *had* to record it. Wanna listen?" Cassandra scooted closer on the seat, leaning against his shoulder as she held up the phone, tilting it back and forth as she teased him with the offer.

"Okay, fine. Let's hear it."

Five minutes into the insanity of the couple shouting at each other, talking about someone's cousin who was pregnant again, she felt Logan chuckle, his ribs bouncing lightly where she leaned against him. It wasn't much, and he was still broadcasting his stress on all frequencies, but at least it was something.

Whatever it was, it would pass. Eventually everything did.

The universe was giving him a hard time at work right now, but things would change. Ups and downs were just a part of life, and even if Logan didn't believe that… she could believe it enough for the both of them.

And, no matter what, they were guaranteed to hear a terrible version of Katy Perry's 'Firework' over the next hour, and there was nothing better than that for distracting someone from the rough parts of life.

CHAPTER 17

LOGAN

*H*e was a failure.

That was really the only conclusion to draw from the catastrophe of the past few weeks. If he was a stronger leader, if he was better at *his* job, then none of these mistakes would have been made.

Mistakes that were adding up fast.

As he sat at his desk, staring out the office windows at the L.A. skyline, the only voice he could hear in his head was his father's. Calling him a disappointment, an embarrassment to the family name... a failure.

Whitney Asset Management had survived the devastating stock market crash in 2008 under his father's hand, and while times had been hard, he'd led the company and emerged out the other side with a brand that the wealthy on the West Coast sought out even more than before.

His grandfather had built the beginnings of the company in the years following World War II, starting with nothing to end up as a successful businessman launching Whitney Asset Management in California before many of the East Coast finance names had even given the area a second glance.

His father may have been an absolute bastard… but at least he'd been successful.

Just like his grandfather.

And then there was him, Logan Chisholm, the downfall of the family legacy.

Lifting the bourbon from the windowsill, he poured another glass over the remnants of the ice and took a drink. It burned down his throat, sweet and smooth, until it joined the rest of the bottle in his stomach.

The last time he'd felt like this had been Yale. When alcohol had eventually stopped being enough and he'd tried every drug he could find, trying to find the one that would make him feel better. It wasn't until someone gave him a baggy of pills his senior year that he'd finally felt a surreal bliss that felt like the answer… until he'd found out what it was.

Vicodin.

He'd tossed himself in rehab over winter break, spent weeks detoxing on everything, and he'd sworn he would never get that low again. He wouldn't go out like his mom had.

But, how did he fill the hours when he was stressed or angry or over-tired? Drinking.

Just like his father.

He was twice-cursed. Damned to follow in their footsteps no matter how much he wanted to be different… and he did. More than anything he wanted to be someone new, someone better. He wanted to feel better.

He wanted to stop hating his life.

Staring at the warm gold of the liquid in the light of the setting sun, he had the sudden urge to throw it out. Pour it on the floor and go home.

"To Cassandra," he mumbled to himself, spinning around in the chair to set down the glass and grab his phone from the desk. Clumsily, he texted her, fixing each typo as he made it until he finally had something simple and light, free of all the bullshit: *Want to hang out tonight?*

That was good.

Much better than *'I think I'm having a mental breakdown, will you come keep me company?'* or *'I need to see you, please come over.'* Desperation wasn't sexy. None of his bullshit was sexy, and the last thing he needed to do was scare her off.

Ding.

Cassandra had texted him back, and he swiped back to it as quickly as he could, but his stomach dropped. *I have my dinner tonight with the Elite Brand Management Group! I might be able to sneak away for lunch later this week?*

Sighing, he picked up the glass of bourbon and took another swig. Of course Cassandra was busy. He'd even known about the dinner... he'd just forgotten. Everything was going wrong, and it made it hard to think straight.

Ding.

Another text. *Shit, I have meetings with the agency until Friday. But we'll get to see each other for our Nutcracker date Friday night! Vanessa is excited we're going to be there, and I'll make sure I send some fun pictures until then.*

Peach emoji. Tongue sticking out emoji. Kiss emoji.

Logan tossed the phone back onto the desk, turning back to the skyline outlined in burnt orange as the winter sun dipped toward the horizon. It was chillier tonight, and the cheesy Christmas lights across town were starting to come on, turning the landscape below him into myriad colors. Everyone was excited for Christmas. All his employees were making plans, taking time off, and he felt like the captain of the Titanic. Doomed to go down with the ship while everyone climbed aboard the lifeboats to escape.

Cassandra deserved a lifeboat. She deserved someone better.

Someone that wasn't a failure driving his life, and his family's company, into an iceberg.

Thunking the glass back on his desk, he sneered as the bourbon sloshed out of the glass, dripping onto his desk as he snagged his phone to text her back. *I hope you have a great night. See you Friday.*

Four days.

He could handle that. Unless everything fell apart between now and Friday... then he'd just let her go. She'd been preparing for that since he showed up at the fashion show anyway. Cassandra had the whole world waiting for her, designers and opportunities across the globe, and he'd never hold her back from that. He'd never weigh her down with his shit.

Everything going wrong right now was his problem, not hers.

She didn't deserve to have his issues laid at her feet.

If this ship was going down, it would be solo.

Just him, with no collateral damage.

And no Cassandra.

CHAPTER 18

CASSANDRA

"*A*ren't you ready yet?" Abelita asked, leaning on her doorframe, but Cassandra kept hovering her fingers over the keyboard on her phone.

She felt like she needed to text him back. To apologize for having such a packed schedule because of everyone's Christmas vacations.

"Earth to Cassandra!" Abelita interrupted her thoughts, waving an arm obnoxiously, and she looked over at her with a sigh.

"I heard you! I'm just worried about Logan."

"Why?" Abelita scoffed as she crossed her arms. "The man is rich as fuck and has plenty of things to entertain him that are *not* you. He's probably racing his Maserati down Sunset or something."

"I doubt that," Cassandra replied. "He's not like that."

"Sure, he showed up here in clothes worth thousands of dollars because he's secretly destitute and just wants to impress you."

"Oh my God! Shut up!" Groaning, Cassandra lay back on the bed, still holding her phone as she tried to think.

"Okay, girl, I can see you're actually upset about this. I'm listening." Abelita sat down on the edge of the bed, flicking her arm softly. "Talk."

"I don't know, I just feel bad about not seeing him this weekend."

"You're seeing him on Friday," she retorted, another layer of exasperation appearing in her voice. "Come *on*. Elite manages so many designers that you want to get involved with and Roberta worked her ass off to get you into this dinner. She even sent you over this sexy-as-fuck dress to wear!"

"I know," Cassandra admitted, hearing the whine in her voice as she lifted the phone and looked at his text again.

It was too short. Too... empty.

He hadn't even made a comment about her promise for some sexy pictures.

"You realize that the people at this dinner are, like, *the* people to know if you want to break into high fashion," Abelita said, interrupting her thoughts again as she went over to the dress hanging on her closet door. "There are girls who would gladly shank you to get in there and the follow-up meetings that always happen after."

"Thanks for the comforting commentary."

"Hey, you love me because I'm honest with you." Hopping back onto the end of the bed, Abelita jostled her and she sat up, glaring at her friend. "You need to get ready. You've got to leave in like twenty minutes, Cass."

"I know!" she snapped, groaning again as she shifted to the edge of the bed and stared down at the phone in her hands. "Is it weird that I want to go see Logan instead?"

"Oh shit..." Abelita muttered, moving over until she was sitting beside her. "You really like this guy, don't you?"

Cassandra shrugged a shoulder, but as she stared at the short text... Logan was all she could think about. If she were honest with herself, he'd been all she could think about for weeks.

The spark between them, the fire, was undeniable. The sex was incredible. But it was more than that... when he let his guard down around her, when he finally took a breath, he could be so damn funny, so charming. When he wasn't watching every word that came out of his mouth, Logan was incredibly sweet. He cared with everything he had, had jumped through every hoop she'd put in his path trying to slow him down — and she didn't even want to anymore.

The realization hit her hard. Harder than she'd even imagined when she'd thought of the worst-case scenario of dating Logan Chisholm.

She wasn't trying to hold him at arm's length anymore.

She *definitely* liked him. A lot.

And she had the distinct impression that another L-word might be hiding just behind her latest realization. It wasn't just that she'd accepted dating Logan as a possibility, accepted that *maybe* they could make the long-distance bullshit work.

It was that she might actually *want* it to work.

"Fuck, Cass, how deep are you into this guy?" Her roommate wasn't judging her, she could tell by the tone of her voice. Abelita never played games, it was one of the reasons she adored her so much, her blunt demeanor made everything easier... except this.

"I think I'm pretty far in," Cassandra whispered, and Abelita wrapped an arm around her waist, hugging her from the side.

"Well, he's head over heels for you, so... I don't think you're going to have much trouble there."

"What?" Cassandra sat up straight, looking at her friend who shrugged, smiling a little.

"I got to talk to him that day when you were getting ready, and even when I put him through the ringer, he never backed down. He's got it bad for you and seemed willing to do pretty much anything if it meant he could keep you interested." Abelita rubbed her back. "All I'm saying is that if you want Logan, he's going to be there on Friday. Hell, he'd probably be waiting for you if you didn't see him again until after the New Year."

"I don't know…" Standing up, Cassandra started pacing, unable to put the phone down. "Maybe I should just go talk to him. I can be a little late to—"

"NO!" Abelita pushed off the bed, grabbing Cassandra by her arms. "If you blow off Elite Management you might as well kiss the idea of *ever* getting signed to one of their campaigns good-bye. Tonight is about your future, Cass. Trust me, Logan is going to be there tomorrow, or Friday, or whenever you're able to see him."

"You really think so?" Cassandra fought the urge to chew on her thumbnail as she wobbled the phone back and forth in her hand.

"Yes, I do." Shoving her toward the dress, Abelita snapped her fingers. "Now get dressed! I'm calling you a Lyft now. Give me your phone."

"Fuck, fine." Handing over her phone, she went to put the dress on, trying to think of exactly how she'd tell Logan what she was feeling when they saw each other. It's not like she had concrete words for it yet. It wasn't quite the big L-word… but it wasn't far from it either. He checked all her boxes, and he'd been telling her for weeks that they could make the long-distance thing work. It would just take more planning, more flying home, but it wasn't impossible.

And Logan was worth it, she was absolutely sure of that.

The universe had aligned to bring them back together, given her the time to see who he could be in her life, and she wasn't going to ignore it.

CHAPTER 19

CASSANDRA

She'd tried to make time to see Logan throughout the week, but nothing had worked out. Every day had seemed to last forever, and by the time she was home — she was exhausted, but he'd been understanding. Wishing her luck, telling her to rest after the long days.

Even today she'd been meeting with Roberta, and others at the agency, talking about her schedule for the new year, and the offers that were already coming in from her meeting with Elite Brand Management. None of them were final, of course. She'd still need to walk for the designers, but the company had a lot of sway for ad campaigns... and they liked her. That was what Roberta kept repeating all week.

They loved you.

You did great.

Your portfolio wow'd them.

Cassandra had even called her parents the night before to tell them about it, and she normally tried to keep their expectations lower. They were her biggest cheerleaders, and as soon as they knew about a possible next step in her career, *everyone* knew. Her brothers, their wives, the entire extended family and all of their friends.

But this felt real. It felt possible.

It meant more shoots, more travel, more runway shows — more success.

All of the things Logan had said she deserved, all of the things Logan wanted her to do, and he'd still said it wasn't a problem. He'd even mocked her at Black Light for doubting his ability to problem-solve around the travel issues.

Well, now he was going to get his chance.

Tonight, was supposed to be about Vanessa, about seeing her perform the Sugar Plum Fairy in *The Nutcracker*, which was a major role for her friend, but Cassandra wasn't sure she'd be able to keep the excitement in until after the ballet.

Logan wasn't a big ballet fan though, so telling him before the show wouldn't be stealing Vanessa's thunder. It would probably make the night that much better, because he'd know how she felt. He'd know she wasn't second-guessing them anymore, and then tonight they could *finally* spend time together, have some fun, and then figure out how to handle her ever-intensifying schedule.

Unlocking her phone, Cassandra checked her text messages first. He still hadn't replied to her today, but he was probably trying to get as much work done before the ballet. Whatever was going on at work was clearly stressing him out, so maybe the good news would help him relax and enjoy the evening.

Smiling, she switched over to the Lyft app to check their progress toward his house. Just another few minutes and she'd be able to talk to him. In person.

She spent the rest of the ride trying out different phrases in her head. Nothing was guaranteed, and she didn't want it to sound like some kind of weird proposal, but she needed him to know she was in this. She was willing to try dating him even when all the insane travel started again.

If only it was as easy as scrawling on a piece of notebook paper *'will you be my boyfriend? circle one.'* School had definitely been easier with conversations like this one, but once she'd made her mind up, she was sure.

The universe had spoken pretty damn loudly. Aligned all the stars, and Logan had more than put in his fair share of effort. Now it was her turn.

"Here we are," the driver said, and she tapped the five stars as soon as it appeared.

"Thanks! You were great!" Climbing out, she held the door for another second, smiling broadly as her excitement spread. "Have an amazing night!"

"You too," the guy said, waving at her as she closed the door and watched him turn around in the big driveway.

Hurrying up the steps to his door, she knocked, and then froze because she could hear Logan shouting inside. If there weren't such a chill in the air, she would have waited, but considering her legs were only covered in tights, she decided to knock again, louder.

Come on, Logan.

Leaning close to the door, Cassandra pressed her ear to the wood, catching another round of shouting. She rolled her eyes, hoping he wasn't yelling at Laura again, and then she tried the handle. To her surprise, it opened, and she slipped inside, shutting it behind her as Logan's voice boomed from the living room around the corner.

"How did you idiots miss these assholes talking to our clients? *HOW* did you fuck up this bad?"

Damn.

She'd known he was having a rough time at work, but it clearly hadn't improved. At least she was the bearer of good news tonight, and stepping away from his job for the night would help him.

"That's right! You're going to research every single

complaint they had and figure out how the hell to get them back!" Logan paused, and she hovered awkwardly at the edge of the wall, wondering if she should sneak out and pretend to still be outside or not. "I don't give a fuck about your vacation. *This* is your vacation now! Get it done!"

Something slammed down, rattling objects, and Cassandra chewed on her bottom lip, feeling her excitement dimming in the face of his mood — but she wouldn't let this ruin their night.

"Motherfuckers!" Logan shouted, and she snuck back to the door, opening it.

"Logan?" she called out, deciding that it would be better under the circumstances for him to think she'd missed his work drama.

But he didn't respond to her.

Shutting the door, she walked around the corner and into the living room. He was sitting on one of his couches, laptop open on the large coffee table in front of him. His head was in his hands, fingers burrowed into his hair as he muttered under his breath.

"Hey, you okay?" she asked, and he looked up at her like it was a dumb question — which, to be fair, it kind of was. Smiling, she took a few steps closer, ignoring his attitude. "I think I have something that might cheer you up."

"Right," Logan groused, scooping up a glass from the table before he leaned back on the couch to drink from it.

"Come on, Logan. I know work has sucked, but we're gonna go on our date, see Vanessa perform in the ballet, and then when we get back… I think we can come up with a few ways to distract you." Grinning, Cassandra moved to the end of the couch, leaning on the arm to try and get his attention. "Pssst, earth to Logan?"

"I'm not in the mood, Cassandra." Another sip, the ice rattling in the glass as he finished it, and then he leaned forward to slam it down on the table, immediately reaching for the bottle to refill it with more muttered curses.

"Okay, then tell me what's going on." Sitting on the arm of the couch, she wanted to reach out and hug him, comfort him, but he definitely didn't seem open to that right now.

"It doesn't matter," Logan mumbled, taking another drink, and she ran her eyes over the bottle of whiskey, wondering just how far into it he was.

"Obviously it does, Logan. You've been upset for over a week, and I'm trying to be here to help—"

"You *can't* help, okay? You can't. Hell, the idiots I have working for me apparently don't even know what to do!" More whiskey, another growl as he shook his head, glaring at the laptop. "Fucking idiots!"

"All right," Cassandra said, raising her hands in defeat. "Then we won't talk about it anymore. We'll go to see Vanessa perform, distract you from all this shit, and just let it go for tonight."

"No."

"What?" Standing up, she adjusted her purse on her shoulder, waiting for him to look at her, but he wouldn't. "Logan, you have to fucking talk to me. I came here wanting to—"

"I don't want to talk about this shit with you!" he shouted, finally looking at her, and she crossed her arms, trying to remember that he was upset, stressed.

"Fine. Let's just drop it and go to the ballet."

"I'm not going to the goddamned ballet, Cassandra! Jesus Christ!" Logan huffed, polishing off another glass of whiskey in front of her. "Just go without me."

"No." Dropping her purse on the large coffee table, Cassandra spread her arms. "If we're not going to the ballet, then we're going to talk about this. Tell me what's going on at work."

"What would you know about issues like this? You're a

fucking model," he sneered, leaning forward to pour more into his glass, and for a moment she couldn't even respond. Too many emotions were at war inside her, too many to count… but anger won out.

Clenching her jaw, Cassandra straightened her back and tried to keep her voice as even as possible. "First of all, you don't get to talk to me like that. Ever. Second, you can *choose* how to deal with shit like this, Logan. Bad things happen to everyone. All the time. And if all you do is focus on the bad things that happen to you, then what's the fucking point of waking up in the morning?"

He shook his head, not even looking at her, and so she kept going.

"*This* is your problem, Logan! You have to start looking at the good shit. Your badass car, your nice house, the fact that you have enough money to basically do anything you want! If today sucked, if this week sucked, if this whole fucking month sucked, figure out something that will make it better that *isn't* downing an entire bottle of whiskey. Stop wallowing in your bullshit and choose to see what you have!"

"You wouldn't be saying that if you'd just lost millions of dollars," Logan replied, and he didn't even give her a glance. Not a single look. Not even a vague attempt at an apology.

"Well, you lost a lot more than that tonight, Logan." Shaking her head, Cassandra scooped up her purse from the table, staring at his profile as he glared at the empty air in front of him. "You might as well lose my number too."

Turning, she went for the door, trying to keep her steps as even as possible, because some part of her was still hoping he'd come to his senses. Run after her and apologize for being so heartless, so cruel… but she never heard him say a word, and by the time she shut the door her eyes were already burning with tears.

She fumbled with her phone, requesting a Lyft as she walked

down his driveway toward the road. Her hands wouldn't stop shaking, still running on the adrenaline that had rushed through her when he'd basically called her an idiot. The words had felt like a slap, crushing the excitement she'd shown up with just minutes before when she'd thought things would work out for them. That they'd defy the odds because the universe was on their side.

But the universe had pulled the rug out from under her feet and proceeded to kick her while she was down.

I should have trusted my instincts.

If I had... it wouldn't hurt this much.

CHAPTER 20

CASSANDRA

"Oh my God! Why didn't you tell me last night?" Vanessa asked, her tinny voice strained with sadness through the little speaker.

"I didn't want to ruin your night." Cassandra shrugged, pulling her knees up to her chest as she leaned back against her headboard, holding the phone in front of her.

"Oh, honey, you could have told me! I mean, shit, I even asked you where Logan was!" Groaning, Vanessa sighed. "I'm so sorry."

"It's okay."

"Fuck that, it's not okay at all! I can hear it in your voice, Cass, you're not okay with this."

"You're right," she said, her voice cracking as another wave of tears hit her. Sniffling, she dragged the tissue box onto the bed and tried to bite down on the urge to start sobbing again. She'd barely slept since she'd come home from the ballet, and she felt like hell.

"Cass... talk to me. Are you *sure* it's over? Maybe you guys just had your signals cross and—"

"He basically called me an idiot, Vanessa," she said as she swiped at her eyes again. *Stupid tears wouldn't stop.*

"He didn't!" Vanessa growled. "I'm gonna fucking kill him! HE'S the idiot! What the fuck did he say?"

"Something about me not being able to understand his work shit because I'm 'just a fucking model.' I've been trying to get him to talk to me about it… but at least now I know why he wouldn't." Sniffling, she felt the ache in her chest like a physical pain, and it wasn't going anywhere.

"That sonuvabitch…" Muttering more curses and threats, Vanessa eventually came back to the phone. "This doesn't make any sense! The way he looked at you at Black Light was… fuck, this makes no sense at all. I can't believe it."

"Well, he said it to my face," Cassandra replied, laughing bitterly as another cry slipped past her lips.

"Sweetheart… God, I'm so sorry. He's a fucking idiot."

"Maybe it's for the best?" Cassandra said, trying to look on the bright side, but her voice broke again as she continued. "I mean… it's not like it would have worked out between us anyway. I always thought that once I started traveling this would just fall apart, and I thought I was prepared for that. I… I just didn't expect it to hurt this much."

"He shouldn't have told you that he'd make it work if he wasn't really in this for the long haul," Vanessa added, trying to be a good friend, but it just didn't matter. She'd let herself believe that they could make it work, that they could figure out a way to keep their relationship going once she started traveling again — and apparently Logan was just trying to figure out how to cut ties with her.

"Well, he made it pretty clear last night that I'm not right for him," Cassandra whispered, tearing the tissue in her hands into tiny pieces.

"And, like I said, he's a fucking idiot."

"Yeah…" Cassandra shrugged, unable to forget the way he'd

spoken to her. The empty look in his eyes. It kept replaying over and over in her head. "At least I won't be able to sit here and sulk about it for long. I fly out to do Christmas at my parents' house in a few days, and I'll be so busy there with my family and all my nieces and nephews that I should be pretty distracted."

"That will be good. Being distracted will be helpful." Vanessa sighed. "Look, I have to be at the Dudorov soon for practice for tonight, but after they let us go, I'm going to come by and see you. Okay?"

"Okay," Cassandra said, sniffling. "Thanks, girl."

"Of course. I've always got your back. See you later today."

"See you then." Ending the call, Cassandra let her phone drop onto the sheets that were twisted into knots around her. She'd tried to sleep, but it hadn't worked. Whatever little bits of sleep she might have grabbed weren't restful, and she could feel how puffy her face was from crying.

Good thing all my shoots are done.

Turning the little TV in her room back on, she tried to zone out on the screen. It was some movie with people fighting, and no romance to be seen... just what she needed right now.

An hour later, the good guys and the bad guys were having a massive shoot-out on the TV. Explosions and racing vehicles and big men carrying big guns, but the sound of Abelita's scream was more than loud enough to be heard over the latest pyrotechnics.

"Abelita?" Cassandra shouted, sitting up in bed, but her roommate burst through her door a second later with a huge grin on her face.

"THEY CALLED MY AGENT!" Abelita screamed, dancing in place as she twirled in a quick circle.

"WHO?" Cassandra asked, trying to calm her racing heart.

"Victoria's Secret!" This time when Abelita let out a joyous scream, Cassandra joined her, jumping out of bed to grab her roommate in a big hug.

"This is amazing! What did they say?"

"Just that I'm going to their next call in January, but I've never made it this far in the process before! Oh my God, what if they pick me? What if I get to model for their Spring Catalog?" Abelita was practically bouncing on her toes, and Cassandra just yanked her into another hug, squeezing her tight.

"I am so fucking happy for you! You deserve this so much!"

"You told me not to give up on it, to keep believing in it, and — AHH! I just can't believe it!" Abelita pulled back, staring at the phone she held as she pushed a hand through her hair. "It doesn't feel real. It totally doesn't feel real."

"Well, I don't think your agent would fuck with you over something like this. She knows how important it is to you." Smiling, Cassandra held on to her friend's excitement like a life raft, but as Abelita's gaze swept the room the joy drained from her face slowly, a crease forming between her brows.

"Have you been crying?" Leaning in, Abelita scanned her face, then stood up straight. "You have! What the fuck happened?"

"Nothing," Cassandra said, fighting the tears that wanted to surface again as her friend stared at her. "Let's just focus on your good news, okay?"

"Screw that, we won't know anything about that until January." Moving past her, Abelita picked up the almost empty tissue box and shook it. "Talk to me, Cass."

Chewing on her lip, Cassandra tried to keep the tears in, but they overflowed anyway, and she melted back onto the bed as she started crying again. Abelita listened while she explained what had happened, how Logan had ended things between them so harshly, and unlike her usual reaction… she didn't go off. Didn't shout or interrupt. Abelita just offered a new tissue occasionally, listening, and it was what Cassandra needed as she tried to process the heartbreak — because that was exactly what this was. Heartbreak.

She wasn't sure when it had happened, when Logan had shifted from a sexy guy she could have fun with at Black Light to something more… but he had. The emotional connection had snuck up on her, creeping in every time he joked with her, every time he smiled, every time he did something so unexpectedly sweet. Strengthened by the way he'd pushed her for a date and then took her breath away on the dancefloor. And all of his dominance, his easy sadism, his playful nature in the bedroom — that had just been the cherry on top. Logan Chisholm had done everything he could to make her fall for him, jumped through every hoop she'd put in place trying to avoid breaking his heart… and he'd ended up breaking hers.

"That's it. I'm making you pancakes," Abelita said, climbing off the bed. "This needs pancakes."

"I don't think we have any mix left," Cassandra said through another sniffle, blowing her nose in the latest tissue her room-mate had pushed into her hand.

"Well, then I'll order some. Urgent delivery." Lifting her phone, Abelita started tapping away as she moved to the doorway. "And I'm going to get another box of tissues. Then we're going to veg out today."

"That sounds nice," Cassandra admitted, looking up at her friend as she paused at the edge of her room.

"I just need to say this, and then I won't say another word. I promise."

"Go ahead." Cassandra dropped her hands into her lap, smiling at the serious expression on Abelita's face.

"Fuck him. Fuck him up the ass with a baseball bat. That fancy-suited asshole didn't deserve you anyway." Abelita pointed at her. "You were too good for him. *Way* too good for him, and when he finally pulls his head out of his ass and realizes that, I hope he gets a major case of permanent limp dick from the serious depression his dumb ass falls into."

"You done?" Cassandra asked, unable to *not* smile at the serious tone in her friend's voice.

"Almost. I hope his impotent, stupid fucking face loses all that money he's so damn proud of and ends up on the streets, wearing thrift store shit, where the only chance he has to see your gorgeous self is on a billboard, hundreds of feet above him."

Even though her chest hurt, and her eyes burned from crying for so long, Cassandra still felt a small laugh roll up, and she let it out. Shaking her head, she smiled through the tears as she looked at her friend. "Thanks, Abelita."

"Anytime, and *now* I'm done. Maybe." Waving her phone back and forth, Abelita spoke over her shoulder as she headed into the kitchen. "I reserve the right to continue this rant if I need to!"

"Deal!" Cassandra called back, and then she slumped back into her pillows. Her bed was covered in crumpled tissues, an empty water bottle, and another half-full one, along with the remnants of the cereal bowl she'd had sometime around three in the morning. The clothes she'd worn for their 'date' the night before were still crumpled on the floor by her closet, and part of her wanted to clean up, to wash her face and brush her teeth... but she just slid deeper under the covers instead.

She could let herself sulk for a few days.

Get it all out of her system so she wouldn't taint her family's Christmas.

Then she'd be on the road again. Traveling for all the new shoots Roberta had her scheduled for, and in time she'd forget about Logan Chisholm.

It sounded good in her head, but the dull ache behind her ribs disagreed. After all, they'd spent ten months without seeing each other, four months without talking, and he'd still been on her mind. Lurking there whenever she found herself even slightly interested in some random guy... but that was before she'd known what he really thought about her.

This time she'd just go out with the random guy. She wouldn't think about him anymore.

Nope, I won't think about him at all. Curling up around one of her pillows, Cassandra turned her face into it, wiping the tears away as they started falling again, because as much as she wanted that to be true... it felt like a lie. And she knew she didn't want some random one-night stand.

She wanted that spark she'd felt with Logan. That electric hum that buzzed through her nerves every time he kissed her. She wanted the connection she'd thought they had... because she'd never felt it with anyone else. And if she were being honest with herself, she didn't think anything else *could* feel like this did. For a short while she thought she'd found someone who accepted her, wholly and completely. All of her nuances, all of her sass, all of her kinks... her life, her world, her career... all of her.

But it had been a lie.

And her heart was definitely broken.

And that just wasn't something you walked off in a few weeks, or months.

Another wave of tears hit her, and she muffled herself with the pillow, hating the pain in her chest and the weak sounds that left her lips. Sniffling hard, she dug out the last tissue from the box and blew her nose, staring down at the tear-stained pillowcase. At the pathetic nest she'd built for herself to wallow in her sadness.

"Damn you, Logan," she mumbled, biting down on another broken sound. "Why did you make me fall for you?"

CHAPTER 21

LOGAN

*H*e was dying.

That was the only explanation for the blinding pain behind his right eye, and the wave of nausea that knocked him flat when he tried to sit up.

"Fuck…" he groaned, trying to open his eyes, but everything was too bright, blindingly painful. With a stomach-churning shift, Logan rolled onto his side where the light mercifully faded. Blinking, he squinted at the leather in front of his face and tried to figure out where the fuck he was.

His brain felt like someone had run it through a blender filled with knives, but eventually two brain cells managed to bump together to give him a single word. *Couch.* He was on the couch. His couch. In his living room.

That was better than the alternatives. Like a hospital bed, which he probably needed, or a jail cell, which he should be in if he'd driven last night.

What the fuck happened last night?

Grunting, he tried to sit up again, but only succeeded in shifting his body a few inches closer to the armrest before he gave up and draped his arm over his eyes. Lying on his back, fighting the urge to empty his stomach on the carpet beside him, he tried to remember getting home the night before.

Everything had fallen apart at the office. *That* he remembered clearly.

Not just two clients leaving for Berringer Holdings, but seven. Big accounts. One after another, and the whole building had been panicking. Tens of millions of dollars and several long-term accounts that his father had never had trouble holding onto. It had been chaos, and no one seemed to have a good answer for how the fuck it had happened.

He'd started drinking at the office, and then he'd left because—

Cassandra.

Fuck, fuck, fuck, fuck.

Rolling off the couch, he caught himself on his hands and knees, and even though the room seemed to slant dangerously to one side, he sat up enough to look over the coffee table. Blinking through the blinding sunlight, Logan found his phone and groaned when it didn't light up at his touch.

Dead.

"Goddammit," he growled under his breath, dragging himself upright with more help from the couch than should have been necessary. Stumbling, he went for the kitchen, hip-checking a table on the way, which only added to the various aches and pains rolling through him. Leaning against the slightly dimmer kitchen counter, he plugged the phone in, then rested his cheek on the cool granite.

He couldn't tell if he was still drunk, or completely hungover, or somewhere in-between — but no matter what, it was hell.

What the fuck did I do last night?

They'd had their date planned. The ballet. He remembered leaving work so he could get ready, but he'd spent the whole drive home on the phone. More excuses, more bullshit, and he'd opened his laptop again to review the emails flying around, and then...

"Oh God." Logan shoved himself upright, bracing his hands on the counter to stare at the dead battery symbol on his phone. "Come on, come on, come on."

Cassandra had come over, all dressed up for their date, and he'd been shitfaced. Yelling at people on the phone... and then he'd yelled at her.

And she'd left.

She left.

Groaning, he flipped open several cabinets until he found the one with the glasses. Quickly filling it with water, he drank it down. Refilled and did it again.

Cassandra left.

He'd said something terrible to her. He could remember the look on her face. Angry and hurt. But he couldn't remember what he'd said, because he'd been too fucking drunk.

"Idiot," he growled, rubbing his face, trying to make his brain work right, but everything was misfiring. Hell, he could barely stand upright.

He hadn't done something like this in years. Not since Yale. When the pressure was insane, and his father wouldn't stop reminding him of everything on the line if he fucked up in school.

His father.

That was exactly who he was acting like. Drunk, shouting, alienating everyone around him, and in general being a complete asshole. He used to hate coming home from school or lacrosse practice, trying to sneak to his room before his dad noticed him, because if he did it always ended in a shouting match. How stupid he was, how useless, how he'd never live up to the family name.

And, apparently, he'd been right.

He wasn't just fucking up at work, he'd messed up the only good thing in his life.

The screen lit up on his phone, and he grabbed for it, cursing under his breath as it took its sweet time turning on. As soon as he could, he swiped to his contacts and called Cassandra.

It rang, and rang, and rang... voicemail.

"Shit," he growled, hanging up to try again. And again. And again. Finally, the phone went straight to voicemail when he dialed, and he slammed his hand down on the counter, trying to compose himself as her voicemail greeting came across the line. Her sweet voice asked him to leave a message, but he was sure that she wouldn't sound like that if she'd actually answered. The beep had him opening his mouth to speak, but he froze. "Hey," he started lamely. "I... I don't really... Look, I'm sorry about last night. Just call me back. Please."

Leaning on the counter, he sent a few texts to follow up.

I'm sorry for last night.

Please call me back.

Or just text me.

His thumbs hovered over the keyboard, wanting to figure out the right words to say that would make her respond... but he could barely think straight. Sighing, he dropped the phone back to the counter and went in search of ibuprofen and coffee.

WHEN HE OPENED the fridge for the half-and-half a while later, he saw the lonely carton of eggs he'd bought for her to have breakfast in the mornings. The bread on the counter was meant to go with it, and he decided that toast would have to work for his hangover because he didn't think he could stomach anything else.

Taking a seat at the island in the kitchen, he stared at the phone charging on the counter, willing it to ring, or buzz, or...

anything. Anything that would show he still had a chance, but thirty minutes later when he forced down the last bite of toast, she still hadn't reached out.

"Because you fucked it up," he muttered.

Moving to the phone, he scrolled through his texts from her. She'd been looking forward to seeing him, said she had something exciting to tell him — and now he'd probably never know what it was.

The night was coming back to him in pieces. An argument he'd had with one of his VPs over the phone, the rage-filled email he'd drafted, re-written, and then re-written again before he'd hit send.

He'd need to go look at that to see how much damage he did there.

Mostly, he kept remembering the look on Cassandra's face. The way it had changed from shocked to hurt to angry. All the warmth and joy just draining out of her, because of him. He'd always worried that he'd taint her with his darkness, his negativity, but he never thought he'd lash out at her.

Cassandra was everything he wasn't. Kind, warm, optimistic… happy. If he was less of an asshole, he'd just walk away. Let her go on with her life.

But he couldn't.

He couldn't let her go.

Swiping out of her message, he went back to his contacts and tapped a name he never thought he'd actually call. It rang twice before he heard, "Wyatt Strickland speaking."

"Hey, it's Logan. Logan Chisholm, we met at—"

"I know who you are, Logan," Wyatt said, rescuing him from the awkward introduction.

"Good. Well, I…" Clearing his throat, Logan turned in the kitchen, leaning back against the counter as he tried to figure out what the fuck he was doing. "I know we don't really know each other very well, but I fucked up."

"I heard." Wyatt's crisp response had his stomach dropping. "Wanna tell me your side of the story?"

Logan let out the breath he hadn't even realized he'd been holding, rubbing a hand over his face as he nodded at his empty kitchen. "Yeah, thanks."

At first he wasn't sure how much he wanted to tell Wyatt, but as soon as he started talking about losing the clients at work, how stressed he'd been the past few weeks as Berringer Holdings continued to cut the legs out from under him… he just couldn't stop. He told Wyatt about what the losses meant to their bottom line, and how it might mean lay-offs in the first quarter, which would only jeopardize his company's position further. And then he talked about the drinking. How he knew it had been getting worse, but he'd thought he was handling it… until Cassandra showed up last night.

"What's worse is I can't even remember what I said to her that made her leave. I just remember her face, and her saying something about choosing to be happy — but, fuck, I was so drunk. I don't even remember her getting here." Logan turned back to the kitchen counter to brace his hand on it. "She's not taking my calls, or responding to my texts, and it's not that I even blame her. I just think I really fucked up here, Wyatt. No, I *know* I really fucked up, and I know we don't know each other very well, but you're the only person on the planet that I can even sort of call a friend who might be able to help me dig my way out of this shit."

The silence stretched on the phone, and while Logan had appreciated Wyatt listening without much commentary and only a few small questions about the work shit, now he needed the guy to talk.

"Wyatt?"

"I'm here, Logan, but…" Wyatt blew out a long breath. "You definitely fucked up. Bad."

"I know," he groaned, clenching his jaw as he stared up at the ceiling.

"Just so you're aware, Cassandra and Vanessa have already talked, and the version of events I got was that she tried to help you with the trouble at work, and you called her an idiot."

"WHAT!" Logan shouted, not believing he'd ever say that to her. Not even if he was plastered.

"I think the phrase had something to do with her 'just being a model,' but Vanessa was pretty pissed when she told me about it, so who knows. This is a pretty miserable game of telephone to be involved in, if I'm honest."

"I don't think she's an idiot. At all. I swear." Growling under his breath, he muttered a curse. "I mean, I've been keeping all the work shit to myself because I didn't want to burden her with it."

"You mean you didn't want to explain it to her?" Wyatt asked, and Logan felt the stab of truth in the statement.

"It's just complicated."

"You didn't seem to have any issue telling me about it," Wyatt pointed out, and Logan felt his temper rising, but he shoved it down. Wyatt wasn't the bad guy here. The man was helping him, and if *anyone* was the bad guy... it was Logan.

"You're right. I should have just told her about it."

"Probably would have kept you from this situation. At least... maybe you wouldn't have called her an idiot. But, apparently, you're not a very friendly drunk, so before you do anything else, maybe you should start by putting the liquor away." Wyatt sighed, and Logan could tell he was waiting for him to agree.

"Yeah, I think that's a good idea. I'll do whatever I can to fix this, Wyatt, but right now she won't even talk to me." Shoving a hand through his hair, he gripped it in his fist, fighting the urge to just start screaming, or breaking shit. "How the hell am I supposed to make this right if she won't even talk to me?"

"Look, Logan, I don't know if I can help you. I'm not going to make any false promises here, but... I'll try. Okay?"

"That's more than I deserve," Logan muttered.

"You're not going to get any arguments from me," Wyatt replied, but there was no humor in his voice. "Cassandra is a sweet girl, and a very good friend of the love of my life. She deserves to be treated better than that, and if you can't—"

"I can," Logan said. "Wyatt, I promise you, I will never do something like this again. I can be a better man than this. I will be."

"Good. I'll see what I can do. Work on getting your shit together today, Logan."

"I will. Thanks, Wyatt."

"Bye." The call ended before he could reply, but Logan didn't blame the man. He'd crossed a lot of lines in one night, and the only reason Wyatt was likely even talking to him was that he hadn't tried some insane BDSM session while he was shitfaced and angry.

No, instead he'd apparently just called Cassandra an idiot and let her walk out of his life.

Leaving his phone on the counter to charge, Logan returned to the living room and sighed.

The bottle of Elijah Craig bourbon had been unopened yesterday, but it just had a couple of inches left in the bottom now, which explained just how plastered he'd been before he finally passed out. Grabbing it, he walked over to the bar and upended it into the sink.

For once, the smell of it didn't even tempt him.

As he emptied bottle after bottle down the drain, all he had to do was remember how hurt Cassandra had looked and the urge to take a swallow disappeared. He wasn't thinking about the cost of the liquor, or the way each of them tasted... no, he couldn't think about anything except whether Cassandra would ever give him the chance to make this up to her.

The shit going on at his company was a nightmare, but the idea of losing her was definitely worse.

She'd tried to get him to understand that so many times. That there was more to life than working, that he needed to *enjoy* his life. Hell, one of the only things he could remember her telling him before she left was that he needed to choose to be happy. To focus on the good things in his life, and as he emptied another fancy bottle into the sink, he looked around his house and started to understand what she'd meant.

He was fortunate, and although he'd always known that on some level, he'd been raised to focus on everything wrong in his life. To analyze every failure, every misstep, every error, and ensure it didn't happen again.

To not embarrass the family name.

But, in the end, that shit didn't matter. His job was an obligation, a requirement, a way to support himself — but Cassandra was his future.

The only future he wanted or cared about, because there was no other option.

For the first time in his life, there wasn't another woman waiting on the sidelines that he could see himself with, no other possibilities for what could be 'next' for him. There was only Cassandra. The only one he wanted to be with today, tomorrow, or ten years from now. She was the only woman he'd ever felt this way about, this strongly. The only woman he'd ever—

Fuck.

He loved her.

The word appeared in his mind, but it didn't send his heart racing. There wasn't the slightest hint of panic, but the weight of it still hit him like a punch to the chest, knocking him down another peg. He'd been an asshole to the only person who actually believed in him, who truly believed he was capable of more… of being a good man.

Being better.

Being *happy.*

It wasn't even a choice anymore. No matter what it took, no matter what he had to do… he was going to show Cassandra he was sorry. He'd do whatever he had to, *anything,* as long as she believed he'd never speak to her like that again, that he'd never violate her trust the way he had.

Because he loved her, and at the very least he wanted the chance to say that to her face.

And he wanted to be worthy of her love in return.

CHAPTER 22

CASSANDRA

"Your dad is putting up another inflatable out front," her mom said through a laugh, and Cassandra felt herself smile.

"What's this one?"

"A big abominable snowman. I swear it's ten feet tall!"

"The kids are going to love it though," Cassandra replied, remembering how much her niece and nephews loved the huge collection of Christmas decorations her parents put up every year.

"Oh, Zach and Kiera are already here, so their boys have been having a field day. They're outside right now helping him put up this massive beast!" Laughing, her mom said something away from the phone, and then came close again. "Apparently Zach has to speak with—"

"Hello, little sister!" Zachary shouted into the phone, and Cassandra rolled her eyes.

"Hi Zach, are you behaving yourself?" she asked, knowing he'd probably been driving their mom crazy all day by trying to help.

"Me? I'm the good one, remember? You and Terrell were the troublemakers," he argued, but he couldn't hide the laugh.

"Riiiiight." Smiling, she leaned back on the couch, enjoying the sound of her mom laughing in the background. "Listen to that, not even Mom believed that lie."

"I'm reformed," he retorted, and she could imagine her oldest brother's broad smile. "When are you going to be here anyway?"

"Just four more days, I promise."

"Too busy being a world-famous model to hang out with us? I get it." He was joking, and she knew it, but other than the 'world famous' part… it wasn't far from the truth. Her job kept her away from her family more than she'd like.

"I'll be there soon enough to keep you from driving Mom crazy. She's not *that* old, you know. She can do things for herself."

"See? This is just more proof that I'm the best kid." Zach laughed, and then there was a commotion in the background. "It's Aunt Cassandra. Okay, okay, here's Alex."

"Aunt Cassandra! Papa got the biggest decoration EVER!" Alex shouted into the phone, as unable to control his volume as her brother, but at least Alex was cute. Five years old and already more than a handful.

"I heard! Nana said it's the abominable snowman."

"YES! It is HUGE!" Alex yelled. "Oh, Nana says I can have a cookie. I love you, bye!"

The phone fumbled for a second, and then her mom came back on the line. "Hey sweetheart, it's me again."

"Sounds like you guys are already busy," Cassandra said, wishing she were already there. *Just a few more days.*

"We are. Darian and Alex are already planning some last-minute requests for Santa, and they helped me bake cookies today. Terrell should be here tomorrow with Sarah and baby Layla… and then we're just missing *our* baby girl!"

JENNIFER BENE

"Mom," she groaned, but she couldn't suppress her smile.

"What! You will *always* be my baby girl. I don't care if you're taller than me!" Her mom laughed a little, but it faded along with the background noise. "Okay, so I've stepped outside for a minute. What's going on, Cassandra?"

"Nothing!" she answered, sitting up straight.

"You sound off, honey…"

"I'm okay, I promise." Cassandra tried to put as much energy into her voice as she could, but it didn't work.

"You're not okay. What is it?" her mom pressed. "Did something happen with the stuff Roberta was working on? The jobs with the Elite Management people?"

"No! Everything is good, really. I just miss you guys." Cassandra sighed. "I'm definitely looking forward to being home for a bit… and eating your cooking." She laughed a little, but her mom didn't return it.

"Are you *sure* you're doing all right?"

"Mom, I'm fine!" she said, but the guilt ate at her instantly. It was a lie, a total lie, and she was sure her mom knew it.

"Okay, honey. Well, we're looking forward to having you home for Christmas again. Maybe you can come again for your dad's birthday in March?"

"I'll definitely tell Roberta about it so we can try and plan a gap for me to fly back. Let's talk about it when I get home, okay?" Smiling, Cassandra tried to sound normal, but she wasn't sure what normal sounded like. It had been days since she felt normal.

"That'll work, honey. I love you very much."

"I love you too, Mom. Please tell Dad to be safe and that I love him too." Cassandra smiled, but it felt bittersweet. "Oh, and I guess tell Zach he's okay before you give my love to Kiera and the kids."

"There's my baby girl!" Her mom laughed. "We'll see you

196

soon. Don't forget to text me your flight info before you leave L.A."

"I won't. See you soon, Mom. Bye!" Cassandra tapped the end call button as soon as her mom said goodbye, and the little voicemail button on the screen taunted her. Glancing at Abelita in the kitchen, she tapped it and picked the latest voicemail Logan had left for her, holding it to her ear so her roommate couldn't hear.

'Hey Cassandra... I know I don't have any right to keep calling you, and it's probably not helping my case any, but I just want you to know that I really am sorry. For all of it. I was an idiot, and I should have just told you about all the shit at work. I know it doesn't mean much now, but — fuck. I miss you.'

Hearing his voice was hard, because as dumb as it was... she missed him too, and a big part of her wanted to call him back. He'd been a complete asshole. Shut her out and then blown up at her like it was somehow her fault.

But all the feelings were still there.

Lurking just under the surface, just on the other side of her lingering pain and anger.

Without thinking about it, she tapped the next voicemail on the list.

'I know I fucked up. I know it. I poured out all the liquor in the house, and I... I don't want to be like my father. I won't be. Just call me back, let me explain the shit at work. It's not an excuse, I'm not making excuses, I— I'm sorry. I never meant to lose you.'

The tears were burning her eyes again, and she bit down on her lip, trying to hold them back, because she wanted to believe him. Hell, if she were honest with herself... she already believed him. He sounded sorry, and Logan wasn't the type of man to apologize even when he needed to, but he'd called and texted again and again to say he was sorry.

But he'd also shut her out. Assumed she wouldn't understand the issues he was having at work. Insulted her when she'd tried to help.

And she was still going to be traveling most of the year.

His job was obviously too stressful, too consuming, and it wasn't like hers was any better. She didn't get to choose her schedule, or the locations. If Roberta landed her a job, she had to go... and Logan was going to be here in L.A. Dealing with whatever shit was going on at work, and even after this issue went away, there'd be more. He ran a fucking company, and that wasn't going to change.

No matter how much she missed him, or the way he made her feel, her thoughts always came back to the first one she'd had when he surprised her outside Runway.

They weren't going to work, because their lives were too different.

And it wouldn't matter that his touch set her blood on fire if they never got to see each other.

Cassandra wiped at the tears on her cheek, idly scrolling through the list of voicemails, and she went back to one before everything had fallen apart.

'Hey gorgeous, I just wanted you to know that I'm keeping count of every bratty comment you send over text, and you're already at eleven. Eleven what? Well, I'm not going to tell you that until I see you, but I'm going to make sure you remember what happens to naughty brats.'

That tingling rush ran over her skin, focusing between her thighs with a needy pulse as she remembered him spanking her before they'd watched *Die Hard*. By then she'd been up to seventeen, and he'd made every single swat count, leaving her ass stinging when he let her sit up—and then he'd told her to watch the movie. Refused to touch her, kiss her, *anything*... at least for a while. His willpower had wound down before the movie ended and they'd started making out on the couch.

The memory was bittersweet now. So damn tempting, just

like the low purr in his voice when he'd threatened her with a punishment, but she couldn't—

"Cass!" Abelita snapped at her, smacking the phone out of her hand, and it bounced off the edge of the coffee table before landing on the floor.

"What the hell, Abelita!"

"You were listening to his fucking voicemails again, weren't you?" Her roommate seethed, crossing her arms as she glared down at her. "I told you to erase those. It's just dragging this shit out for you."

"I'm not talking about this," Cassandra muttered, picking up her phone to set it on the table, relieved that it wasn't cracked.

"He broke your heart, Cass! That asshole doesn't deserve a single minute of your time, or the space on your phone he's taking up with all of his stupid voicemails." Abelita pointed at herher expression serious. "He's not worth it, and you know it."

Rolling her eyes, Cassandra kept her mouth shut, because she didn't want to fight about this. It was pointless, because they'd never work out. It just wasn't meant to be.

"You need to delete them," Abelita repeated, walking back into the kitchen to keep cutting up fruit.

"I will! I'm just not ready, okay?"

Her roommate sighed heavily. "What's the point of listening to them over and over? What's he even saying? *Oh, woe is me, I was a dumbass, forgive me?* Fuck that."

Cassandra groaned, and then her phone started ringing and buzzing on the coffee table.

"If that's him don't you dare answer it!" Abelita shouted from the kitchen.

"It's Vanessa! Oh my God, rein in the friend-rage!" Muffling a frustrated scream, Cassandra answered the phone. "Hey, Vanessa."

"Hey girl... how are you today?"

"I'm doing okay." Cassandra shrugged, leaning back on the couch to stare at the little Christmas tree in the corner.

"Abelita still on the rampage?" Vanessa asked, and she could hear the grin in her voice.

"Definitely. He-who-must-not-be-named is an off-limits topic."

"He's an asshole!" Abelita called from the kitchen, and Cassandra flipped her off from the couch, immediately getting a finger in return along with Abelita sticking out her tongue. "Right back at'cha!"

"Well, then we'll just have to speak in code." Vanessa laughed. "Be honest with me, how are you feeling about him?"

"It doesn't really matter, does it? I mean, even if I talked about it, even if I listened to what he had to say, at the end of the day we're still dealing with the same core problems."

"And what are those?" Vanessa asked, and Cassandra sighed.

"One second, I need to go to my room because *someone* gets annoyed with me if I even discuss this." Rising from the couch, Cassandra went to her room as Abelita planted her hands on her hips.

"I'm just trying to protect you!" her roommate called out just as she shut the door.

"I know!" Cassandra yelled back, groaning as she dropped onto her bed. "I swear, Abelita is one of my best friends, but she's *ruthless*. If it were possible, she'd have already hired a hitman."

"She loves you," Vanessa said, laughing a little. "But, seriously, tell me what you meant. What core problems would you guys have?"

"The same stuff I've been saying all along," she answered, waving an arm toward her ceiling. "He's here in L.A. with his company, which is obviously a huge fucking source of drama and issues for him… and I'm traveling. I *have* to travel for my job, and he *has* to be here for his. It doesn't matter how great we can be together when he's not being an asshole if we're never actually able to be together."

"Didn't he say he could problem solve the travel stuff when we were at Black Light?" Vanessa offered, and Cassandra appreciated that her friend was being more reasonable than Abelita... but it just didn't matter.

"He kept saying that, but it's not like we ever sat down and talked about it. I mean, apparently he never talked to me about *anything* that was a real problem, and what kind of relationship is that?" Cassandra sat up, crossing her legs on the bed. "I'm being serious. A relationship has to be about more than just amazing sex. If he can't talk to me about the hard stuff, if he can't lean on me when he needs to... then that's not real. It's just an extended booty call. A fuck-buddy."

"I really don't think that's how Logan sees you, Cass."

"Yeah, well, it doesn't really matter now, does it?" she grumbled, hating the sour tone in her voice as she plucked at her comforter.

"So... are you done with him? You don't think you might want to at least talk to him about what happened? Maybe get some closure?" Vanessa's voice was tentative, cautious, and the exact opposite of what Abelita had been telling her for the past two days.

"I don't know, Vanessa..." Sighing, Cassandra had to admit it was tempting. She did want to talk to Logan, if only to clear the air. To not leave things so shredded and raw. But... "It won't really change anything. Even if we talk, all the other shit is still true, and if I accept his apologies, he's going to expect things to just go back to how they were, and they *can't*. I mean, I'm about to leave for my parents' house for Christmas, and then I might come back to L.A. for New Year's... but then I'm in London the second week of January. My travel schedule is getting packed with jobs, and I'm really lucky that Roberta is getting me in front of so many designers and companies. There's no way I'm going to fuck any of that up on the off-chance that Logan and I might be something."

"I don't think Logan ever expected you to change your modeling stuff. I mean, I didn't get that impression when we were all at the club together. Has he ever acted like he wanted that?"

"No!" Cassandra groaned, rubbing her forehead where she was definitely getting a stress headache. "Just the opposite really. He's been so fucking supportive of it, he seemed so *proud* of what I was doing — which is why it made me so angry when he threw modeling in my face! I mean, he doesn't get to have it both ways. He can't be proud of me *and* think it makes me too stupid to talk to him about his work issues."

"That was definitely a dick move," Vanessa acknowledged.

"A major dick move." Shaking her head, Cassandra dragged her iPad over, waking it up to look at her digital calendar app. Flipping through the months, she saw so many jobs scribbled in. Days blocked out in different places around the world. London, New York, Milan, Paris, Hong Kong. Round and round the globe, and she could already see how little she'd be back in L.A. And even when she *was* home, it's not like she was on vacation, there were meetings with Roberta and other obligations.

It was impossible.

It had always been impossible... She'd just been too damn hopeful to accept it.

"Anyway, none of that really matters in the end. It doesn't matter how much chemistry we had together, or what I might have thought we could have together. Honestly, it doesn't even matter that he was an asshole, because even if I forgive him, we're still going to be on two very different tracks in life, and neither of us are changing them anytime soon."

"Okay..." Vanessa said, her voice quiet. "But, can I ask you something that you probably won't like?"

"Ugh… what?" Cassandra sighed, preparing for whatever was going to come out of her friend's mouth.

"Ignore reality for a minute. Your job, his job, all that shit. If you both lived here and — fuck, I don't know, worked at a bakery or something, do you think you guys could work it out? Would you even want to work it out?"

"That's not the situation, Vanessa."

"Yeah, yeah, I know," her friend said. "Just go with me for a second. If you just think about Logan, *just* him, would you try and fix this? Would you call him back?"

Sighing, Cassandra leaned back on her pillows. She wanted to tell Vanessa how stupid the idea was, because it wasn't reality, but when she closed her eyes, she could still feel the way her lips tingled when he kissed her. She could remember how his whole face changed when he laughed, and how ridiculous he could be when he actually relaxed. She remembered him bringing her a scarf from his closet the first night she slept over. The way he danced. The way he swung a paddle. The way it felt to wake up with his arms around her.

"It's not possible, Vanessa, but in your fictional little world… sure. I'd probably call him back and see if we could fix it." She shrugged even though her friend couldn't see her. "But it doesn't really matter, does it?"

"I just wanted to know, Cass." Vanessa sighed. "I'm really sorry this happened."

"Me too," she answered, blinking back the haze of tears.

"Look, I'll catch up with you later, okay? I want to see you again before you leave town."

"Sure," Cassandra said, smiling a little. "We'll figure something out. Talk to you later."

"Bye, girl." Vanessa hung up, and Cassandra sighed, but it quickly turned into a groan as her bedroom door creaked open and Abelita peeked her head in.

"This is a no-yelling-at-Cassandra zone," she said, pointing at her roommate. "If you're still being bitchy, go back in the living room."

"I'm not going to yell at you," Abelita replied as she pushed the door open the rest of the way. Crossing her arms, her roommate just looked at her for a minute, eyes narrowed and face pinched as she stood there in silence.

"What is it?" Cassandra asked, exasperated with her friend's over-the-top protectiveness.

"Listen, I was eavesdropping—"

"Abelita!" Groaning, Cassandra threw her hands up, but her roommate waved at her to shut up.

"Ugh, yes, I'm *so sorry* I was eavesdropping," she said, clearly not apologetic at all. "But I heard what you said… so, was he really supportive of your modeling?"

"Yeah, he was."

"And you really liked him? Abelita asked, and for the first time in days there was no venom in her tone when she mentioned *he-who-must-not-be-named*.

"If you were eavesdropping, then you already know it doesn't matter what I think of Logan. It's like I told you a few weeks ago when all this shit started… we wouldn't work out even if he got his head out of his ass and managed to apologize enough for me to forgive him." Shaking her head, Cassandra dropped her phone on the bed beside her. "So, don't worry, you won't have to deal with me pining over him forever. I'll get over this, it's just not going to be today, okay?"

"I don't expect you to just bounce back, Cass. I never expected that. I just hate him for doing that to you. For saying that shit and breaking your heart, because you don't deserve it."

"Thanks," Cassandra said, giving her roommate a half-hearted smile. "I know you're just showing me that you love me."

"I absolutely do," Abelita replied, walking over to sit in front of her. "And, no matter what, I've got your back, okay?"

"I know." Reaching over, she pulled her roommate into a hug, wishing that she could just snap her fingers and feel better. She hated feeling like this. Sad, mopey, empty. It wasn't her, and more than anything, she wanted to feel like herself again, but that would take time. Time, and surrounding herself with the people who loved her.

Even the ones who acted kind of crazy when they tried to show it.

CHAPTER 23

LOGAN

The phone vibrated on his desk, and he answered, immediately switching the call to his headset so he could keep working.

"Hello?"

"Hey, Logan," Vanessa said, her already irritated voice coming across the line, and he sighed as he lifted his hands from the keyboard.

"If you're calling to yell at me again, I'm happy to listen, but I've got a work call in twenty minutes, so it's going to have to be more concise than yesterday."

"Ha. Ha." She mocked, muttering under her breath for a second before her voice became intelligible again. "Look, I have no idea why I'm even trying to help you. Well, no, that's not true. I'm doing this for *Cassandra*, because for some unknown reason she's still got feelings for you."

Logan sat bolt upright in his chair, his heart pounding. "You talked to her? She said that?"

"Yes, I talked to her, and… not exactly. I mean, I can tell she's still got feelings for you, but you royally fucked up here. It's not just about you being a Grade-A douchebag to her, it's that by being a complete asshole you just reminded her of all the *other shit* she was already stressing about with you two." Groaning, Vanessa muttered a few curses. "Look, apologizing to her isn't going to be enough, Logan. She's taking this as some kind of sign that things would have never worked out between you two."

"What! Why?"

"Because your stupid fucking job is here, and hers is *everywhere*. You knew she was already worried about traveling and how that would make things super hard for you guys to maintain any kind of relationship, and by being a complete dickless idiot to her, you destroyed any faith she had in you guys being able to work past that."

Logan sighed at the repeated insults. It wasn't that he didn't deserve them, but he'd heard most of them during Vanessa's rant the day before that had lasted over an hour. Although, he was slightly impressed by her creativity.

The information she was providing him was useful, though.

"So, *yes*, I fucked up that night, but she's more focused on the travel stuff again?" he asked, trying to not sound as excited as he felt.

"That's what it sounds like. Basically, you're on two different tracks in life, and neither of you are going to change that anytime soon... so it's just not possible." Vanessa actually managed to soften her tone as she continued. "Even though you're a jerk, I still wish I had better news."

"I'm not giving up, Vanessa," he said, and she sighed heavily.

"Well, unless you plan on changing your life substantially, I'm not seeing any way you can fix this," Vanessa retorted. "But, for the record, I tried to get her to talk to you, and it seems like she's thinking about it, so... maybe she'll call. Then you guys can at least clear the air about your nuclear-level fuck-up and get some closure."

"I don't want closure." Logan shook his head, leaning on his desk. "I don't want to lose her."

"Yeah… maybe you should have thought about that before you went on a binge and yelled at your girlfriend."

"I know I messed up!" he snapped, slapping the desk. "Do you really think I'm not sitting here every minute of every day regretting what I did? She's all I can fucking think about! I keep replaying that look on her face in my mind, over and over, and I hate myself for it. I hate myself for hurting her, for being such a goddamned idiot that I didn't do everything in my power to keep her close, to let her know how much she meant to me. But I'm not giving up now. I love her, and I don't care what I have to do, what I have to change to make this right, but I'm going to fucking figure it out."

Silence filled the line, and he clenched his jaw, cursing himself for losing his temper.

"I'm sorry, Vanessa. I shouldn't have snapped at you like—"

"You love her?" she asked, and he realized he'd said it out loud.

"Yeah, I do." Logan took a deep breath, feeling it shudder on the way out as he tried to calm down, to think clearly. "That's why I can't just let this go, Vanessa. I can't just let *her* go. I know I've made mistakes. I know I'm so damn far from perfect that it's stupid to even expect her to give me a second chance, because she deserves someone so much better than me… but I have to try. I can't just give up. Not on her."

"Dammit, Logan…" Groaning, Vanessa paused for a long moment. "Okay, listen, if you can come up with something before she leaves town — and it better be something fucking genius — then Wyatt and I will try to help. *If* we can."

"Thank you," he said, feeling his heart racing again as the possibility hovered in front of him. "I really appreciate your help, both of you."

"Just don't fuck this up, okay?" she said.

"I won't."

"Good," Vanessa retorted, letting out a breath. "Well, good luck. I have no idea how you're going to fix this, but... I think you could make Cassandra happy."

"As long as I'm not a dickless idiot?" he offered, and Vanessa actually laughed.

"Exactly. Just call us if you come up with something."

"Hopefully I'll call you soon. Thanks again, Vanessa." They hung up a moment later, and he grabbed the notepad on his desk, flipping it to a new page to scribble down notes from their conversation. Every little piece of data Vanessa had provided could make a difference, and he didn't want to forget it. He kept writing even when he'd exhausted their call, making notes on every concern Cassandra had ever shared, and he was trying to remember what her roommate had told him in their kitchen when the phone rang.

"Shit," Logan grumbled, taking a sip of his water before he sat up in his chair and answered the call from his COO. "This is Logan."

"Hey. How's your afternoon going, Logan?" Jared Parker asked, but he could tell his COO was less than excited about being on the phone for work so close to Christmas.

"Pretty good, and I don't plan on keeping you on the phone long. I know we both have things we'd rather be doing right now," Logan replied.

"Really?" After a brief pause, Jared laughed a little. "Okay, that's different."

"What's different?"

"You. I mean, no offense, but you sound different. Happier. And I can't remember the last time you were worried about how long a meeting would take." Jared chuckled again. "Christmas spirit got to you?"

"Let's go with that," Logan answered, smiling a bit. "So, I know things have been chaotic, and we definitely didn't end the year how we wanted to, but I think the only way we're pulling out of this is if we hit the first week of January running."

"All right, and what are you thinking?" Jared had left the field open, not mentioning a single suggestion, and Logan felt a little frustrated, but he pushed it down.

"To be honest, I asked for this call because I wanted to see what *you* thought about what we need to change in the new year to ensure something like this doesn't happen again."

"You want my opinion?" Jared sounded more than a little surprised, and that was pretty much everything Logan needed to know about himself as a leader.

Fuck.

"Yes, I do," he said, trying to sound calm and confident. "Clearly my choices lately haven't been the best, and you're in your position for a reason, so let's talk about what we can do differently next year to turn this ship around."

"Well, Logan, I have to admit this is nice to hear, but I'm not sure how much change you're looking for." Jared seemed to hesitate, but he continued with, "I mean, are we talking about small tweaks or big changes?"

"If we need big changes, I think now is the time, don't you?" he asked, feeling the stress of all of his failures creeping up on him. "I want your honest opinion."

"Exactly how honest do you want me to be, Logan?"

Chuckling, Logan sighed. "I'm not going to fire you, if that's what you're worried about."

"That is good to know, and I think I'll take it as my first point." Jared took a deep breath, letting it out slowly. "Listen, Logan, you know I worked with your father the last few years he was in charge, and he had a leadership style that was... not very appreciated. When you took over his position, I know that I, and many others, were hoping you'd bring change."

"And I didn't," he filled in.

"Right. The micro-management has increased, not

decreased. Our advisors feel less empowered to take action on accounts without decisions running up the chain, sometimes all the way to your desk. And, in some ways, you've got our employees more scared of getting fired now than when your father was in charge."

"Shit," Logan muttered, leaning back in his chair as he scrubbed at his face.

"I know you took things on pretty young, but you've never had to do this alone, Logan. You've got a lot of knowledge in the boardroom, and in the upper ranks of our organization, and right now it doesn't seem like you're open to any of it." Jared was using a gentle tone, almost fatherly, except that he sounded nothing like his father. But he was practically old enough to be. Jared Parker was almost twenty years older than him, and when he thought back over the years since his dad had died, he couldn't really argue with the man.

"You're right," he said, shaking his head. "You know, when I first took over as President and CEO, the only thing I was worried about was not embarrassing my family name. Not damaging my father's legacy. If I'm honest with myself, I think that's been my number one concern all along. Not the actual health of the company, or our success, and I'm sorry I haven't made better use of what you and the others have to offer."

"Okay… not to be rude, but were you abducted by aliens? Body-snatched? And if so, what have you done with Logan Chisholm?" Jared chuckled, and Logan joined him, letting his stress go a little as he continued to laugh.

"I deserved that," Logan admitted, smiling as he looked over the photos on his bookshelves. *So many empty, lonely pictures. So much wasted time.* "Recently I had someone I care about make it very clear to me that I have to change some things. Not just about myself, but about how I live my life, and I know that has to include Whitney Asset Management."

"Well, I owe them a gift basket, because I think this is the first real conversation you and I have ever had." Jared was smiling, he could hear it in his tone, and Logan had to admit this conversation felt much different than any other he'd had at the company. It felt better. Easier.

"I'll see what I can do about passing that along. Now, if you don't mind, I'd really like to come up with some central ideas for change that we can pass along to the board for them to look over during the holiday. Let them add their ideas to the mix, and then after Christmas we can do a virtual meeting to review them and see what can be implemented quickly."

"No holds barred?" Jared asked.

"Give me your best shot," Logan replied, grinning, and he leaned forward to his laptop to take notes.

HE'D TOLD Jared that the call would be short, but they'd been on the phone over two hours when they finally hung up. The changes they'd discussed were big. If even half of them were implemented in the new year, Whitney Asset Management would feel like a completely different company.

They'd be empowering their advisors to make decisions in the best interest of the clients, without needing layers of approval, which aligned with the new customer-controlled angle the industry had taken in recent years. It would also mean that Logan, and other leaders, wouldn't be holding up key clients from taking action with their investments.

And *that* had apparently been how Berringer Holdings managed to steal their clients.

All the hours he'd spent shouting at people, writing angry emails, fuming and raging... and the people around him had known why it was happening, but they'd been too afraid to tell him.

It was a foundational concept in every leadership book. *You get more done through others than you can ever do yourself.* And Logan had definitely forgotten that, if he'd ever even truly understood it to begin with.

But, for the first time, he felt hopeful that the company might pull out of its tailspin.

Change wouldn't be easy, but Jared had assured him that the primary goals they'd outlined would be things the employees and the leadership would support. Everything else would just take time.

Setting aside his laptop, he grabbed the notes he'd scribbled down after his call with Vanessa. He'd written 'roommate' with two underlines before Jared called, and he tried to remember where he was going with the idea.

What had her roommate told him before they had coffee?

"Spontaneous!" he shouted, writing the word down quickly as he thought back to Cassandra's sassy roommate. She'd taken great joy in dressing him down, but in the end, she'd given him some tips on how to impress Cassandra.

One had been about being spontaneous, *interesting.*

"What else did she say?" he muttered, resting his head in his hands. Then it hit him, and he wrote as quickly as he could. Cassandra's roommate had echoed things that Cassandra said to him often. *Not everything has to be perfect. Sometimes things are just better when they're unplanned, disorganized.*

Living his life by his father's rules had almost steered the company into disaster, and had made him so rigid, so focused on being perfect, that he didn't even know how to actually *live.* If he wanted a chance in hell of getting Cassandra to give him a second chance, he'd have to show her that he was ready to really live his life. To enjoy it. Hopefully with her.

The pictures on the bookshelves distracted him again, reminding him of the conversation he and Cassandra had about them. About friends, and loneliness, and so many other things that had never crossed his mind until she'd entered his life.

As he stared at them, another memory popped into his head, and he smiled as an idea formed.

It would be ballsy, definitely not perfect, and very spontaneous coming from him — and if he was lucky, it would be interesting enough to get her attention.

That's all that mattered.

Getting her attention one more time so he could try for a second chance before he lost her for good.

CHAPTER 24

CASSANDRA

*T*he bar was surprisingly crowded for three days before Christmas, but Cassandra appreciated the distraction, which was the whole point of this little 'girls' night out' Vanessa had planned.

"What do you want next?" Vanessa asked, having to practically yell over the music and the crowd.

"Another chardonnay!" she shouted back, wincing at the noise.

Abelita reached over to grab Vanessa's shoulder, finishing off her vodka soda as she pointed at the bar. "Wait, I got this round!"

"Thanks!" Vanessa answered before shifting her seat a little closer to Cassandra and lowering her voice. "Are you having any fun at all?"

"Yeah," Cassandra lied, smiling at her friend as she twirled the stem of her wine glass, trying to feel that rush that encouraged her to let go, have fun, enjoy herself... but it wasn't there. She'd been pouring all her energy into being happy for Abelita's news on the Victoria's Secret call, which she sincerely was excited about, but all she really wanted to do was lie in bed.

Not healthy.

"I know that's not true, but I'll let it slide," Vanessa said, bumping her with her shoulder as she smiled. "After all, the universe works in mysterious ways, and it *is* Christmas time. Maybe you'll get your own little Christmas miracle?"

"Maybe," Cassandra replied, rolling her eyes a little at the idea. She believed that good things happened when you focused on them... but Cassandra had absolutely not been putting out good vibes into the universe lately. It was more of the pity-party-of-one type of energy, which she was okay with. After she spent a week with her family, and got back to her routine with work, she'd feel better.

"Well, good evening!" Wyatt said, stepping past another table to stand next to Vanessa. She smiled and looked up at him, accepting his quick kiss, and Cassandra waved at him.

"Glad you could come, Wyatt! Vanessa said you were still running errands. Christmas shopping?" she asked, laughing a little when he sighed.

"You caught me. I'm very good at planning for absolutely everything... except figuring out the perfect gift for this naughty girl." His voice dropped a little on the last words, and he winked at Vanessa when her wide eyes sought his.

"You were doing *that* kind of shopping?" Vanessa asked, clearly a little nervous, but Cassandra knew she was excited too. They were a perfect match. The luck of the roulette wheel had been on their side... just like Cassandra had thought it had been for her.

Shaking her head, Cassandra smiled at their playful banter, turning to help Abelita set the glasses on the table when she returned.

"Oh, hey, I didn't know someone else was coming!" Abelita said, lifting her hands apologetically. "I just grabbed a round, but if you'll tell me what you want I can—"

"No, no, it's okay," Wyatt said, waving a hand. "I can grab something in a bit when I'm ready."

Cassandra felt her phone buzz inside her little purse as she took a sip of her wine, listening to Abelita and Wyatt introducing themselves. She was about to mention that Wyatt supported the Dudorov Ballet when her phone buzzed again... and then again.

And again.

Rolling her eyes, Cassandra opened the flap on her purse and tugged out her phone, glancing at the Instagram notifications on her screen. She'd thought it might be Logan called again, but it wasn't, so she set the phone face down on the table.

But when she looked up, everyone was staring at her.

"Did I miss something?" she asked, just as Wyatt leaned down to say something in Vanessa's ear, and her eyes went wide. Huffing, Cassandra stared at her friend. "What!"

"I think you should check what's happening on your phone," Wyatt said, pointing toward it on the table.

"Why?" Cassandra picked it up, tapping the screen to wake it up, and again to expand the list of Instagram notifications. They were all from the same user, 'notprincecharming0219.' Scrolling down, she tapped the oldest notification and when it appeared on her screen, her breath froze.

Logan?

She leaned back in her chair, as she stared at his face. It was a selfie of him, half-smiling, in front of the bar in his living room. All the bottles and glassware were gone, replaced with picture frames. Lots and lots of picture frames. Scrolling down she read the post he'd made with it: '*My name is Logan Chisholm and I've never used Instagram before today, but someone I care about very much does use it... and I thought this might be the best way to show what I learned about myself because I met her.*'

"What is this?" she asked, her heart pounding as she looked

up to see Vanessa covering her mouth with her hands, and Abelita rolling her eyes.

"Just keep reading!" Vanessa said, clearly holding back tears as Wyatt took the seat beside her with a small smile, reaching over to rub his girlfriend's back.

Glancing at Abelita made her roommate sigh. "Go on."

"You knew about this?" she asked, and Abelita shrugged.

"Vanessa told me what the idiot had planned. Just… go on. Read."

Turning her gaze back to the screen, she clicked on his username and started at the bottom of his feed. The entire idea of Logan being on Instagram seemed impossible, but there he was. Face and name for all to see on a *public* feed. Anyone could see this. His employees, the board at his company, stockholders… anyone. He'd panicked when he thought she was posting an anonymous picture of him with her in a coffee shop!

Scrolling past the first selfie, she found another one of him inside the bar area, a different angle to the shot where his smile looked even less confident. The picture showed empty shelves underneath the bar—all of the bottles were gone—and behind him she noticed the large portrait of him and his father from his study. He'd moved it to the bit of wall beside the shelves for the bar. Shaking her head, she expanded the text for the post: *'When I was younger, I promised myself that I'd never be like my father. That I would be a different man, a better man. Unfortunately, I inherited more of his flaws than I ever wanted to admit to myself. His temper, his stoicism, his inability to communicate, and his tendency to drown everything out by seeking the bottom of a glass. I didn't recognize how much these flaws affected me until I did something that hurt the person I care about. But seeing the consequences of my actions, my behavior, helped me see all the ways my father's legacy has impacted my life.'*

Cassandra scrolled to the next picture as quickly as she could, her heart pounding in her chest as she saw his smile again. *He was still so fucking gorgeous.* Standing in the sunshine, in his backyard… and he wasn't in a suit. He was in a navy sweater that made his blue eyes pop in the bright sunlight. One of his arms was extended in the direction of his pool and the beautiful view of L.A. stretched out into the distance behind him. Underneath the picture it read: '*Someone once told me that I live a charmed life, but I didn't understand what she meant at the time. I knew I was fortunate, that my wealth has allowed me to live comfortably without ever worrying about money… but I've never focused on that. Instead of appreciating my home, my cars, my opportunities, I did exactly what my father always did — I focused on everything wrong instead. If there was a single mistake, a single error, then I was failing. If something wasn't perfect, then it was wrong. I've lived like that for so many years that although I had this charmed life, I wasn't actually living it. I never stopped working long enough to enjoy it. To see the things right in front of me.*'

"Did you tell him to write this?" she asked, looking up at Vanessa as she felt the tears rising in her eyes, but her friend shook her head hard.

"No, no! I don't even know what they say, I swear, I just talked him through using Instagram. How to make posts and save them to drafts so he could… you know, post them now." Vanessa lifted her hands. "I swear. I actually can't wait to read what he said."

"Same here," Abelita added, taking a sip of her drink as she pointed at the phone. "But you have to read them first."

"You talked to him though?" Cassandra pressed, looking back at Vanessa and Wyatt, and her friend looked more than a little guilty.

"He called me," Wyatt answered, shrugging a shoulder. "I know he was an asshole. Vanessa told me all about it, but I have to admit I feel a little sorry for the guy. I think I might be his only friend."

"Logan said you were his friend?" she repeated, still too stunned over everything to process any of it.

"Actually, I think he said he'd *like* to be able to call me his friend, but to be honest, Logan seems pretty out of practice with... everything. Not just friendship."

"But he's trying!" Vanessa piped up, immediately covering her mouth as she shook her head. "I'm not saying that matters. This is all you, Cass, but *please* at least read them?"

"Okay..." Cassandra took a shaky breath, looking down at the screen to find the next post, but it was hard to focus with all the thoughts flying through her head. Had he actually listened to the things she said? Was this real? Did Logan actually understand what had been going on with him?

Did it matter either way?

Biting her lip, she blinked away the haze of tears and saw the next selfie of him, back inside, leaning down in front of the framed photos lining the edge of his bar. All the pictures from his solo travels around the world that had been on his bookshelves, but there were more too. Behind the front row were a few pictures of him and his mom, showing a chubby-cheeked, smiling little boy, and a beautiful blonde woman. A woman he'd lost when he was still just a kid. Fighting the tears and the dull ache in her chest, she read the next post: *'After college I traveled for a while. I've been to so many incredible locations around the world thanks to my charmed life... but I went everywhere alone. I went there to see these places in person, to check them off my list and file them away as 'accomplished,' but that was all it was. A checklist. Not an experience, not living, because I don't have many memories of those trips that actually matter. If I still had someone to share it with, I'd go see these places again. We'd walk the Great Wall of China and stop to just enjoy the views, we'd tour the Gardens of Versailles and take a hundred pictures so we could remember it for years. I'd hike to Machu Pichu in Peru, stroll the streets of Rome, sail the islands in the Aegean*

Sea, climb the Eiffel Tower – I'd go anywhere, as long as she was by my side.'

The next photo was a simple one. Just Logan on his couch, the last place she'd seen him in person, and the accompanying text was just as simple: *'I've been a lot of places and had a lot of opportunities, but it was on this couch that I wasted the best opportunity I ever had. The chance to be with someone who believed in me. Who believed I could be a better man before I had any idea what that might even mean.'*

Scrolling up, Cassandra felt like she couldn't breathe right. Her chest was tight, her pulse racing, and the worst part was the way her optimistic hopeful side was rearing its head. Everything he said sounded so good, so wonderful... but she reined it in and looked at the last photo. It was Logan, outside, on a street in the city. The Christmas lights decorating the storefronts, glowing in multi-colored glory under the night sky. He was wearing the same navy sweater, and she could see the sadness in his half-smile as she clicked the text beneath it. *'There's so much in life I haven't appreciated, that I've taken for granted, and I don't want to do that anymore. I want to really live my life, I want to see the good in life, I want to see the sunlight in your smile again, and I'll wait all night if it means I can have the chance to tell you I'm sorry.'*

Sliding her thumb over the screen, she pulled the picture back into view, staring at his face and then looking closer at the buildings behind him. The names on them.

"Holy shit, he's outside! He's here!" she shouted, looking up at all of them to see Wyatt shrug, chuckling.

"Yeah, I think he said something about how he'd rather sleep outside a bar than miss the chance to apologize to you."

"Oh my God." Standing up from her chair, she looked at Vanessa, who was smiling, unable to contain her excitement.

"Go!" Vanessa urged.

"You know you want to, Cass," Abelita said, and she actually smiled. "For the record, he told Vanessa that I inspired him to do this little Instagram confessional thing."

"What?" Cassandra asked, confused, but Vanessa tugged at her arm.

"Later! You can talk about it later! Go talk to him!" her friend practically pushed her toward the door, but she didn't need the encouragement. She'd wanted to talk to him, to see him, she just hadn't known how she could possibly have the conversation she needed to… but he'd started it. And he'd said more than she'd ever expected, more than she thought he was capable of.

Slipping between the other customers, Cassandra finally made it to the front door and pushed it open, stepping out onto the sidewalk to find him. Logan wasn't right in front of the bar, he was leaning next to a light pole off to the left, staring at his phone. After a moment, he saw her, and she swallowed down the urge to run over and hug him, or hit him, or kiss him, or — whatever. As he walked over, he tucked his phone into his jeans.

Jeans. He's wearing jeans, and a sweater.

When he got close enough, she could tell he wasn't himself. All that cocky bravado he usually wore like armor was missing. Hair all mussed, eyes red-rimmed, but he was still handsome as fuck and so much more approachable in the comfortable clothes. *This* wasn't the corporate asshole who had shouted at her on Friday night… this wasn't a Logan she recognized.

"I'm sorry, Cassandra," he said, his voice that perfect blend of low tones and polished upbringing that she'd been torturing herself with by listening to his voicemails over and over.

But, while the posts he'd made were amazing, and as insane as him actually posting them was, she couldn't just let go of how much he'd hurt her. No matter how much she wanted to feel his arms around her again. Steadying herself, Cassandra crossed her arms and met his pretty blue eyes.

"You're going to have to do better than that, Logan."

CHAPTER 25

LOGAN

*H*is hands were definitely shaking, and he tucked them into his pockets so he wouldn't reach out and touch her — because that's all he wanted to do. After Wyatt had texted him to confirm she was inside, he'd posted the things on Instagram and waited for her to come out. Waited, and waited, and waited until he'd started to convince himself that it hadn't been enough. That his last-ditch effort to show her that he'd changed had failed, and he'd lost her forever.

But then she'd come out.

Beautiful and incredible and standing in front of him.

You're going to have to do better than that, Logan.

Nodding, he didn't even have the vaguest urge to argue, and he was so relieved just to hear the sass in her voice again that all he wanted to do was kiss her. But he wouldn't, he hadn't earned that.

"You were right," he started, clearing his throat as they moved to the edge of the sidewalk so others could pass more easily. "I never should have spoken to you like that, and it was stupid anyway. I have *so much* respect for you, Cassandra. For how hard you work, for how talented you are, and I lashed out like an asshole because I was miserable, because I was *drunk* — and I know that's a shit excuse. I'm not even trying to use it as an excuse, because it's inexcusable. My father was an absolute bastard when he drank, and when I woke up that day... that was all I could think about. How much like my father I'd been when I lashed out at you for something you had nothing to do with, something you'd tried over and over to *help* me with."

Groaning, Logan rubbed a hand over his face, shoving his hair back from his forehead as he looked at the tense expression on her face. Brows pulled together, that soft lip tucked between her teeth... but she was listening. That's all that mattered. She was listening to him.

"I absolutely hate myself for what I did. I hate who I let myself become in trying to fill his shoes, to run my family's company like he had, but... I don't want to be that man, Cassandra. I don't want to grow old and die bitter and alone and angry at the world like he did."

"What do you want?" she asked, her voice almost too quiet to be heard over the traffic and the bustle of people.

"The same thing I've wanted since Roulette. *You.* I want you, Cassandra, and I know I don't deserve you. You are beautiful, and light, and full of so much goodness that I feel like I taint you just by being near you but... *fuck.* I—" He took a breath and made sure to look her in the eyes as he laid down the biggest gamble of his life. "I love you, Cassandra. I can't imagine my life without you in it. I don't want to take another photograph alone. I want *you* in them with me. I want to build a life with you and *enjoy* life with you."

"Logan..." she said, her arms dropping to her sides with a sigh, but he raised his hands, wordlessly pleading for her to listen a minute more.

"Listen, I don't know how good I'll be at enjoying life, but I swear to you I will do my best if you'll just give me the chance to show you who I can be, who you make me want to be." He stopped, running out of all the phrases and ideas he'd thought through over and over, and all he could do now was hope it would be enough as he dropped his gaze and forced his hands back into his pockets. "I'm sorry I cut you off, I just... I just wanted to tell you that."

Cassandra shook her head slowly, looking out at the traffic and the others on the sidewalk as she seemed to struggle with what to say. He knew exactly what he wanted to hear, but something about the sorrowful look on her face told him it wasn't coming.

"I believe you, Logan. I can tell you're sorry, that it was a mistake, and I really appreciate that you did all this to show me how sorry you are. I mean, hell, you made a fucking Instagram account with your real name and your face just to tell me everything because I wouldn't take your calls!"

"I don't blame you at all for that," he replied, smiling a little.

"Yeah..." Sighing, Cassandra bit her lip again, and he could swear that she was about to cry, her voice cracking a little as she continued. "But... Logan... this was never going to work. *Us.* I'm about to leave to be with my family for Christmas, and after that I'm heading back to London for my first shoot of the new year. My travel schedule is just as crazy next year as this year, even more so, and we're going to end up in the same situation we were after Roulette. You wanting to meet up, me never being in town, and both of us disappointed."

Sniffling, she swiped at her cheeks, brushing away the few tears that managed to escape, and he took a step closer, hands leaving his pockets on instinct because he wanted to pull her against him. To wrap his arms around her and tell her everything would be okay.

He'd made her cry enough already. Vanessa had made that very clear.

"So, while I appreciate your apology, and I want you to enjoy your life... I can't be a part of it," she finished, her voice breaking as she turned away from him, taking a step the other direction, but he grabbed her wrist before he could think twice about it.

"Cassandra! Wait, please," he said, pulling his hand back as soon as she looked at him again.

"Logan..." Her voice was full of pain, and he knew he'd put it there. Vanessa had been right about it. If he'd ever had a chance of Cassandra believing in them, of her seeing a future with him as a possibility, his actions had ruined it — but he wasn't giving up. He couldn't.

"Look, I wasn't kidding that I want to start enjoying my life." Spreading his arms, he laughed a little, hearing the bitterness in his voice. "I've spent the last couple of weeks blaming everyone *else* for the issues we've had at the company. For the accounts we've lost, the money we've lost... but it was me. I was running the company into the ground because I was trying so damn hard to be like my father. Tough, knowledgeable, infallible, and I forgot that I had an entire team of people with experience and ideas that could have helped me. But I'm not doing that anymore, Cassandra. I had a long talk with my COO about everything that needs to change, and I'm one of the biggest issues. *Me.* My micro-managing, my insistence on being involved with everything so that I can control it. And I'm done."

"You're not done, Logan," she said, wiping at tears again as she shook her head.

"I am! For *years* all I've done is work. Day and night. I've been burning the candle at both ends, never stopping for even a minute to step back and really fucking see my life. You were absolutely right when you said that all I've done is focus on the bad. The mistakes. The problems. The issues. I haven't looked at any of the *good* in my life, not ever. Not until you. Not until I saw the sheer joy you live your life with... and then spent a few days without it. Then the truth was pretty clear... I've been burned out for a long time."

226

"I agree with you, and I'm glad you see this stuff now, but that's not the issue here." Cassandra crossed her arms again, her shoulders curling in as she focused on the ground, and it killed him to see the lights catch on her tears.

"Cassandra, I have spent my entire life worried about living up to my father's legacy, and I worked so hard trying to impress him, to not embarrass him... that I forgot how much I never wanted to *be* him. I forgot that I wanted to be different, to be better, and I'm going to be. I'm not going to try and follow in his footsteps anymore, and to start with—" He took a steadying breath, trying to get his heart to stop slamming against the inside of his chest. "To start with that means I'm not going to be at work 24/7 and I'm going to travel. Hopefully to see you, if you'll have me."

"You can't leave your job, Logan!" she snapped, groaning as she scrubbed at her cheeks again.

"You're right! I can't walk out on the job. It would tank the company. Hundreds of people would probably lose their jobs, and I won't be responsible for that... but I don't have to be President *and* CEO of Whitney Asset Management. Just because my father and my grandfather were, it doesn't mean I have to, and my COO has already agreed to take over the role of President — as soon as the rest of the board approves it, but something tells me they'll be celebrating as soon as I'm not in the room." He chuckled a little, but Cassandra wasn't laughing. "As CEO I'll still have responsibilities, but Jared will take on most of the day-to-day stuff, and I'll be able to take a week here and there and *not* be here in L.A. I'm grateful I have my job, but of all the things in my life that I need to be grateful for... you're number one on that list for me, Cassandra. And I'll do whatever it takes to prove that to you."

"My hours on shoots are insane. Early mornings, very late nights, it's—"

"Worth it," he said as he moved a little closer, and this time she didn't step back. "I don't care if I only get you for one meal, or for a few hours a night. I don't care if all I do is take care of you when you're tired... if you'll let me. But I want to fight for us. For what I think we can be."

"And what do you think we can be?" she asked, looking up at him as she allowed him to slide his hands over her waist.

"I think we can be forever."

When Cassandra reached for him, pulling him into a kiss that felt like an electric current attached to his spine, he was pretty sure he could have levitated. Right then and there, on the sidewalk outside of a bar in Los Angeles.

There was absolutely nothing better than having her in his arms. Nothing in the whole world.

CHAPTER 26

CASSANDRA

*S*he barely remembered getting back to Logan's car. They'd been making out like kids on the sidewalk, not giving a flying fuck who saw them — but eventually he'd asked if she wanted to go somewhere else... and she'd chosen his place.

Dealing with Abelita could be done in the morning.

On the drive to his house, Logan seemed like a completely different person. More animated, warmer, although he hadn't lost the commanding side of himself. Asking her about her schedule, making plans before she even had a chance to process that he was really doing this. He was actually going to change his world so she could be a part of it.

Who really did that for someone else?

It felt impossible. A real Christmas miracle, just like Vanessa had predicted, and she wasn't going to ignore it when the universe lit up a runway this brightly. She'd felt it before she ever went to his house that night, the inkling that he could be so much more than just a date, or a boyfriend... he'd felt like a possible future.

And he felt the same way.

He'd said he loved her.

He'd said they could be *forever*.

What else was she supposed to do except kiss him? It's all she'd wanted to do since she was standing in front of him. The shadow of scruff on his cheeks just begging her to touch, to remember what it felt like to feel him against her again.

"I want you to know, that I will never violate your trust like that again," Logan said, pulling her out of her thoughts as he turned down his street.

"Learned your lesson?" she asked, grinning, and he squeezed her hand a little tighter.

"Yes, I believe I have." He chuckled, looking at her with a smile she'd never seen before. So free, so… happy. "But, if I ever fuck up near that bad again, please feel free to slap me and tell me I'm an idiot."

"I'll keep that in mind. Although… I'm pretty sure Abelita is ahead of me in line to slap you, and Vanessa might be close on her heels."

"Oh, I'm well aware of what Vanessa thinks about me. I think her favorite phrase was either 'Grade-A Douchebag' or 'dickless idiot,' but both of them were effective," he said, and she couldn't help laughing.

"I guess I'll have to tell her she has to stick to 'Grade-A Douchebag' because you are many things, Logan, but you are definitely *not* dickless." Grinning, she felt the rush of heat up her chest when he looked over at her like he wanted to pull the car into a random driveway and bend her over the hood. Fortunately, it was only another minute or so before they were at his house.

"Finally," he growled, slamming the car into park before he caught her by the back of the neck and pulled her into another kiss. *This* would have never been acceptable on the sidewalk. This kiss was a half-step from ripping her clothes off in the car, and while his garage was secluded, his bed was way more comfortable.

"Inside," she gasped when their kiss broke for a moment, and Logan stared at her like he was afraid to stop touching her. "Please?"

"God, I love when you beg." He shoved open his door, and she followed, letting him take her hand to pull her into the house. The plan was to make it upstairs, but she yanked him to a stop when she saw the Christmas tree.

It had to be fifteen feet tall, fully decorated, and lit up with soft white lights that reflected off all his windows like a hundred stars trapped in his living room.

"Logan this is beautiful, did you do this for me?" she asked looking over at him.

"I was hoping you'd come back here before you left town, and I know it bothered you that I didn't have any decorations up."

"So... you did this?"

"Well, I paid someone to do it. I'm not even sure where I'd buy a Christmas tree, to be honest. But that doesn't matter," he replied, and then he scooped her off her feet, tossing her over his shoulder.

"LOGAN!" she shouted, laughing as the world inverted, and her purse landed on the floor.

"You can look at it in the morning, I promise." A sharp swat to her ass had her focus back on the very attractive dom carrying her up the stairs, but she stole one more glance at the beautiful tree before it disappeared.

"You're ridiculous," Cassandra said through her laughter, just before he dropped her onto the bed. Every nerve-ending in her body was lit up like the fancy new tree downstairs, glowing with need, and more than ready to feel him on top of her again... but he was just standing there.

"You are so beautiful," he whispered, running his fingers

down her leg in an almost reverent touch. "And smart," he added, slipping her heels off to set them on the floor. "And so much better than I can ever hope to be."

"That's not true, Logan." She reached for him, but he caught her hand, kissing each of her fingers before he let go.

"It is, but since it's only beneficial to me if you believe that... I'll drop it." Smiling at her, he reached for the bottom of his sweater, and then froze. "You know, we don't need to—"

"Take your damn clothes off." Rolling her eyes, she sat up to pull her blouse over her head, tossing it off the side, before she sent her bra after it. Then she lay back, unzipping her skirt as Logan finally threw his sweater to the side. It still felt like too long before he was kissing her again, a low chuckle rumbling in his chest as he inched down her neck.

"I think I'm the one who's supposed to give you the orders." A nip over her collarbone had her back arching as he soothed it with a lick.

"Just trying to keep you out of your own head, sir," she answered, grinning as he caught her nipple gently in his teeth before teasing her with his tongue. "Since you tend to make bad decisions when you spend too long in there by yourself."

"Really?" Logan looked up at her, eyebrows raised, and she laughed.

"Am I wrong?"

Shaking his head, he muttered something just before he nipped her other nipple just a little harder than the first, pulling the first gasp from her lips. The pain was a tingling rush, a hum in her veins, and no one got that better than Logan. No one had ever understood her needs as well as he did. It was just one of the reasons why thinking of losing him had been so heartbreaking, why her whole world had felt wrong when she thought he wasn't in it anymore.

She hadn't lied to Vanessa that sex wasn't everything in a

relationship, but *fuck* was it important, and while Logan had plenty of issues... this wasn't one of them.

"I swear to you," he whispered against her skin, kissing his way slowly down her stomach, his hands gliding over her thighs as he nudged her knees wider to fit his shoulders between them. "I will never put this in jeopardy again."

"Having sex with me?" she asked, grinning when he looked up at her with a heavy sigh.

"That, absolutely, but also us." Logan pinched the tender skin on the inside of her thigh, and she gasped, whining as he twisted for another long second before he let go. "Because I love your smart mouth." Another kiss on her lower stomach. "I love your independence." Another kiss, even lower, dangerously close to where she wanted his mouth so desperately. "I love how strong you are, how kind you are, how much you care for other people."

"You're killing me," she whined, squirming in his grip as he tightened his hold on her thighs, his lips teasing between her thighs everywhere *except* where she needed it.

"Are you listening?" he asked, pinching her thigh again until her hips bucked, and she gasped, a needy sound leaving her lips.

"Yes, sir!" Cassandra tried to focus as he wandered further away, his kisses trailing to the insides of her thighs, brushing the places he'd already given her tastes of pain.

"Such a good girl," he purred, and then he dragged his tongue through her folds, pulling a greedy moan from her as he switched his hold to her thighs to spread her wider. "I love that about you, too. How you can be such a sassy little brat one minute, and such a very good girl the next."

"Oh God," she groaned, fisting the comforter as he teased her clit with flicks of his tongue before returning to long licks and skin-tingling nips.

"I may not deserve you, but I'm going to do my very best to be worthy of you," he whispered, and she propped herself up on her elbow, reaching down to grab his hair just as he moved to lick her again.

"You don't get to decide who deserves me, Logan. I do. And I wouldn't be here in *your* bed right now if I didn't think you did."

His eyes were a wide, vibrant blue as he stared at her for a moment in shock, but that didn't last long. A second later he narrowed his gaze, caught her wrist, and twisted just enough to make her release him before he pinned the offending limb at her side.

"That may be true, Cassandra, but I will point out that one of the more important parts of your statement is that you're in *my* bed right now." Turning his head, he bit down on her thigh, and she whined through her teeth as he held on long enough to turn the spike of pain into a throbbing pulse before he finally let go. She could see the impression he'd left behind when he lifted his head, smirking at her in that devilish way. Placing a gentle kiss on the mark, he looked up at her again. "Going to be a good girl for me?"

"I might be able to handle that, sir," she answered, grinning when he yanked her hips to the edge of the bed and started to *really* taste her. It didn't take long before she was squirming, fighting the rising tide of pleasure as heat rushed through her in waves timed to each devious flick of his tongue and bone-melting focus on her clit. When he slid two fingers inside her, she arched off the bed, so close to coming that she shouted something unintelligible before he forced her hips back down.

"Don't come yet," he growled, and she whimpered, because he wasn't slowing down at all. Everything was too much, completely overwhelming, and just when she thought she'd lose the battle, he sat up, pulling his hands away from her as he ripped open the bedside table.

"Please, sir!" she begged, watching his expression turn dark as he tore the condom wrapper. "Please fuck me."

"You know what that does to me." Logan rolled the condom

on just as he moved between her thighs. Tugging her ass to the very edge of the bed, her pushed her legs apart as he lined up. "Say it again."

"Please fuck me, sir," Cassandra repeated, looking up into his eyes, and he leaned over her, hand wrapping to the back of her neck as he claimed her mouth in a fierce kiss just as he slammed deep. She broke the kiss with a gasped cry, moaning along with him as he slid back and thrust again. "God, I missed this."

He took her mouth again, the glorious friction between her thighs bringing her back to the edge as he filled her in steady, hard thrusts that rocked her against the bedding. Trailing kisses down her throat, he started to move faster, teasing her closer and closer to bliss as he whispered, "I love you."

The words alone almost sent her over, but she focused on the warm rush in her chest. It felt like she was glowing, and she wrapped her arms around him, pulling him closer. "I love you too, Logan."

That next kiss was practically bruising, tongues brushing just before he nipped her lip, tasting it for a moment before diving in again. A low groan rolled through his chest as he thrust deep and held still, ending the kiss to lean his forehead against hers. "You don't have to say it back right now. I just wanted you to know, because I swore I wouldn't keep anything from you again."

"You really are an idiot," she said, grinning as she brought her hands up to either side of his face. "I think I've loved you since the night you danced with me." Lifting her hips, she squeezed him inside her, reveling in the rumble in his chest as his eyes fluttered closed for a second. "And then you did other things with me, and for me… and I think I knew then, I just wasn't ready for the words."

"I'm an idiot, huh?" he asked, smiling back at her as he slammed deep. "But not a *dickless* idiot?"

"Yes, sir," she moaned, and he laughed, kissing her again

before they lost themselves to the need to move. Every thrust inside her was perfect, summoning just enough of an ache to have her brain filled with tingling sparks, turning into electric bliss as he leaned up and started to rub her clit in merciless circles.

"Good girl. Come for me. I want to watch you come," he commanded, but it wasn't like she had much of a choice. She was already lost to the rising tide of ecstasy, her breath catching just before everything went blindingly bright and incredibly perfect.

"Logan!" she cried, arching as she wrapped her legs around his hips, trying to hold onto something as he leaned over her again, pressing her into the bed with each powerful drive of his hips that only wound her higher. It was never ending, a constant buzz of trembling aftershocks as he wrapped his hand over one hip, fingers digging in hard enough to ache as he held her still.

"Fuck, fuck, fuck," he groaned, breathing hard against her ear just before he pushed deep and held, his cock twitching inside her as he moaned her name in a way that she wanted to memorize forever.

"Oh my God." Everything was hazy, her body still squeezing him in waves as she shivered through another aftershock, and he moaned against her shoulder, nipping her.

"Be still," he growled, a command that just made her let out a breathy laugh as she squirmed again, and he groaned.

"This is *your* fault, sir."

"Such a brat." He swatted the side of her ass, but that only made her hips jerk again, and he cursed under his breath. "You are amazing."

"As are you, sir," she replied, smiling at him when he finally lifted himself onto his elbows to look down at her.

"Thank you for giving me a second chance."

Squeezing him inside her again, she rolled her hips, and his eyes closed on a hushed moan as his grin spread. "This wasn't just for you, Logan. I wanted to be with you. I wanted us to work out... I just couldn't see how it was possible."

"I wouldn't have let anything stop me," he answered, pressing another kiss to her lips before he slowly eased out of her and stood up. "Stay right there."

"Yes, sir," she said, giving him a quick salute, and he chuckled softly as he walked toward the bathroom. A moment later he came out and went into his closet, returning with one of the silk hair wraps he'd bought her — or he'd sent someone to buy. There was no telling with Logan, but what mattered was that he cared enough to do it.

Hell, apparently, he loved her.

And she loved him.

CHAPTER 27

LOGAN

*W*atching Cassandra put her hair up for bed was going to be one of his favorite parts of their nightly routine, whenever they were together anyway. There was something hypnotic about how she moved her hands. So incredibly feminine and delicate, but with all the confidence she lived her life with every day.

"What are you doing?" she asked, smiling at him over her shoulder.

"Watching you."

"Being a creeper at this point seems a little late in the game, right?" Cassandra finished and turned toward him, laughing at her joke as he sighed.

"You think I'm creepy?"

"No, I think you're hot, and amazing in bed, and although you can be a spectacular idiot at times… you're also pretty wonderful." Wrinkling her nose at him, she leaned in to kiss him before shifting to move the covers down.

"You just bring out the best in me," he answered, and she laughed, rolling her eyes.

"Oh my God, you and your *lines*. So damn smooth." Her long

legs went under the covers, and he already knew that he wanted to spend tomorrow licking and kissing every single inch of her. He wanted to memorize her for when they couldn't be together.

The thought was like a painful jab between his ribs, and so he shoved it away.

He'd spent ten months away from her. Fantasizing about her, dreaming about her, unable to do anything with the subs at the club because it wouldn't have felt right when he was thinking of her. A couple of weeks here and there were nothing by comparison, especially since she was his again. *Really* his, because she loved him too, even if he really didn't deserve it.

Maybe someday he would.

Rearranging the pillows, he was about to lie down when he noticed she was still sitting up, staring down at the comforter, toying with her fingers.

"Everything okay?" he asked, trying not to think of the sudden pit in his stomach that suggested she may have changed her mind.

"I have a question, and I don't want it to be weird."

"*That* is not the best way to start a conversation after sex," he replied, comforted by the way she grinned at him, giving him a look that told him it wasn't about that.

"It's actually about the Christmas tree downstairs. You really put it up for me?" Cassandra didn't look at him when she spoke, instead she kept her gaze down, picking at the nail polish on her thumb.

"Yeah, did it bother you?" Shifting in the bed, he leaned back against the headboard, watching her profile. "I only did it because you said—"

"No, that's not it. I really appreciate you doing that for me, it's sweet... I just wondered why you didn't already have one." Waving a hand, Cassandra shrugged. "You don't have to tell me."

Sighing, Logan leaned forward, grabbing her around the waist to tug her back to him, tucking her against his side. "I will always answer any question you have. No matter what it is," he said, but then he held up a finger. "*Unless* it is a surprise for you, and then I reserve the right to torment you with the information until I decide to give it to you."

"So rude," she said, but she was chuckling as she nudged him with her elbow.

"But, to answer *this* question, Christmas was never a very big deal in my house." Logan dropped his head back to the headboard, staring up at the ceiling as he sighed. "Before my mom died, they used to do a big Christmas party every year. The whole bottom floor of the house was decked out. Multiple trees, all the ribbon and wreaths and holly and evergreens. It was wild."

"Were the parties fun?"

"I didn't get to go. I was a kid, so I had to stay in my room and out of the way." Shrugging, he traced a finger down her arm. "After she passed, my father didn't do them anymore. He went to other people's parties, and I think he might have had someone put up a tree that first year, but after that he just didn't bother."

"That's horrible!" Cassandra said, sitting up to turn and look at him. "You didn't celebrate Christmas at all? Santa Claus and all that?"

"I mean, I was twelve or thirteen, so it wasn't a big deal. I kind of thought I was too cool for it anyway, you know?" He interlaced their fingers, gently tugging her back to lean on his shoulder. "But that's why Christmas just isn't something I think about. I mean, it's hard to ignore since it's *everywhere* this time of year… but it just wasn't a big deal in my house."

"Did you ever have a good Christmas? Like when your mom was alive?" she asked, squeezing his fingers, and he tried to remember. When he was little, he did like looking at all the decorations, and the biggest tree was always in the large sitting room. That room was perfect every year because it was where they would have all the furniture moved or rearranged for the party. Unfortunately, on Christmas, his parents were usually hard to find. His father would be busy, his mom would be sleeping, and it would just be him and whatever person they'd hired to watch him. But then he remembered something.

"Yeah... I'm not sure how old I was though. Still pretty young. I came downstairs and my mom was awake, and she had a camera to take pictures as I opened the presents she'd put under the tree. She was so excited, and we had milk and cookies for breakfast, and then she turned on some channel that was playing Christmas movies, and I sat with her on the couch while she fell asleep." He smiled a little, remembering how they'd been covered in a big blanket, and he'd been holding some toy while *Rudolph the Red Nosed Reindeer* played. Just him and his mom, his father nowhere to be found, and until she'd gone back to sleep, she'd rubbed his back. "That was probably my best Christmas."

"That's it. You're coming to my house for Christmas."

"What?" He sat up, and Cassandra turned to face him with a big smile.

"Yep. It's not like you can't afford a last-minute plane ticket to Massachusetts."

"*That* is absolutely not what I'm concerned about," he said, shaking his head. "I cannot just show up at your parents' house for Christmas."

"Yes, you can," she argued, and he was so tempted to bend her over his lap and spank some sense into her... but knowing Cassandra, that would probably only encourage his little brat. "When my oldest brother Zach was dating Kiera in college, he just brought her home one year. They stayed a couple of days and then went to her parents' house, and he was only twenty-one. He hadn't even graduated yet."

Brothers, right... hell no.

"You just agreed to start talking to me again *tonight*, Cassandra. There's no way in hell that I'm—"

JENNIFER BENE

"Do you love me?" she asked, looking at him with a serious expression that made him clench his jaw.

"Yes," he pushed through gritted teeth.

"And you said we were a *forever* thing, right?"

"I did, but—"

"*And* I have a feeling that the idea of me ever being with anyone else makes you feel a little... itchy?" A smile teased her lips.

"My palm is getting itchy, Cassandra."

"You said you'd answer my questions," she teased, and he groaned.

"You know the answer to that question is yes, except if anyone else touched you I might pay someone to make them disappear," he growled, and she grinned victoriously.

"Then there is absolutely no reason why I shouldn't bring the man I love to Christmas so he can see what a real family holiday is like." Cassandra laughed a little, her grin turning wicked. "And my family's Christmas is definitely an experience."

"You're insane," he said, knowing it was pointless to fight this. She was headstrong, independent, and he'd already admitted he'd do anything for her.

Apparently, that included a Christmas with her family.

"We'll get you a ticket in the morning," she replied, leaning over to kiss him, and he couldn't resist the urge to kiss her back.

"Is your dad going to want to kill me for touching his little girl?" he asked, letting the defeat show in his voice as Cassandra shimmied under the covers, and he reached over to flick off the light.

"Maybe."

Logan groaned. "Do you *want* to get me killed?"

"No! Trust me, they act tough, but they're all sweet on the inside. Honestly, between my mom, my dad, and my brothers... you're going to want to impress Mom the most." Cassandra pulled his arm around her waist as she settled down. "Her opinion would be the final one, but I'm the baby of the family, and they all just want me to be happy."

"Just more incentive to never fuck up again," he muttered, breathing in the lingering scent of lotion on her skin, mixed with the barest hint of her perfume, and whatever it was that made Cassandra so incredibly delectable.

"That's right," she said, and he could hear the grin in her voice as he squeezed her tighter to his chest.

"I'm going to need a Christmas miracle," he mumbled, and she laughed softly.

"Actually, I think we both already cashed in our miracle this year. You're going to have to do this on your own."

Fuck.

EPILOGUE

LOGAN

*C*HRISTMAS *E*VE
    "He did not!" Cassandra said, laughing with her brother and his wife in the living room.

"I swear! They were completely wilted. Just *dead*," her sister-in-law answered, still cracking up over the story.

"Wait, wait, let me explain," her brother, Zach, interrupted, talking loud enough to be heard over them. "It was our anniversary, and I went to the florist shop over my lunch hour and picked up these ridiculously expensive roses, an actual card, and stopped at Target to replace the headphones she dropped in the pool this past summer. I happened to leave the flowers in my car, and I didn't know you weren't supposed to do that! So, yeah, by the time I got home that night, they didn't look as nice."

"They were dead, Cassandra. I mean, completely wilted! Nothing could have saved those roses," the woman said, and the girls continued to crack up while the two boys played. Whatever it was, it had them both shouting and laughing, adding to the noise, while Logan hovered at the edge of the dining room, trying to stay out of the way.

He felt completely out of his element, and the last thing he wanted to do was volunteer for a cross-examination with her family, which he'd successfully avoided for about thirty-five minutes so far.

Just four or five more days of this, and he'd be home free.

It wasn't that her family seemed to dislike him. In fact, arriving at the Moreira house hadn't been anywhere near as traumatic as he'd expected. When Cassandra got out of the car, her entire family had poured outside to welcome her home, and then they'd cheered and laughed even louder when he climbed out the other side. With all of them talking at once, he had no idea how Cassandra kept track of all the questions, but the basics got out.

His name was Logan. *Yes,* he was her boyfriend. They'd met in February — although she didn't mention where. *Yes,* he was older than her, but *no,* she didn't care.

And she loved him.

That had brought a raucous response of cheers and hugs, and Logan had been pulled forward into a hug from her mom, a firm handshake from her dad, and some back-slaps and handshakes from her brothers and their wives with some high-fives from the two boys who names he couldn't quite remember... but there had been a lot of names.

Their house was beautiful, a two-story in a spacious neighborhood, and it was clear that they were very into Christmas. The lawn was covered in big inflatable and wooden decorations, there was a Santa, sleigh, and reindeer on the roof, and even in the daylight he could tell the whole place was covered in Christmas lights.

He hadn't seen anything like it in person. Ever.

Inside was just as festive. Warm and comfortable, with the walls covered in family photos and normal decorations mixed in with those for the holiday, and he'd taken a peek at some of them while trying to stay out of the way.

It was just… a lot to take in. Even without a house so full of people.

Cassandra's parents were obviously there, along with both of her brothers, their wives, and three young kids. Two boys and a little girl. When people were up and moving around, it seemed like there was nowhere to stand that wasn't in someone's way, and so after he'd carried their suitcases up to Cassandra's bedroom, he'd retreated to the dining room while she rushed around catching up.

He knew it wouldn't last forever though.

"Hiding in here?" Cassandra asked, smiling at him from the doorway that led to the kitchen where her mom and the other sister-in-law were busy cooking dinner.

"To be honest, yes. I am definitely hiding." He shrugged when she walked over to slip her hands around his waist, and just feeling her next to him seemed to lower his heartrate a bit. "This is nice though."

"Well, don't get used to it. Everyone wants to meet you." Slowly removing her arms, Cassandra reached for his hand and pulled him into the living room as she whispered, "I promise it's going to be okay. They're going to love you."

Logan just offered a weak smile, because he definitely didn't have her optimism. Sure, he was trying to be a different man, a better man, but he was at least a few months — or a few years — from mastering the ability to summon optimism on a whim.

If that was ever possible.

"I found him!" Cassandra announced, pulling him to one of the couches, but she mercifully put him on the outside so she could serve as a buffer between him and her middle brother, Terrell. "What are we watching?"

"The kids picked *Elf*," Zach said, putting the DVD in as he looked over at them on the couch with a grin that definitely reminded him of Cassandra planning to be a brat.

Shit. It runs in the family.

246

Logan stayed tense until the movie started and everyone was looking at the screen, or their phones. The summons to the living room hadn't turned into some kind of inquisition, which was a huge relief, even though he still felt like it was coming. It was only a matter of time.

Cassandra squeezed his hand, leaning on his shoulder, and he tried to breathe normally, to calm his pulse, because being panicked around her family was guaranteed to make a bad impression.

"You're doing great," she whispered, and he couldn't help but chuckle softly, because that was *absolutely* not true.

"I haven't really talked yet," he whispered back, and she rolled her eyes. Leaning closer, he whispered right into her ear, "That's six."

Her wide eyes when he sat back up made him grin, and for a second he actually felt a little calmer, a little more in control. "You wouldn't," she mouthed, and he grinned.

Cassandra shook her head, a hushed laugh leaving her as she leaned on his shoulder and they settled in to watch the movie.

CASSANDRA

"Okay, so now you move five spaces," Darian explained, pointing at the board game on the floor as Logan moved his cardboard character to the appropriate place.

"Now I draw a card?" Logan asked, looking at her seven-year-old nephew as if he really didn't understand the game.

"Yes, one of these because of the symbol you landed on."

"Oh, thanks," he said, drawing the appropriate card to add to his pile as he passed the die to Alex.

Watching him sitting on the floor in jeans, a sweater, and socks was surreal enough. Seeing Logan play some weird boardgame based off one of the shows her nephews loved, and pretend he needed Darian's help to understand it — that would have seemed impossible a week before. But... here he was. All the way across the country, in her parents' house, sitting on the floor with her nephews.

Maybe they'd earned another Christmas miracle after all.

"So, he's cute," Kiera said, bumping Cassandra with her hip as she smiled.

"True," Cassandra acknowledged with a laugh.

"You guys meet at one of your modeling events?" she asked, and Cassandra remembered the exact story they'd come up with. Only to be deployed if necessary.

"An afterparty, actually. People who had sponsored the event were invited, and Logan's company had been one of the sponsors."

"Right, he said he's a CEO during dinner." Kiera shook her head, blowing out a long breath. "Well, all I have to say is... damn, girl. Apparently, I should've been a model."

Cassandra rolled her eyes, but the grin was impossible to hold back. "He's pretty great. Not perfect, but no one is."

"Pfft. Anyone who seems perfect *definitely* isn't," Kiera said, crossing her arms as she watched her boys on the floor. "Although this guy seems pretty damn close. What exactly is his flaw?"

"Kiera..." Cassandra groaned, and her sister-in-law laughed.

"Sorry, it's just, he looks like *that*. He runs his own company, which means he definitely has money. He's keeping my boys entertained and *sitting still* on Christmas Eve, and he got you to fall in love with him." Kiera spread her hands as she shrugged. "Seems pretty damn perfect."

"Did Zach tell you to come over here and dig for dirt?" she asked, eyeing her sister-in-law.

"Nope. This is all my curiosity, although, fair warning, your brothers are talking in the front room, and I'm pretty sure it's about Logan." Kiera gave her a knowing look, and Cassandra decided to not take her eyes off Logan anytime soon. Her sister-in-law leaned closer, dropping her voice to a whisper, "Come on, tell me... is it the sex? He's gorgeous but just can't bring it home?"

Cassandra burst out laughing, drawing everyone's attention, including Logan's, but she waved them off as she shoved Kiera's shoulder. "Um, no. I can assure you that is absolutely *not* an issue. Trust me."

Groaning, Kiera crossed her arms again. "Totally not fair."

"You married my brother!" Cassandra reminded her, and Kiera just smiled.

"I know, and I still love him to death, but that doesn't mean a woman can't shop with her eyes," she answered, and they both started laughing again.

"Cass!" her mom called from the kitchen, and Cassandra sighed.

"Do not let my brothers corner him, okay?" she said, poking Kiera in the side before she walked into the kitchen.

"Hey, babygirl, I feel like we haven't got to have any time together today," her mom said as she pulled her into a hug. She had to lean down, but it was more than worth it to feel her mom's arms around her — which she missed more than she liked to admit as she traveled throughout the year.

"I'm sorry, Mom. It's just been chaos. Did you need more help cleaning up?" Cassandra asked, looking at the kitchen, which already looked brand new again.

"Nope, I just wanted to talk to you."

"About Logan?" Cassandra finished, smiling at her mom as she leaned against the counter. "Go ahead."

"I'm not prying or anything. I know you kids have your own lives to live and all that, and your dad and I want you to... I'm just curious why you've never mentioned him to us."

"I just didn't want to get your hopes up over anything until I was sure," she replied, hoping that answer would satisfy her mom, because there was no way in hell she could tell her the truth. About Black Light, what she'd *thought* their relationship would be, or the messy fight they'd had.

"Are you saying I can get my hopes up about him now?" her mom asked, eyes twinkling with mischief, and Cassandra laughed.

"I mean... I hope so? We love each other, he's rearranging his work schedule so he can fly around the world to see me while I'm working, and—" She felt the heat in her cheeks as she stopped herself short, but that wasn't going to fly.

"Aaand?" her mom prompted her, a smile spreading across her face.

"He might have said that he feels like we're a forever thing."

"Do you think he's going to ask you to marry him?" There was *way* too much excitement in her mom's face, and Cassandra very quickly shook her head.

"Whoa, whoa, we've only known each other since February, Mom, and this year is the first time we're going to try him coming out to see me all over the place." She shrugged, glancing back at the doorway before she looked at her mom again. "So, no, not this year, but... someday? Probably? At least, that's what it feels like, but I'm not in a rush. You know that."

"I know, I know. Your career is your focus right now, and you know how proud we all are of what you've accomplished." Her mom reached over to pinch her chin lightly. "I just want to know you're happy. Does he make you happy?"

"Yes, Mom, I promise he does. I've never felt like this before... about anyone." Cassandra grinned as her mom let go, clapping her hands together with emotion welling in her eyes. "Oh, Mom, don't cry. Come on."

"I'm not," she said, waving Cassandra off as she grabbed a tea towel off the counter to dab her eyes. "But does this mean you're not staying the full week? Are you heading to his family's house after Christmas?"

"Nope, we're all yours," Cassandra answered, but she could see the confusion on her mom's face. "He doesn't have any family left. It's why I wanted to bring him here this year. Christmas wasn't a big thing in his family growing up, and if I left him back in L.A., he would have been by himself."

"You have the best heart," her mom said, pulling her down to press a kiss to her cheek before she dabbed at her eyes again. "Okay, well, it's time for Christmas Eve. Help me gather everyone in the front room?"

"Yes, ma'am!" she said, saluting her mom as she went back to the living room, only to see Logan standing off to the side with *both* her brothers in front of him.

Walking over to Kiera, she smacked her arm, and her sister-in-law laughed. "What! He needs the Moreira family welcome."

"I'm going to kill you!" Cassandra whispered at her as she marched up behind her brothers and shoved them apart, giving Logan some breathing room. "What are you guys doing?"

"Nothing," Zach said, grinning, and Terrell just chuckled, running a hand over his hair.

"You do *not* get to corner my boyfriend and harass him. I'm not in high school, and he's not taking me to prom." Poking Zach in the chest, she raised the finger a little to point at his face. "And you don't want to piss me off."

"Ooooo, Cass is gonna tattle on us to Mom!" Zach replied, laughing.

"Or maybe she'll pour Kool-Aid on our stuff again like she did when she was nine," Terrell added, and she stifled the urge to scream.

"They just wanted to make sure I treat you well," Logan said, smirking a bit, probably at the crap her brothers were saying.

"See? Logan's fine," Zach said, dropping a hand on Logan's shoulder. "And he can hold his own, right?"

"Absolutely," Logan replied, glancing over at Zach, who was probably two or three inches taller. "I've dealt with worse."

"Oh shit," Terrell said, laughing as Zach playfully shoved Logan's shoulder.

"All right, Logan. I'm glad our baby sister has someone with a spine, because otherwise she'd steamroll right over you," Zach added, grinning at her until she smacked him in the stomach.

"Don't forget, I know where you guys actually went two years ago when you told your wives you were going to the Celtics game." That was all it took for both of her brothers to drop their smiles in an instant.

"You wouldn't dare," Zach whispered.

"That's low, Cass," Terrell added, but she just shrugged.

"Your choice, guys. Think you can play nice with Logan or should I have a chat with Kiera and Sarah?" Crossing her arms, she saw them both relent as they glared at her before turning to nod at Logan.

"We meant what we said though," Zach said, but he lifted his hands and backed away when she poked him in the ribs.

"Love you, Cass." Terrell winked then headed into the front room where the rest of her family was already gathering.

"I'm really sorry about them, Logan. Kiera was supposed to make sure they didn't corner you and—"

"It's fine," Logan said, pulling her into his arms, and she sighed as she set her chin on his shoulder.

"What did they say to you?" she asked, and he squeezed her a little harder.

"Guy stuff. Just trust me, they weren't assholes about it, okay?" Leaning back, Logan smiled at her, and she could tell he wasn't upset. "They just wanted me to know how important you are to them, and your parents, and I told them how important you are to me."

"You did?" Cassandra felt that warm, buzzy feeling in her chest again as he pressed a kiss to her cheek.

"I did, and I think they might have even believed me."

"Cassandra! Logan!" her mom called from the front room, and she grinned.

"So, tell me, how do you feel about singing?"

"What?" he asked, and this time she saw a little fear in his face, but it only made her laugh as she dragged him to the front room.

LOGAN

Family traditions weren't a completely new thing to him, but the ones the Moreiras had definitely were. They'd sang every Christmas carol he knew, and quite a few he didn't, while Cassandra's mom played the piano. Her mom wasn't a concert pianist, but that's what made it so... wholesome.

No one was expected to be perfect.

Every mistake just brought a few laughs before everyone continued, and the only ones with a decent singing voice were Cassandra's dad, her brother Terrell, and his wife Sarah. Everyone else just did their best, and although it had taken a few songs for him to start singing loud enough for anyone to hear, they cheered for him when he joined in on *Jingle Bells*.

Afterwards, everyone got to open one present a piece, and Cassandra's mom had even put a gift bag in his lap. Inside was a pair of socks, an apple, an orange, and a small note that read: *'We're glad you joined us for Christmas, Logan. Thank you for making our baby girl shine bright. Merry Christmas.'*

He hadn't expected to feel emotion swelling in his chest, but he'd managed to clear his throat and blink away the stinging in his eyes before he embarrassed himself in front of Zach or Terrell. It was just... completely unexpected. Other than little gifts from people at work and some of his clients, he couldn't remember the last time he'd received an actual gift from someone who didn't somehow associate him with making them money.

Then everyone had gathered in the living room again to let the little ones watch *Santa Radar* on TV. It was ridiculous, and completely fake, but Cassandra's nephews were completely wrapped up in it, and had to be dragged away from the television to go to sleep before Santa arrived.

As Cassandra's brothers helped get the kids in bed, he went back to the front room to look at their Christmas tree again. There was nothing perfect or organized about it. Some of the ornaments looked store-bought, while others were clearly handmade — arts and crafts from Cassandra and her brothers growing up.

The presents underneath the tree were also a hodge-podge of colors. Different wrapping papers, some with ribbon, some without, some in bags with tissue paper sticking out of the top. Even the room itself wasn't perfectly matched. The cabinet on one wall was a different wood than the table between two upholstered chairs, and nothing matched the piano tucked against the wall, but just a couple of hours before it had been filled with singing and laughing and jokes from years before.

"What are you looking at?" Cassandra asked, walking up behind him, and he turned to smile at her, noticing how all the Christmas lights reflected in her eyes, turning them into sparkling honey.

"All of this," he said, gesturing around the room. "You know... you said I live a charmed life, and I'm not arguing that in general, but in this case, I think you may have had it backwards. All of this— *this* is the kind of Christmas I've seen on TV and in movies, and I thought it was all bullshit. Just Hollywood painting a pretty picture of what everyone wishes the holidays were like... but you have it."

"Logan..." She moved closer to him, winding her arm around his waist, and he let his drape around her shoulders, holding her close as his eyes continued to move over the little ornaments, especially the ones with pictures tucked inside them. Capturing Cassandra at different ages through the years, an annual testament to just how much her parents loved her.

"It's okay. You don't have to say anything." Turning, he slid his hands down her arms until he could switch to her waist, pulling her just a little closer. She had a slight frown, the tension focused between her eyebrows, and he had a pretty good idea of what she was thinking about.

His family, the Christmas stuff he'd shared with her, but none of that really bothered him. He'd moved on from wishing he had different parents a long time ago.

All he could think about now was how lucky he was to find her, to fall in love with her, to earn her trust enough that she would bring him here, around the people most important to her. To give him a *real* Christmas, around people who love each other.

"I just wanted you to know that I get it, and I love you even more for bringing me here."

"I love you too, Logan," she said, smiling at him a little as she closed the gap between them. "I have to admit though... I was definitely worried you'd panic and bail back to L.A. Especially after my brothers said whatever they did."

"They just told me how much they love you, and it's true. Everyone here loves you. They love each other."

"It's a family," Cassandra filled in, and he chuckled a little.

"I know." He shrugged, glancing out at all the decorations on the front lawn, glowing warmly in a multi-colored rainbow of Christmas joy. "I guess I'm just saying thank you for wanting me to be a part of your family this week."

"Only this week?" she asked, pressing more firmly against him as her lips came dangerously close to his. "Logan, if you think you're getting off that easy... you have no idea what you're in for."

He chuckled, squeezing her tight. "If I'm lucky enough to be with you, to be a part of this family, years from now. Then I'll admit you're right about me."

"About what?"

"Well, if I'm still with you, singing carols in this room ten, fifteen, twenty Christmases from now… that will definitely be a charmed life. Because I'll have lived it with you."

He kissed her before she could sass him, or crack another joke, and instead he got the softest moan from her lips as she wrapped her arms around his neck, letting him take control of the kiss. It was as close to perfect as he could imagine. Probably because it had been messy, disorganized, a little crazy, but completely filled with love.

And what more could he ever want?

THE END

ABOUT THE AUTHOR

Jennifer Bene is a *USA Today* bestselling author of dangerously sexy and deviously dark romance. From BDSM, to Suspense, Dark Romance, and Thrillers—she writes it all. Always delivering a twisty, spine-tingling journey with the promise of a happily-ever-after.

Don't miss a release! Sign up for the newsletter to get new book alerts (and a free welcome book) at: http://jenniferbene.com/newsletter

You can find her online throughout social media with username @jbeneauthor and on her website: www.jenniferbene.com

ALSO BY JENNIFER BENE

The Thalia Series (Dark Romance)

Security Binds Her *(Thalia Book 1)*

Striking a Balance *(Thalia Book 2)*

Salvaged by Love *(Thalia Book 3)*

Tying the Knot *(Thalia Book 4)*

The Thalia Series: The Complete Collection

The Beth Series (Dark Romance)

Breaking Beth *(Beth Book 1)*

Fragile Ties Series (Dark Romance)

Destruction *(Fragile Ties Book 1)*

Inheritance *(Fragile Ties Book 2)*

Redemption *(Fragile Ties Book 3)*

Dangerous Games Series (Dark Mafia Romance)

Early Sins *(A Dangerous Games Prequel)*

Lethal Sin *(Dangerous Games Book 1)*

Standalone Dark Romance

Imperfect Monster

Corrupt Desires

The Rite

Deviant Attraction: A Dark and Dirty Collection

Reign of Ruin

Mesmer

Jasmine

Crazy Broken Love

The Institute: A Dark Anthology

Standalone BDSM Ménage Romance

The Invitation

Reunited

Standalone Suspense / Horror

Burned: An Inferno World Novella

Appearances in the Black Light Series (BDSM Romance)

Black Light: Exposed (*Black Light Series Book 2*)

Black Light: Valentine Roulette (*Black Light Series Book 3*)

Black Light: Roulette Redux (*Black Light Series Book 7*)

Black Light: Celebrity Roulette (*Black Light Series Book 12*)

Black Light: Charmed (Black Light Series Book 15)

Black Light: Roulette War (*Black Light Series Book 16*)

BOOKS RELEASED AS CASSANDRA FAYE

Daughters of Eltera Series (Dark Fantasy Romance)
Fae *(Daughters of Eltera Book 1)*
Tara *(Daughters of Eltera Book 2)*

Standalone Dark Fantasy Romance
One Crazy Bite

BLACK COLLAR PRESS

Did you enjoy your visit to Black Light? Have you read the other books in the series?

Infamous Love, A Black Light Prequel by Livia Grant
Black Light: Rocked by Livia Grant
Black Light: Exposed by Jennifer Bene
Black Light: Valentine Roulette by Various Authors
Black Light: Suspended by Maggie Ryan
Black Light: Cuffed by Measha Stone
Black Light: Rescued by Livia Grant
Black Light: Roulette Redux by Various Authors
Complicated Love, A Black Light Novel by Livia Grant
Black Light: Suspicion by Measha Stone
Black Light: Obsessed by Dani René
Black Light: Fearless by Maren Smith
Black Light: Possession by LK Shaw
Black Light: Celebrity Roulette by Various Authors
Black Light: Purged by Livia Grant
Black Light: Defended by Golden Angel
Black Light: Scandalized by Livia Grant

Black Light: Charmed by Jennifer Bene
Black Light: Roulette War by Various Authors
Black Light: Brave by Maren Smith

Black Collar Press is a small publishing house started by authors Livia Grant and Jennifer Bene in late 2016. The purpose was simple - to create a place where the erotic, kinky, and exciting worlds they love to explore could thrive and be joined by other like-minded authors.

If this is something that interests you, please go to the Black Collar Press website and read through the FAQs. If your questions are not answered there, please contact us directly at: blackcollarpress@gmail.com.

WHERE TO FIND BLACK COLLAR PRESS:

- Website: http://www.blackcollarpress.com/
- Facebook: https://www.facebook.com/blackcollarpress/
- Twitter: https://twitter.com/BlackCollarPres

GET A FREE BLACK LIGHT BOOK

Enjoy your trip to Black Light? There's a lot more sexy fun to be had. All of the books in the series can be read as standalone stories and can also be enjoyed in any reading order.

Get started with a FREE copy of *Black Light: Rocked* today. Your fun doesn't need to end yet!

14049161R00149